The Father,
the Son and the
pyjama-wearing
Spirit

THE FATHER, THE SON AND THE PYJAMA-WEARING SPIRIT

Dominic Garcin

Garnet
PUBLISHING

THE FATHER, THE SON AND THE PYJAMA-WEARING SPIRIT

Published by
Garnet Publishing Limited
8 Southern Court
South Street
Reading
RG1 4QS
UK

www.garnetpublishing.co.uk
www.twitter.com/Garnetpub
www.facebook.com/Garnetpub
blog.garnetpublishing.co.uk

First Edition

ISBN: 9781859643679

British Library Cataloguing-in-Publication Data
A catalogue record for this book is available from the British Library

Typeset by Samantha Barden
Jacket design by Garnet Publishing
Cover images Twisted clock face. Time concept © liseykina and A depressed
teenager walking towards the light © kwest, courtesy of Shutterstock.com
Author photo by Will Gaffney

Printed and bound in Lebanon by International Press:
interpress@int-press.com

Professor Joy Small
Head of Psychiatry
Pasteur Hospital
Royston
Hertfordshire
SG22 3HO

14 March 2012

Dear Publisher

Re: Enclosed manuscript

I'm not really a writer. I'm a psychoanalyst, but I urge you, in the interest of human progress, to publish the enclosed record of the most singular case of my career.

I am fully aware I'm likely to be struck off the medical register if you publish the record, but I'm willing to accept that consequence if it means the case of a super-bright philosophy student, Gian Paolo Friedrich, is brought to the attention of the world.

I'm aware – as a psychoanalyst – my passion to see the case study in print could be Gian Paolo's obsessive-compulsive behaviour rubbing off on me but, as a mature woman brought up in the Catholic faith, I prefer to think it has more to do with vocation.

If you're unaware of Catholic teaching, I should explain I was brought up to believe every person has a calling and, if we exercise conscientious discernment, we'll know when God is telling us what He wants us to do with our lives.

Until my treatment of Gian Paolo for an obsessive fixation on the metaphysical, I believed my vocation was to become a great psychiatrist and help humanity understand itself better. Although I've achieved that in some small measure in my career, my discernment is now telling me my knowledge, personality and experience have in fact been preparing me all along for a completely unforeseen final destiny: that of being the presenter of Gian Paolo's ideas to mankind.

But before I break with every professional ethic I've ever held dear and ask you to read this account of our analysis sessions together, let me solemnly assure you the only fiction in what I've written is Gian Paolo's surname: I've given him my maiden name of Friedrich in order to prevent his family being unequivocally identifiable. The rest is truth.

My one request of you is that you present Gian Paolo's case to the wider world so it can judge whether what he says is simply the irrelevant fantasies of an obsessive or the clearest insight of any man yet into the secret of life.

Yours most sincerely

Professor Joy Small
Head of Psychiatry
Pasteur Hospital

CONTENTS

Session 1: the family

Monday 17 May 2010

The consultation room where my sessions with Gian Paolo Friedrich were conducted is also used for analysis of psychologically disturbed children. It contains shelves of toys, a sink where children engage in water play and two south-facing windows, overlooking the hospital's field six floors below. It also has a camera in the ceiling directly above a seating area with two sofas and a square table containing a built-in microphone.

On the day of Gian Paolo's first session with me – on a morning when he should have been taking final exams for his master's degree in philosophy – spring sunshine was streaming through the windows, giving the room a creamy glow.

Having read the preliminary notes on his admission form, I was expecting a relatively unchallenging case where a young man's anxiety over important exams was generating disturbing symptoms: severe concentration loss and prolonged lapses into deep daydreaming.

The technique in such cases is simple: allow the subject to speak freely until the ideational material generating anxiety is brought into consciousness where it can be dealt with practically. In the case of most students, this is a three- or four-session process that ultimately involves: removing the pressure of exams by having them deferred; boosting the individual's security through a stay in the familial home; finding a boy or girlfriend.

In conducting Gian Paolo into the sunlit room and onto a sofa, I was struck by the contrast between the azure blueness of his eyes and darkness of his thick, wavy hair. So it was with real disconcertment I looked up from my papers at the start of our session to find emerald-green eyes fixed on me while an echoing cry rang out from a patient in a distant corridor.

Thanks to my long experience of the analytical situation, I was able to avoid displaying any surprise, but I couldn't help feeling deeply distracted as I introduced myself and gave the formal preamble about what Gian Paolo should expect from our sessions together. I then asked how he was feeling.

He gave a half smile and, as he said: 'I'm not sure I know where to start', I felt another pang as his eyes returned to blue.

Deciding to keep a watching brief on what I was seeing, I said in as even a voice as I could: 'Why don't we start with your family?' And keeping my eyes fixed on his, I added: 'How is your relationship with your parents?'

'In the case of my father, it's a disaster. As for my mother, I feel like I'm invisible.'

'Can you explain "disaster"?' I said, as another echoing cry sounded somewhere in the hospital.

'My parents divorced when I was about three,' he said, then he explained that from that time he'd only ever seen his father on the occasional birthday or Christmas. Then, when he was seventeen, he and his father had rowed and stopped talking altogether.

'My brother continued to see him from time to time, but I lost all contact,' he continued. 'That is, until I tracked him down again just after my twenty-third birthday.'

'I see,' I said. 'And why did you get back in touch?'

'I don't know, really. It just seemed the right thing to do,' he said. Then he told me how his father, Claudio, and mother, Alice, had married very young and, because of their poor education and naivety, the marriage had been a mess and ended in divorce after nine years and three children: Gian Paolo, his elder brother Aldo and his five-years-older sister, Renata.

'I might sound cold towards my father,' he continued, 'but I can honestly say, I find it difficult to see him as anything other than a vain egotist, full of silly ideas – especially about men and women.'

As Gian Paolo continued to talk about his family, his resentment towards his father became increasingly apparent.

'In some ways, of course, it's an advantage not growing up with the stupidity of a parent like him,' he said. 'But there's always this hole. Like not having him on the sidelines when I was playing rugby; or him not seeing how well I was doing at school.'

'You wanted someone to be proud of you, of course,' I said. 'But do you think his absence has any deeper significance?'

'I'm not sure,' he said. 'But I do know it caused me a lot of confusion.'

'Confusion? Why do you say that?' I said.

'Because I didn't know if my sister Renata and I were really different from other children, or whether we just felt we were because of the single-parent thing,' Gian Paolo said. 'It confused us both until we were older and could understand we truly were different. Although we didn't call it being different. We said we were "newer".'

'Newer?' I said, amused at the term but keeping my tone neutral.

Gian Paolo glanced to the far side of the room then back at me, and said: 'Do you think I could have a drink of water, please? I'm incredibly thirsty.'

'Of course,' I said and, crossing to the water cooler in the corner, I added: 'Newer is an unusual description for a person. Can you explain what it means?'

'Well, it's quite complicated,' he said as I filled a paper cup with water.

'Just do your best,' I called over my shoulder, watching the air bubble up from the cooler's bottom. Then, when I turned to cross back to the sofa, I was suddenly faced with a huge camel standing just before the table, chewing impassively.

A blink and the camel was gone, but the complete unexpectedness of the vision made my heart thump and it kept thumping as I moved back to where Gian Paolo was sitting.

Accepting the water from me, he said: 'I guess newer means the latest thing – the newest model in human development.' He then drained his cup in one and continued: 'I know that sounds quite a claim. But we were just kids when we first discussed it, so it wasn't like we'd had time to build up some complex about being superior or anything like that.'

Settling back into my place, I said: 'So this newness makes you superior?'

'Well, not exactly superior,' he said. 'Just different – able to do more things. Or perhaps I should say, feel more things.'

'What sort of things?'

'Well, the main feeling is one we called "there".'

'"There"?' I said, allowing myself a little smile.

'Yes. It's hard to explain, but it's kind of like your imagination is in a very specific space where someone else is and you can share your existence for a while.'

'You mean you and Renata had a kind of telepathic under-standing?' I said.

'Not really. It's more about sharing your whole self than reading minds,' he said. 'It's like when a song really grabs you and even though the person singing is a complete stranger, you're so in tune with what they're saying, you feel you can touch every emotion they've ever felt.'

'I'm not sure I understand,' I said.

Gian Paolo looked to the ceiling a moment and said: 'Imagine you're working at close quarters with someone to hang a picture, say, and you're both straining hard to hold it in place and knock in a nail when the other person hits their thumb with the hammer. And you almost say ouch before they do.

'Well, Renata and I used to be like that, only we'd have much more complex experiences.'

'But you and Renata don't do this any more?'

'No, she died from a brain tumour when she was eighteen.'

'I'm sorry, I didn't realise,' I said and, making a note on my pad, I added: 'Was she the only person you ever felt "there" with?'

'Yes. It doesn't work properly with my brother Aldo, or at all with anyone else.'

'And you're confident "there" is a real feeling and not, say, a game Renata led you into? A game of imagination maybe?'

Leaning forward, Gian Paolo said: 'Look, I know it's difficult to believe someone can bring new feelings into the world, but I promise you what Renata and I experienced wasn't just a game.'

'But if it really is a new feeling,' I said, 'you should be able to make me feel it too in some way.'

'Maybe, but first, let me see you put a feeling into words. Let's say "cold",' he said. 'Tell me on this nice sunny day what it's like to feel cold.'

'I think I know where you're leading, Gian Paolo, but it's you who should talk in these sessions rather than me.'

'I understand that,' he said. 'But this is a very important point if you're going to make a correct diagnosis. I mean, if you think the new feelings I describe are delusional, then you'll end up thinking I'm psychotic. Whereas if you can see they're real feelings, you'll understand the help I need from you to get humanity to change its relationship with God.'

Hearing another cry echo in a distant corridor, I said: 'Okay. Cold is when you hunch up your shoulders and tense your body and your fingers and toes go numb. Then you lose sensation in the tip of your nose and it runs and your teeth chatter.'

'Yes, those are all symptoms of cold, but what does cold *feel* like?'

'Well, cold feels like... well, cold I suppose!' I said and laughed.

Gian Paolo nodded and said: 'Okay. On that basis, I can describe the symptoms of "there", but I'm not going to be able to make you actually feel it.'

'All right! Let's try the symptoms.'

Sitting back, he said. 'The first really distinct "there" I can remember is when I was about six.' He then told me how when Renata was in her first year at secondary school, she had made good friends with a very attractive, round-faced girl called Sue who'd visited their house several times and always made a big fuss of Gian Paolo because she thought he was cute.

'I was very in love with her – in a six-year-old way,' he said, then recounted how Sue would often arrive in a turquoise and brown, retro-patterned mini-dress with a white plastic belt and spend ages talking fashion and music with Renata while they played vinyl records on the old turntable in the living room.

He described Sue as having straight, chestnut hair cut in what used to be called a 'pageboy' with the fringe almost touching the curl of her heavily mascaraed lashes. 'I thought she was the most beautiful human being I'd ever seen,' Gian Paolo said, 'and whenever she smiled, I thought my heart would burst.

'Then, one day in February, Renata came home from school and – before she'd even closed the front door – I heard a desperate call from her inside my head,' Gian Paolo continued. He then told me how he immediately left the TV programme he was watching and met her in the hallway.

'She was heading straight for the kitchen,' he said. 'And, as we looked at one another, I felt myself "there", in exactly the space her mind was occupying, and I caught all her feelings of finality and incredulity, and fear, and bitter sorrow, and stunned realisation, and importance by association and awesome wonder. All feelings I couldn't possibly have initiated myself – not at six years old.

'Anyway, I remember her standing with her hand on the kitchen door and I asked: "Who's gone? Where have they gone?" Then she tried to smile, but her lips trembled and I said: "It's Sue, isn't it. Sue's dead."

'She nodded and went into the kitchen to tell Alice, our mother,' Gian Paolo continued, then explained Sue had been hit by a car the previous night and died in the ambulance taking her to hospital. He also told me how Renata's teacher had called her whole class together that morning to give them the news.

'When Renata came back from the kitchen,' he said, 'she sat next to me in the living room and, while Aldo watched television, we held hands for ages, feeling "there" and sharing ourselves.'

Folding his arms, he added: 'I know all that probably doesn't bring you much closer to what "there" actually feels like, but all I can say is it's the closest you'll ever get to fusing streams of the God that come into the world through us.'

'I see,' I lied and, after jotting a note on the nature of "there", I continued: 'I know you said you've never experienced "there" with anyone but Renata, but have you ever tried it with anybody else?'

'God, yes!' Gian Paolo exclaimed, tossing his head back. 'All the time… all the bloody time.'

'Is that before or after Renata's death?'

'Both.'

'And what normally happens?'

'What normally happens is I creep people out!' he said, rubbing his temples. 'You see, I can't help reaching out and trying to be "there" with people. For me not to reach out would be like someone normal saying they're not going to be lifted by stirring music or feel a heart-tug when they see a crying child.

'It's just when someone else feels strongly, they reach out physically, but I do it with my whole mind. And that's what creeps people out,' he said, moistening his lips.

'I see,' I said, noticing he had a bit of salad leaf between his teeth. 'And creeping out involves what exactly?'

'Well, it pretty much follows the same pattern,' he said, then he told me how people tended to see fleeting visions and hear imaginary sounds.

Recalling my chewing camel, I said: 'Hallucinations you mean?'

Gian Paolo thought a moment then said: 'Hallucinations are when you imagine something because of some impulse inside you, right?'

'Yes.'

'Then "hallucinations" is probably wrong. You see, what people imagine when they're around me is actually prompted by me reaching out to them – not their own impulses.'

'Are you saying you're controlling people's minds?'

'God, no! I'm just reaching out to them – trying to see if they can enter a "there space" – it's they who come up with the funny imaginings,' he said. Then, looking thoughtful, he added: 'I guess it's something like the "means of representation" in Freud's "dream-work".'

'You've read Freud?'

'Plenty. But let's not go there!'

Smiling, I said: 'Okay. But why do these fleeting perceptions creep people out? Most of us have visions as children, and they never entirely go away.'

'It's creepy because, whenever I spend a lot of time round someone, the visions just happen more and more,' he said. 'It actually stops me having a proper relationship with anyone.'

'But can't you control the reaching out?'

Shaking his head, he told me he'd often tried, but it always ended in failure. 'It would be like if you said you weren't going to smile at anyone, or would only speak if spoken to,' he said. 'You can manage it for a while, but then you bump into someone in a supermarket and, bang! – you say "sorry" and smile.'

'This is very interesting,' I said. 'Has anyone ever told you exactly what it is they see in a vision?'

Gian Paolo looked skyward then told me the person he could think of who'd had the most visions was a girl he'd dated from one of his A-level courses seven years ago. She told him that whenever they made love, she would always imagine strange scenes in corners of the room, such as someone on an operating table or being given mouth-to-mouth resuscitation, or having treatment in a dentist's chair. She also imagined on occasions she heard music or children crying.

He then told me how, one night, he and the girl had been making love on a duvet in front of the gas fire in her bedroom and, while he was absorbed in kissing her throat and admiring her skin in the glow of the flames, she suddenly opened her eyes and said: 'Who the hell's playing the radio?'

Gian Paolo told her he couldn't hear anything, but she placed a quietening hand on his chest and said: 'Shhh! Listen,' then she sung what she thought she was hearing: 'Get the fire brigade, get the fire brigade before the building starts to really burn' – from the 1960s song by The Move.

'But,' said Gian Paolo, 'there wasn't any music and that was really creepy!'

He then explained they'd had a chat about it later and she'd said she was thinking of going to see a therapist because she must be developing a sexual problem if every time she made love she saw weird visions and heard non-existent music.

'I said she should wait a while before going for help. Then I stopped seeing her and crossed my fingers she'd find somebody else soon and just get back to normal.'

Checking the wall clock, I said: 'And what about you? What happens to you when someone you're with experiences these hallucinatory perceptions? Do you know they're experiencing them?'

'No. It's like I say, I'm not a mind reader or anything like that,' he said. 'All I get from reaching out are fragments of feeling; an overall mood – a kind of emotional atmosphere, if you like.'

'I see. And when did you last reach out to anyone?'

'Well... please don't be mad,' he said, 'but I've done it a couple of times in the last twenty minutes.'

'With me you mean?'

'Yes.'

'And what sort of "emotional atmosphere" did you detect in me?'

Gian Paolo crossed his legs and said: 'Do you really want an answer? I mean, is it relevant?'

'If I'm to make a correct diagnosis, I'd say so – yes.'

Taking a deep breath, he said he'd met with strong feelings of absence and devastation – the sort that only come from the loss of a person one's loved for many years. He then suggested my husband had died and the death was recent enough to still be affecting me. He also said he'd detected the loss was mixed with affection for something small I felt maternal towards – such as a dog, or a new baby in the family.

'I also met a vague feeling of weariness,' he continued. 'A kind of indignity at being treated unjustly or disrespectfully. Maybe because you're being worked too hard.'

'Go on,' I said.

Uncrossing his legs, he said: 'That's it really. Just fragments, like I say.'

I pondered a moment whether I should give him feedback on what he thought he'd detected in me. On the one hand was the basic politeness of letting someone know how they've done in meeting a challenge; on the other, was the danger of driving him deeper into a fantasy world by confirming his supposed detections were actually incredibly accurate.

Erring on the side of caution, I decided to say nothing about my husband's death two and a half years ago or me buying a cat I'd become attached to. I also kept my counsel on the tiresomeness of health department bureaucrats pressing me to provide ever-increasing amounts of cost-benefit analyses and management data without appreciating the contribution the unit's work was making to the advancement of science.

'Okay,' I said, making a show of looking at my watch, 'I think we should perhaps close this off for now and book a session for the day after tomorrow. Maybe then we can talk about your other "new feelings". I think you said there are others?'

'Yes. The main ones are what Renata and I used to call "floaty" and "cyclonic".'

Allowing myself another little smile, I made a note of the terms and said: 'Right. Let's book another session for Wednesday. Can you make that?'

'Yes, of course. Thank you very much.'

'Meanwhile, I can give you a medical certificate or a letter so you can arrange a date with your college to re-sit the exams you're missing today.'

'A letter would be great,' he said. 'Thanks very much – for everything.'

As I led Gian Paolo from the analysis room and along the corridor to the unit's reception desk, I told him in our small talk I would be speaking at a conference in London the next day, discussing the psychological health risks of potential genetic-modification treatments in humans.

While the receptionist entered Gian Paolo's Wednesday session in the appointments diary, and I made a note I needed to write a letter, he told me he had read I was an authority on the treatment of psychological problems in people whose bodies had been scientifically altered. 'It's one of the reasons I needed to come to you,' he said with a smile that revealed the bit of salad again.

Checking my own teeth with a swipe of the tongue, I said: 'Oh?'

'Yes,' he said and explained he'd read my case studies of organ-transplant recipients in some detail, then added: 'If I'm truthful, it's not an accident that it's you I've come to see.'

'Really? And how did you know I would see you and not one of my team?'

'I just had a feeling, but we don't need to talk about that now, do we?'

'No, I'm sure it can wait,' I said.

We then shook hands and, as I watched him head down the corridor to the lifts, I called out in a cheery voice: 'See you Wednesday.'

He waved and, having watched him enter a lift, I returned to my office and, on a sudden impulse, I closed the door behind me and hurried across to the window overlooking the car park at the front of the hospital.

After a short wait, I saw him emerge onto the path leading from the hospital's main entrance, cross the car park and make his way through the gates, onto the pavement outside. I expected him to go to the bus stop a few metres to the left but he crossed the road instead, to the expanse of open grassland opposite.

When he'd walked about fifty metres, he sat down with his legs stretched out and his head hung back. The May sun was shining full in his face and, just as I was envying him his chance to sunbathe, I saw a falling body – with a bloodied head – flash past the window. It was dressed in one of the paper hospital gowns patients wear in the operating theatres.

My heart thumping, I pressed my face to the glass to check where the body landed but I didn't have the angle to see the ground directly below. I could, however, see plenty of people walking in the car park and watched out for who would be first to rush to the body.

After waiting what seemed an eternity while everyone just carried on as normal, I left my office, took a lift down to the ground floor, then made my way out to the car park. The coolness of the dark shadow cast by the hospital sent a chill through me and I felt goosebumps form as I hurried towards where I reckoned the body would have fallen.

I then looked up to my sixth-floor office window to check my bearings and, sure I was in the right place, I looked all around me. There was no sign of a body.

Applied science

After several minutes fruitlessly looking for evidence of a body, I left the car park and went to the staff canteen for a cup of coffee, which I brought back to my office to drink while I regained my composure. I then created a new document on my PC and began writing up my notes of the session with Gian Paolo Friedrich.

My initial view of the case was that Gian Paolo had taken part in an incestuous relationship with his sister at a very early age and I typed: 'The feeling of sharing oneself – which Gian Paolo said he experienced at six years of age – is too closely aligned with the sense of union occurring in post-coital afterglow for there not to be a strong possibility the aetiology of his delusions lies in him having entered into a sexual relationship with Renata.

'Consistent with this possibility is the superiority Gian Paolo feels is the result of his self-sharing since there is strong likelihood the superior feeling is an over-compensation for guilt he would experience from the incest.

'To defend itself against the anxiety generated by this guilt, his ego could have reverted to magic thinking and, making use of the unmediated imagination of the six-year-old mind, he could have succeeded in transfiguring the incest into a virtuous act by telling himself it was the natural result of magical new feelings that made him and his sister special.'

Taking a sip of coffee, I re-read what I'd just written and, although I felt it made sense psychoanalytically, I couldn't prevent a voice in my head challenging my assumptions. After all, there was physical evidence of what had happened in the session that needed checking if I was to be as rigorous as I should.

I picked up the phone and dialled the laboratory assistant's number.

'Hello. It's Joy,' I said. 'I need a quick favour, please.'

'Hello, professor,' said the assistant, Addeel. 'How can I help?'

'I finished talking to a patient in the main consultation room about twenty minutes ago and I was wondering if it would be possible to send me the video file – or at least the early part of it – as soon as possible please.'

'It shouldn't be a problem,' said Addeel. 'I just need to save it to the shared drive and send you the link. Give me a few minutes.'

'That's great, Addeel,' I said. 'Thanks very much.'

I then drained my coffee, left the office and made my way to the geriatric ward up the corridor, where I found the senior duty nurse drinking tea at her desk. She hurriedly put her mug down as I entered. 'Don't worry, Jane,' I said. 'It's nothing serious. I just wanted to ask if you were on duty at around ten o'clock this morning.'

Jane wiped tea from her lip and said: 'Yes. I've been here since eight.'

'Good,' I said. 'I'm trying to find out if there was a patient crying out in one of the corridors shortly after ten. Then again a few minutes later.'

Noticing her frown, I quickly added: 'I'm not making a complaint or anything. I just want to check how I heard a cry – so I can see if we've got a soundproofing issue.'

Shaking her head, Jane said: 'No, there's definitely not been any crying out. I haven't left the floor all morning and there's been nothing – if you don't count the usual moaning and coughing!'

'What about the ward on the far side?' I said.

'Wordsworth, you mean?'

I nodded.

'No, I don't think so. I'd have heard any cries.' Then looking up at me she added: 'It was a sort of shouting you heard, was it?'

'Yes,' I said and, glancing at the coughing patient in an adjacent bed, I added: 'I don't suppose it could have been somebody from another floor could it?'

Pulling a sympathetic face, she said: 'I don't think so. There are operating theatres directly below, but you never hear a sound from them.' She then looked thoughtful and suggested: 'It could have been someone in a lift maybe?'

'But then you'd have heard it too, wouldn't you?'

'Yes,' she said. 'It was just a thought really.'

Thanking her for her time, I went down to the operating theatres. It was clear one hadn't been used in the last few hours and the second was being set up for a caesarean procedure.

Spotting the anaesthetist making her way to the second theatre, I stopped her and asked whether the room had been used earlier that morning for another procedure. She was very confident it hadn't, so I returned to my office and opened the just-arrived email from Addeel Chowderey containing the link to the video file of the session.

As I double-clicked on the film icon the link took me to, the video came to life and, with a quickening heart, I saw Gian Paolo and me enter the consultation room and take our places on the sofas by the table. Seeing him on film made me realise just how good-looking he was, although perhaps a little too pretty and petite for a man.

The moment I specifically wanted to see was imminent: when I first looked up and saw Gian Paolo's eyes had become green. But the distance of the camera from him meant his eyes were too small and lost in shadow for me to see their colour. I continued watching, nonetheless, and saw my explanatory preamble about the analysis process draw to a close. Then I remembered how when Gian Paolo had said he wasn't sure where to start explaining how he was feeling, his eyes had become blue again.

Unfortunately, his eye colour was indiscernible at that point too so I clicked off the video and returned to the document with my case notes. I then typed: 'In continuing in later years to make a virtue of what his ego-ideal thinking could not fail to judge continually was a deep-rooted wrong, Gian Paolo would have been required to develop an ever-adapting complex that would have become progressively more sophisticated and labyrinthine.

'In discussing what he describes as his other "new feelings" at our next session, I will gear my enquiry to determining whether these feelings are part of the same set of ideas surrounding self-sharing or relate to some different neurotic complex with its aetiology in an event other than his incestuous relationship with his sister.'

* * *

Next morning, I caught the train to London and arrived at the city's principal northern terminus with more than an hour to spare before the start of the genetic psychology conference I was attending. The conference venue was a few minutes' taxi ride away but the spring sunshine pouring through the glass front of the station gave me an urge to be outside and I changed course from the steps down to the taxi-rank and headed out to the station's busy forecourt.

Outside, my eye was immediately caught by the mass of sun-filled leaves undulating lazily above a row of dappled tree trunks lining the stone walkway. The sun was shining in a uniform-blue sky, radiating a delicious warmth on my shoulders, and I congratulated myself on having decided against the taxi.

Moving onto the pavement bordering the busy road beyond the station, I noticed two children on the top deck of a passing bus pointing to something ahead of me and grinning. I followed their point and saw a giant chicken handing out advertising leaflets to passers-by, bowing and clucking whenever a leaflet was accepted.

As I came alongside the chicken, I accepted one of the flyers, partly to receive my own cluck, but also to make sure the figure wasn't another vision like yesterday's camel or falling patient.

After a cursory read of the leaflet, I folded it ready to put in the next bin I came across and thought how much my late husband, Brian, would have been amused by the chicken. I pictured his smile and remembered the way he would sometimes hold on to my arm when he laughed, as if he needed an anchor to keep some form of self-control.

Stopping at the kerb of a side road, I waited for the pedestrian crossing's green man to light up and I realised I'd just thought about Brian for the first time since his death without feeling the awful pang of devastated isolation I'd become so accustomed to in the last two and a half years.

Crossing the side road, I caught the pleasant smell of fresh coffee coming from a café and joined the thickening crowd making its way along the main road's pavement. The people around me seemed to come from every walk of life: well-heeled professionals; a couple in radiantly-coloured African robes; schoolchildren with blazers over their shoulders; a tradesman in plaster-spattered overalls; youngsters in sports clothing; a tall man in a peacock-blue turban; fake-tanned blonde girls in noisy shoes.

Then I glimpsed two dour-faced, bearded men with heavy rucksacks on their backs whose upper bodies suddenly seemed to swell then shrink back as if they'd walked past one of the comedy mirrors I used to see at funfairs when I was a girl.

Moving to one side, I stopped to rub my eyes while the two men continued their resolute walk past me. Their lightweight anoraks were heavily spotted under the arms with perspiration and, as I watched them carry on up the road I suddenly felt an intense fear of death.

The feeling wasn't the anxious dread I felt whenever I allowed myself to think the only thing on the other side of life was an empty nothingness. It was more the panicked fear of someone facing imminent death, like a condemned criminal walking to the execution chamber.

Rubbing my eyes again, I chastised myself for letting my feelings run away with me and, as I glanced back up the road and saw the two bearded men disappear among the crowd, all trace of panic evaporated, leaving me feeling slightly abashed.

Taking a deep breath, I resumed my walk and carried on until I arrived at the corner of the road containing the conference venue, where I found a bin mounted on a lamppost. I then discarded the leaflet and several old tissues before moving into the road between two black taxis sitting in a line of stationary traffic and making my way onto the opposite pavement.

As I began walking up the street, I heard shouted chants and caught sight of the tops of placards waving above the heads of the pedestrians between me and the venue. The chants grew louder as I neared and I began to discern bits of slogans on the placards: 'PLAYING GOD'; 'NO DESIGNER BABIES'.

A feeling of annoyance rose in me and I wondered how anti-science protestors could have found out about the conference. It was such a small event with only sixty delegates, all of whom were specialists and had been invited by personal letter. And the invitation had stated details of the event would not be published in any print or web media until after it had taken place.

Covering the final few metres to the front of the conference building, I could see there were around thirty protestors blocking the entrance while a smartly-dressed balding man, flanked by two policemen, was talking heatedly to a protestor holding a megaphone.

Guessing the smart man was one of the event organisers, I approached him and waited for a gap in his angry exchange with the protestor so I could show my invitation and introduce myself. But, before I could catch his eye, I was suddenly driven back by the protestor shouting through his megaphone: 'Man is designed by God! Man is designed by God!'

The organiser caught the amplified shout full in the face and, having taken a reflex step back, he quickly jumped forward and tried to seize the megaphone. Protestors around the megaphone man immediately grabbed the organiser and the two policemen rushed to insinuate themselves between them and him, shouting for everyone to calm down or face arrest.

I watched as the struggle for the megaphone intensified and the shorter policeman's hat was knocked off, prompting him to grab the offending protestor's wrist and, with highly efficient movements, spin him into an arm-lock and steer him away from the crowd while he explained at almost shouting volume he was arresting him for assault. Amid a hail of boos, he then formally cautioned the protestor while the taller policeman tried to separate the organiser from the scuffle and restore order.

The first policeman then made a request into his radio for more officers to be sent to the scene, keeping the arrested protestor in an arm-lock as he did so.

Feeling duty-bound to help, I stepped forward and told the megaphone protestor at a half-shout I was one of the delegates for the conference and if he and his friends stopped it taking place, they would be serving no useful purpose whatsoever.

Dropping the megaphone to his side, the man said loudly with a sweeping gesture: 'Look at this. We've got a white coat come out the woodwork.'

'No one's coming out of the woodwork, my friend,' I said. 'I'm simply trying to attend a legitimate science conference.'

'Legitimate? Don't make me laugh,' said the man, looking round to check people were watching. 'Is it legitimate to treat Man like a laboratory mouse; to keep trying to pervert his nature?'

'Nobody's perverting nature,' I said.

The man turned again to make sure his audience was with him, then he looked me in the eye and said: 'Are you saying your little get-together today isn't about genetically engineering human beings?'

'No,' I said. 'What we're actually talking about are the potential psychological effects of altering one tiny element of a person's DNA for a specific health reason.'

'God!' the man said, 'Can't you just immunise people if you want to protect them? Why do you have to produce Frankenstein people?'

A cheer of support followed his words and, having waited for it to die down, I said as loudly as I could that, despite medicine's best efforts, millions of people died every year from hepatitis, meningitis, measles, diphtheria, diabetes, ebola... I then argued if techniques existed where one could introduce a hormone into the nucleus of a cell capable of fertilising an egg that subsequently went on to grow into a perfectly normal foetus, but with inbuilt immunity, then it was legitimate for science to ask the question 'What are the risks of employing such a technique to save millions of lives in the future?' 'As a Catholic, that seems a very pro-life enquiry to me,' I said.

I could tell from the man's frown he hadn't followed the science but he didn't let that deter him. 'But if you start designing human beings to order,' he said, 'you'll anger God.'

Aware many of the protestors had now hushed, I said: 'Look. I take your point genetic alterations may have spiritual consequences. But unless we use scientific enquiry to examine what those might be, we'll be turning our backs on the greatest life-saving opportunity in history.'

'But there's no maybe about it,' said the man. 'If you turn human beings away from the path God put them on, there will be consequences.'

'Well, perhaps,' I said, 'but I still say it's up to science to find out.'

Most of the crowd was now quiet and more of the protestors had grouped around me and the megaphone man.

'But I, and many other people of faith are telling you now, creating human beings in science's image is evil,' he said. 'You'll be dooming souls to purgatory, just because you won't leave nature alone.' He then glanced around the listening faces and added: 'You have to understand, nature is God's way of showing His will for life on Earth.'

Patting the man's shoulder I said: 'You argue your case very well, my friend. But I think you have to understand scientific advancement is synonymous with Man's advancement.' I then suggested God had made Man the steward of creation precisely because of his ability to practise science.

'After all,' I continued, 'a garden left to itself will never grow as well as one tended by a gardener.'

'You're twisting the argument,' he said. 'A garden can be perfectly healthy without pesticides.'

'Maybe,' I said. 'But ask any farmer how important science and technology are to him and you'll find you can't just leave it to nature to feed the world.'

A woman standing in the crowd said: 'But the world isn't being fed. Thousands of people starve in Africa every year, most of them children.'

'Yes,' I said, 'but that's the fault of politics, not science.'

A man near the woman shouted: 'Fucking scientists! You think you've got all the answers. But you're just destroying the planet. The more you interfere with nature, the more fucked up everything gets.' He then turned to the people gathered round

– who now included some passers-by – and shouted: 'Man is designed by God! Man is designed by God!'

Other people joined in the shout and the first protestor looked me in the eye again and, raising his megaphone, lent his amplified voice to the chant: 'Man is designed by God! Man is designed by God!'

Feeling a touch on my arm, I looked up to see the taller of the two policemen looking at me. 'Good try, doctor,' he said, 'but we need to move back now – until we can get more officers.'

Allowing the policeman to steer me away from the crowd, I said: 'Well, I just hope I and the other delegates can get through at some point.' And unable to contain my frustration fully, I added: 'And it's professor, by the way – not doctor.'

Glancing up the roadway then back the other way, the policeman apologised then guided me towards the smartly dressed organiser, saying to him: 'I think it might be best, sir, if you could get delegates to go and have a coffee or something while we stabilise the situation.'

'Can't we just go in a back way?' I said.

The organiser explained he'd already thought of that but protestors were guarding every entrance.

Exchanging mobile phone numbers with the organiser, I wished him luck above the chants of the protestors then headed back up towards the main road to look for a café. The crowds on the main road's pavements seemed to contain fewer professionals now and more foreigners, poring over maps and pamphlets.

After a few minutes' walk, I found a coffee shop and went inside to join a queue at the service counter. The display cases were full of muffins, toastable paninis, sandwiches and cakes, and I felt sure almost every one of the protestors I'd just encountered would have eaten in a place like this many times without the slightest thought for how what they were eating had only arrived there courtesy of modern farming techniques.

In my mind, that made them like spoiled teenagers: disagreeing with everything their parents stood for while taking for granted how well looked after they were.

Having paid for my latte and a stupidly overpriced apple, I sat down at a small table by a wall, opened my briefcase and took out a hard copy of the slide presentation I intended to give at the conference. Then, when I was halfway through eating my apple and reading the presentation, a voice above me said: 'Yes, professor, but will you ever deliver it?'

I looked up and saw Michael Servo, a geneticist and very dear friend who I'd thought would be attending the conference but had forgotten to talk to about it in our email exchanges of the last few weeks.

Michael had worked with my late husband, Brian, at a pharmaceuticals giant when they'd both just completed their doctorates. The bond they had formed meant they'd remained good friends throughout their careers and Michael had taken a leading role in speaking at Brian's funeral.

'Of all the coffee shops in all the world!' I said, as Michael placed his case onto the chair opposite and plopped his newspaper on the table.

'Not that much of a coincidence,' he said. 'Gerry Thingy told me you'd headed this way.'

'Gerry Thingy?'

'You know, the event manager. Smart suit, thinning hair.'

'Oh yes,' I said. 'I left him with a policeman looking very frazzled.'

'Yes, poor dear. But I expect he gets a fortune for putting a few bums on seats,' Michael said. 'He'll just have to work a bit harder today.'

I smiled and Michael – who was now leaning his hands on the back of the chair – twisted towards the counter and added: 'If it's all right with you, I'll just get myself a coffee. I expect we'll have to kill at least half an hour.' And setting off to join the queue, he called out: 'Would you like anything?'

I said I was fine as he picked his way through the tightly grouped tables with their faux marble tops and black, steel chairs. I then put my presentation back in my briefcase while Michael took his position in the queue behind a bare-legged young woman in a short dress that perfectly showed off her muscular buttocks. She glanced surreptitiously up at him and I couldn't help smiling at the way she then smoothed the dress over her behind, knowing Michael had been actively gay since around the time he'd met Brian twenty-eight years ago.

Although he'd been fairly certain he was gay throughout his teens and early twenties, Michael had been late in fully realising his sexuality because he'd resolved to put it on hold while he studied, and it was only once he'd gained his PhD that he lifted his ban on sex.

He had been raised in a stereotypical, upper-middle-class English family and, consequently, had learnt how to keep the lid on his passions. And even when he had qualified as a geneticist, his eruption of self-expression confined itself largely to showy shirts and brief encounters with men in bars and gyms.

His friendship with Brian was based on a shared passion for lengthy, abstract discussions about science and Brian's complete absence of interest in Michael's sexuality. Brian's uninterest flowed from his lack of desire to explore his own sexuality, which is typical of many less-than-averagely attractive men with a love of study.

Combine this asexuality with natural shyness, and the code of propriety Brian had been brought up with, and it's easy to understand why he was still a virgin at twenty-six, when I met him.

My introduction to Brian came about when I was lecturing at a teaching hospital affiliated to a London university with an expensively equipped gym in its sports and social facility. Michael had been a regular user of the gym – which backed on to the building where he and Brian worked – and, after several frenetically lustful encounters in the male changing area with a young doctor from my teaching hospital, Michael's first serious – although brief – relationship began.

It was thanks to this relationship I was invited to one of Michael's soirées and met Brian, whose eyes lit up with interest as soon as I was introduced to him as '*Professor* Friedrich'. We then spent the majority of the evening talking about whether or not the laws of physics were immutable in view of a theory making headlines at that time, which suggested the speed of light was slowing.

At the end of the night, Brian asked me if I'd like to have dinner one evening and I told him to come to the hospital at 7 p.m. two days later to pick me up. And so began the love of my life.

Michael returned with his coffee and caught me deep in reverie, toying with the bittersweet pain that even now accompanies recollections of my early days with Brian.

'Are you okay?' Michael said, sitting down. 'You look a little tearful.'

Clearing my throat, I took a sip of latte and said: 'Yes, I'm fine, thanks. I just drifted back to some old memories.'

Michael looked into my eyes and, squeezing my hand, said: 'Oh, Joy, you can drop your guard with me. If you fancy a blub, go right ahead. I can always read the paper.'

I held his gaze and said: 'It's all right, Michael. Please don't read.' Then dabbing my eyes with a tissue, I added: 'Why don't you tell me why you're at this conference. I don't think I saw you on the speakers' list, did I?'

'Believe it or not, I've come to listen for once.'

'Oh? Anyone in particular?'

'You for one,' he said. 'And that Korean chap with the modified cows.'

29

I asked if he meant the animals genetically altered to make them immune to mad cow disease and he said: 'Yes, Professor Woo-Park I think his name is.'

I confirmed he had the name right then asked why exactly he wanted to hear what I had to say. 'Surely I've bored you before with my transplant case studies?'

'Strangely enough, you never have,' he said, then he explained he knew they had brought me a lot of fame – or at least what passed for it in our little world – but he'd never read them properly. 'Not so I totally understand them, anyway,' he said.

'So why the interest now?'

Sipping his coffee, he told me he was leading a line of research looking at how measles and possibly mumps could be eradicated by a mutant protein treatment. 'A bit like with the cows,' he said.

My bittersweet pain entirely gone, I said: 'Yes, I've read about it. But I don't see why you'd want to hear what I have to say. Woo-Park, yes, but me?'

Glancing at his chunky watch, he leant forward and said: 'In some ways, I'm less interested in Woo-Park than you.'

'Oh?'

'Yes,' he said. 'You see, we've developed a process for replacing egg nuclei that gives us a ninety per cent success rate in fertilising eggs that go on to the blastocyst stage.'

'Ninety per cent! That's incredible,' I said, and asked when exactly the process had been developed.

'About fifteen months ago,' he said. 'I didn't say anything at the time because it didn't seem such a big deal.' He then explained one of his clinical trials directors had come up with a design for some manipulation tools. 'He's a plastics expert,' he continued. 'Worked on the NASA space programme.

'Anyway, he developed a kind of shoehorn made from spun plastic and we use it with a special pointy tool to squeeze out the nuclei.'

'I see. And that's replaced pipettes, has it?' I said.

'Good Lord, no!' Michael said, popping his eyes. 'Nobody's used pipettes since 2003, my dear! Way too damaging!'

I then asked him what was so different about the shoehorn and he told me it provided such a high level of control that his team's production of blastocysts was up more than seventy-five points on the rates achieved using the old tools.

'It wasn't until we'd had a few weeks of the new "cutlery" I realised what a tremendous breakthrough it was,' he said. 'It's accelerated our whole programme by seven or eight times.'

'I see,' I said. 'So where are you now?'

Leaning closer, he said: 'That's the thing. We're ready to go.'

'Go?'

'Yes,' he said and explained all his tests on mice and guinea pigs had been so successful his team was granted a special licence last summer for pigs and chimps. Those tests were proving incredibly successful too according to Michael and he was now in a position where he could go no further without actually trialling the technology on human beings.

'And we're still talking here about a genetic alteration treatment using a mutant protein?' I said.

'Yes.'

The significance of what Michael was saying suddenly dawned on me and I asked if I was right in thinking that, while the rest of us saw today as a chance to develop a framework for looking at the effects of human DNA alteration, he was actually using the conference to put together an ethics case for a real-world trial.

Michael sat back and, patting his fingertips together, he said: 'Got it in one!' He then took another sip of his coffee and added: 'I'm glad your memories haven't dulled your wits.'

My surprise growing, I said: 'I can't believe you're at real-world stage so quickly.'

Michael gave a theatrically camp bat of the eyelids.

'For goodness' sake,' I said. 'Don't tell our placard-wavers. They'll have you dangling from the nearest lamppost.' Then, smiling at his face of mock horror, I said I could see now why he wanted to know more about my transplant case studies. 'It's the logical next step,' I continued. 'But I can't believe you haven't just looked at them yourself.'

'Well, I sort of have,' he said. 'But I can't really work out if you're saying your heart-transplant woman would have been bonkers whether she'd had the surgery or not, or if the new heart actually sent her cuckoo.'

Taking another sip of latte, I said: 'The conclusion is slightly complicated, I know. But, basically, what it says is the woman harboured a massive amount of unresolved anxiety from childhood.' I then explained this anxiety stemmed from her fear of reprisals for attacks she'd made in fantasy on her mother's body as a child. These attacks were an expression of the rage that had built up in her as a result of sibling rivalry and jealousy over possession of the father.

The reason she couldn't resolve the reprisal-anxiety was, in my view, because girls cannot see inside their bodies and reassure themselves their wombs haven't been mutilated as punishment for attacks on their parents – full reassurance only comes when they have a baby. And, since the woman was not a mother, she was still full of anxiety regarding the integrity of her sexual organs.

Grinning, Michael said: 'Yes, I remember the bit about boys checking themselves by masturbating. Which seems a much better deal!'

'Michael!' I said. 'If you're going to keep interrupting and labelling people as "bonkers" or "cuckoo", we won't get anywhere.'

'Sorry.'

I then summarised the conclusion of my paper by explaining the woman had built up a set of delusions that enabled her to cope with anxiety generated not only by unresolved guilt from fantasy attacks on the mother, but also by the guilty feelings arising from the fact she was only alive because the heart donor was dead. Added to these delusions was a complex of ideas around the scenario that she was a bad-hearted person whose heart had been replaced with that of a selfless and giving human being.

'So you see,' I said, 'the situation was one where neurotic fantasies were bound to lead to severe psychological disturbance.'

Shaking his head, Michael said: 'I'm sorry; I'm none the wiser,' and, taking another sip of coffee he added: 'I suppose my question is: did the physical fact of her having someone else's heart make her ill? And, if it did, does that mean psychological damage is an inescapable side effect of altering someone's insides?'

'The simple answer is yes and no,' I said. Then, spotting that Michael's exasperation was about to overflow, I quickly added: 'Yes, the heart transplant brought on a mental illness. And no, psychological disturbance doesn't necessarily follow changes to the inside of someone's body.'

I then told him, if he'd read my case study of a man who'd benefited from a kidney transplant, he would have seen the paper included reference to studies of children who underwent multiple transplant procedures during infancy and didn't know about it until later in life and, consequently, suffered no discernible psychological side effects whatsoever.

Draining his coffee and returning the empty cup to the table, he said: 'Okay. I guess all I need to do now is work all that into my ethics case.' He then said he also thought my kidney transplant evidence meant he should propose his trial made use of a group of people who knew they'd been genetically altered and some who simply grew up unaware.

'A group!' I said. 'You'll be lucky to get go-ahead for one subject. And then you'll have to wait until they're at least thirty before you know if it's worked.'

Sighing, Michael said: 'I know you're right, my dear. It's going to be a long process. But as long as I go down in history as the man who saved the world from disease, I'm prepared to be patient.' He then gave another of his eyelid bats and added: 'After all, it's not like I'll stake my place in perpetuity with children, is it!'

The sound of a police car's siren reached us and, finishing my latte, I asked if he thought it was too soon to take a walk back to the venue. The siren sound then grew much louder and, as Michael was explaining he felt less inclined to sit through the conference now he'd spoken to me, I realised the noise was being made by several sirens simultaneously drawing near.

Looking out the window, I saw a pair of motorcycle policemen weave their way past, closely followed by a police car and personnel van, slaloming their way round pulled-over vehicles in the main road.

'My goodness!' Michael said, 'I hope that's not because of our demonstrators.'

I said I thought it must be something bigger as a fire engine wailed past with its blue light flashing.

Rising and crossing to the window, Michael watched the fire engine head up the road and said: 'You're right. It's gone past our turning.' And, pressing his face to the glass, he added: 'It's heading to the station.'

Another fire engine then came up the roadway, followed by a police car and rescue vehicle and Michael took his phone from his pocket and said: 'This is looking big. I'll see if I can find a news site with info.'

Deciding I'd call the conference organiser to see how he was doing with the protestors, I took out my phone and saw its 'no signal' graphic was flashing. Meanwhile, Michael made his way out to the street, where he also checked his phone's display before returning to tell me he couldn't obtain a signal either.

Seeing another police motorcycle speed by, I said: 'Perhaps it's bombs and all the phone masts have been turned off like last time – so the bombers can't remotely detonate.'

A thirty-something man at an adjacent table looked up from his phone and said: 'I can't get a signal either. There must be something wrong because I make calls from this café all the time.'

'Oh God! Not more bombs,' said Michael. 'It probably means all the trains will be out again and we'll just have to walk everywhere.' He then looked down to his feet and added: 'I knew I shouldn't have worn new moccasins.'

'We don't know anything yet,' I said. 'Let's see what happens. It might just be a couple of local masts gone down.'

'What network are you on?' said the thirty-something man. 'I'm on O2.'

'T-mobile,' Michael said.

'Vodaphone,' I said.

Pocketing his phone, the man said: 'It must be a bomb then. All the networks couldn't be out the same time.'

'I hate to say it, but I think you're right,' Michael said and, turning to me, he added: 'And these shoes are definitely pinching.' He then crossed to the shop's counter, pointed to a television on a shelf up in a corner and said to the young man at the till: 'Do you think you could switch on the telly please so we can see the news. We think there may be bombs in the area.'

A puzzled look on his face, the young man looked up to where Michael was pointing and said in a Polish accent: 'Bombs? This area?'

'No, not in this café. At least we hope not!' Michael said, then he asked again if the man could put the television news on so we could find out what was happening.

The young man stretched up to the shelf and took down a remote control and after he'd pressed some buttons to no effect,

Michael politely took it from him and zapped the screen into life with one press. He then clicked his way through several channels until he came to one with a carefully-coiffed woman speaking earnestly to the camera while the studio wall behind showed a train company's logo.

As Michael turned up the television's volume, we could hear the earnest woman say how reports were coming in that the number of casualties on one of the two trains wrecked by explosions was believed to be high.

The studio graphic then changed to film of a train pulling into a station while the woman explained police at the scene were now confirming the blasts were almost certainly caused by bombs.

Sighing, I returned my phone to my bag then crossed to where Michael was standing, the TV remote still in his hand.

'That logo they showed – it's my train operator,' I said.

Keeping his eyes on the screen, Michael said: 'That probably means you'll be stranded for the rest of the week.' Then patting my arm, he added: 'Never mind, my dear, you can always stay in our spare room.'

We then heard the TV newsreader say how one of the blasts on my operator's line had occurred less than thirty seconds after the train's departure from the terminus while the other device had gone off on a train still at the platform.

'That should mean it's only a couple of tracks blocked at the station entrance,' I said. 'Hopefully the main line out's still intact.'

'Maybe, but let's get some more info before we count our chickens,' Michael said. 'There could be more to come.'

We then watched the television news for another fifteen minutes without any report of further explosions, so we agreed to return to the conference venue.

* * *

The protestors were still blocking the entrance but there was now just one policeman on duty. The conference organiser was leaning against a pavement railing and, in between checking his phone, he told us he would be cancelling the event since every available police officer was now being deployed in a city-wide resilience exercise and couldn't be spared for his demonstration.

Having decided he would walk the mile and a half back to his office, Michael said goodbye and I returned to the terminus to find out if any trains were running to Cambridge. As I approached the station's forecourt, I could see the whole station façade was cordoned off by police ribbons while officials from the train-operating companies frantically gave information to the clusters of people swarming round them.

By eavesdropping on one exchange, I learnt the terminus would not open until tomorrow at the earliest but there were still trains running from the main station in the east of the city.

I knew services from the eastern terminus ran to towns near Cambridge so I began the walk east and assured myself I'd be able to find a taxi to take me home if I could just reach one of the stations in Hertfordshire.

My assurance turned out to be correct and, having managed to catch a train to Stevenage, I found a taxi at the station rank to take me to Cambridge for what seemed an extortionate sum of money while I sat in the back and ate a sandwich I'd bought ten minutes previously from the station's buffet. The taxi ride took almost fifty minutes, meaning the journey from London ended up taking more than five hours and it was after 3 p.m. when I finally put the key in my front door.

Having been travelling since shortly after 7 a.m. – with my spell in the coffee shop with Michael the only break – I felt incredibly weary.

After hanging my jacket on the banisters and placing my bag and briefcase in the hallway, I went into the kitchen and poured myself a large glass of red wine then took out a box of cheese straws from a cupboard while Sebastian, my cat, rubbed round my legs.

Moving to the living room sofa and enjoying that first delicious sip of Côtes du Rhône, I bit into a cheese straw and scanned the room for the television's remote control. It was perched on top of the TV and, as I crossed to fetch it, I paused to look at myself in the large mirror hanging on the room's chimney breast.

The skin of my eyelids seemed baggier than usual and I recalled the time when, as an eighteen-year-old medical student at the University of Bonn, I'd looked in the mirror of my digs' bedroom and said to myself: 'I know one day you'll be old and wrinkled, but it's hard to see now how such supple skin will ever really look worn out.'

I was probably at the peak of my attractiveness then – such as it ever was. Of course, I wouldn't have been considered a beauty in those days, but I certainly wasn't among the uglies the boys used to make fun of in their student bar conversations.

I was nicely tall and had perfectly almond-shaped, grey-hazel eyes, glossy hair and, although my nose was a little hawkish, it was softened by a gentle spattering of freckles and the fullness of my top lip. Sadly, the freckles were now gone, the hair greyed and lacklustre, and tiny vertical lines were giving my lips a pinched look.

Sighing at the cruelty of age, I also recalled how that session in front of the digs' mirror had ended with me staring so deeply into my own eyes I suffered a panic attack. I'd told myself then it was because of the anxiety of being away from my family for the first time, but I later met a theology student named Lothar – who was also studying philosophy – who changed my mind.

He told me of a passage he'd read in a work by existential philosopher Martin Heidegger in which it said, when faced with itself, human existence was so terrified, it fled into everyday objects so it could hide from the truth of being. To help me understand the passage, Lothar had said I should think what would happen if I sat in a silent room and contemplated every breath I took, paying conscious attention to my lungs filling with air and squeezing carbon dioxide out with every exhalation.

'You won't be able to do fifty breaths before you start going nuts,' he said.

The memory made me smile and, turning away from the mirror, I collected the remote control and returned to the sofa. The twenty-four-hour news channel was full of images of train wreckage at the north London terminus and footage of blood-stained people being stretchered or helped into ambulances.

An interview with a high-ranking Metropolitan Police officer was then screened where he suggested the morning's bombs had been a deliberate attempt to undermine the country's tourism industry. The two train services attacked regularly carry large numbers of foreign visitors to Cambridge and York.

As the interview with the police officer drew to a close, Sebastian jumped on my lap and pushed his whiskers against the hand I was holding my cheese straw in. Suddenly, a shock of electricity burst in me. There on the screen were blurry images of the two men I'd seen walking towards the terminus that morning carrying the heavy rucksacks.

Sebastian continued nuzzling my hand and, the shock still tingling in my body, I began stroking him as I listened to the newsreader explain the faces on the screen belonged to men captured on closed-circuit-television cameras that morning who were thought to be the suicide bombers who'd attacked the trains.

The newsreader then announced a special incident room had been set up by police and a contact number for anyone with information on the attacks was shown on the screen. This number was also available on the news channel's website, along with details of who viewers should contact if they needed to enquire about friends or relatives who might be among the nineteen dead, or one-hundred-plus injured.

Finishing my now flavourless cheese straw, I lifted Sebastian on to the cushion beside me and, picking up my glass of wine, headed upstairs to my study.

Within minutes, I was logging on to the news channel's website and, sipping my wine, I navigated to the pages featuring the morning's train bombings and found mug-shots of the two suspected bombers. I had no doubt they were the men I'd seen but couldn't prevent my mind forming a challenge: 'How could I be so certain, from among the hundreds of faces I'd passed that morning, the two men I'd glimpsed for just a few seconds, were the same pair I was now looking at?'

Was it because their heavy rucksacks had made them look suspicious in the sunny weather, or had I noticed them particularly because of the glitch with my vision when I first saw them?

Whatever the reason, I was certain it was the same men and decided I would ring the incident room so I could at least confirm the pair had been walking in the direction of the terminus at two or three minutes past nine, with about two hundred metres to go to the forecourt.

Happy with my decision, I recalled the sense of imminent death I'd felt as they passed me and how I'd likened it to the fear a death-row criminal would feel walking to his execution. My skin then went cold. 'Oh my God!' I said out loud. The two men had been walking to their death.

Session 2: The Moon

Wednesday 19 May 2010

As I sat at my desk waiting for reception to call and tell me Gian Paolo had arrived for his 10 a.m. session, I realised my feet were tucked awkwardly behind my chair's legs and my whole body was tense.

The thought that had kept me awake until three o'clock that morning was still haunting me: had my apparent empathy with the death-anxiety of two passing suicide bombers been an example of what Gian Paolo had described two days ago as 'there' and, if so, did all his odd-sounding 'new feelings' deserve to be taken seriously?

Crossing to look out the window and down to the hospital gates six floors below, I had a nagging sense I needed to resolve the question before this morning's session began. Then, for the umpteenth time since yesterday afternoon, I focused my mind on what had actually happened as the bombers passed me and, suddenly, the truth hit me: I'd been contemplating a few moments before how I'd been able to think about Brian for the first time in two and a half years without feeling the awful devastation I'd so often experienced since his passing. That's why anxiety about death was on my mind.

A wave of relaxation spreading through me, I chastised myself for having allowed the idea to enter my head for even a moment that yesterday's experience with the bombers was in some way connected with Gian Paolo and his 'new feelings'. I then told myself the reason I'd thought of a death-row prisoner was probably because it provided a good image of dying and finality and, since I was now ready to say goodbye to the death wish I'd been harbouring for the last two and a half years, my mind had simply used the idea as a handy symbol.

By the time reception called me, I felt completely relaxed and, as I walked at a leisurely pace to the consultation room to wait for the receptionist to bring Gian Paolo to me, I found I was actually looking forward to seeing him again.

Making myself comfortable on one of the sofas, I was just checking through my notes of the last session when Gian Paolo arrived looking so pale, I asked him if anything was the matter.

'I feel a bit shaken,' he said. 'I had a terrible time yesterday. Really terrible.'

'Really,' I said, recalling my own stresses in London. 'Tell me what happened.'

Gian Paolo then recounted how on Monday night he'd gone to see a band at a concert venue in the town centre. He'd made the decision to go while he was sunbathing after seeing me in the morning. 'You see,' he continued, 'I started to get this feeling I call "lovey".'

Keen to talk about his 'new feelings' I said: 'Ah! Is this one of the feelings you used to experience with Renata?'

'No. This is something I've only really known in the last few years,' he said.

'I see,' I said. 'Are you okay to talk about it now?' and noticing his slight frown, I quickly added: 'We can talk about your bad day later.'

'Okay,' he said, and sitting back, he explained: 'It comes when I'm happy. It means I start seeing everything and everybody as beautiful.'

I gave a short laugh and said: 'It sounds like the flower-power crowd of the 1960s.'

'Yes,' he said. 'I think it's probably the same sort of thing, except I'm not on cannabis when I feel it – just in a good mood.'

'A good mood,' I said, 'or a euphoric one?'

'Well,' he said looking thoughtful, 'it starts off when I'm just normally happy and builds to a kind of euphoria I suppose.' He then told me how when the feeling came on him, he would go to a shopping mall or busy street, or anywhere he could see crowds. Then he would just stand for an hour or two and watch people go by.

'And what do you watch for?'

'I'll look at the face of everyone who passes,' he said, 'and try to get a glimpse inside them: who they are; what's their history?; are they living in a lonely bedsit?; are they in love?; do they have a secret vice?' He then explained he would try to pick up anything personal about people, no matter how small. And if he could see something intimate, he would feel he'd made a connection, even if it was just for a nanosecond, then he would love them for being them. For being a beautiful, individual human being with their own complicated history and personal feelings and thoughts. He also said he loved them for being the greatest creation God has achieved so far. For being able to love, live, laugh and cry. 'And I love them so much,' he said, 'I just have to stand there until I'm tired and the feeling's spent.'

'I see,' I said. 'And do you think this is a "new feeling" or simply a version of the 1960s peace-and-love thing?'

'I don't know exactly what pot-smoking hippies felt, or what kids on pills feel today,' he said, 'but my "lovey" is sober and sincere.' He then said although 'lovey' relied on him glimpsing an intimate truth about another human being, it didn't want to focus on any one individual.

'I suppose,' he continued, 'you could describe it as a love of an individual to arrive at a greater, universal love of humanity.'

He then said the feeling was about recognising everybody is a breathing receptacle of God and seeing them as being a tangible ray in God's superbness. Seeing their ability to love as their direct power to bring God into the world and realising the truth they know and beauty they possess are actually living, breathing manifestations of God in three dimensions. 'It's hearing their voice and knowing it's God speaking,' he said. 'Seeing their wonderfulness and knowing the reason it looks wonderful is because you're gazing at God.'

'I see,' I said, making a note his metaphysical fixation might include seeing himself as Jesus. 'And what is it about this "lovey" experience that makes you say it's so different to what anyone else has felt?'

Gian Palo looked pensive and said: 'I guess it always has an element of "cyclonic" in it.'

Checking a jotting from the first session, I said: 'That's one of the other "new feelings" right?'

He nodded and said: 'Yes. Cyclonic is probably the one I get most often. It's also probably the one people would find hardest to understand.'

'I see,' I said. 'And can you tell me about it with examples – like we did on Monday?'

'Yes, but it's hard, because it has a lot of different forms,' he said. 'But if I had to sum it up, it's like your mind is a tornado, sucking up impressions at super speed.' He then said when he's watching the crowds go by, he can drink in the presence of someone who passes close to him then do the same again with the next person, and the next, even if they're just a second apart.

'So it's a kind of speed perception?' I said.

'Partly,' he said, 'but there's more to it,' and he told me how the 'feeling' could take him inside himself on a kind of journey to the infinitesimal, as if he possessed X-ray vision and could keep drilling down to tinier and tinier elements of his body tissue.

'I know it sounds crazy,' he continued, 'but, if I close my eyes, it's like I can whiz round my body and create an image of what's happening in every cell.' He then told me how Renata had found her brain tumour by practising this kind of body scanning, long before doctors diagnosed it.

Glad for the chance to talk about his sister, who I suspected was at the root of his problems, I said: 'And had doctors been trying to diagnose a problem with her? I mean, was she ill before she did the body scanning you're talking about?'

'Oh yes. She'd been having fainting fits for years,' Gian Paolo said. 'Doctors said it was anaemia or exhaustion or because she was always partying.'

'And was she a party girl?'

'Not really, it's just she always had boyfriends who took her out,' he said. Then he explained Renata was a very beautiful girl who boys would queue up to date. And they were usually the boys who had motorbikes or played in bands. 'So she did end up drinking in clubs and bars, and sometimes taking drugs,' he said.

'Drugs?'

'Yes, cannabis mainly,' he said. 'But I know she tried LSD a few times too.'

'Really?' I said, and suggested an LSD trip would be incredibly dangerous for someone capable of the kind of extraordinarily sensitive feelings he'd been describing.

'God, yes!' he said. 'I would never dream of it myself.' He then told me how Renata would sometimes take LSD on a Sunday night when she was watching a band then go to school next morning, still tripping.

'And do you think that did her any harm?' I said.

Gian Paolo sucked in his lower lip and said: 'Who can say? There were times Renny could be really spaced out and say things that didn't make sense. But I don't know if that was drugs or her brain tumour – or just because she'd grown up knowing she was different.'

He then said Renata had told him several times how tough her childhood had been because it wasn't until he was six she realised he was different like her. That meant she had felt like she was the only person with genuine 'new feelings' right up until she was eleven.

'Thinking about it now,' he continued, 'I suppose her being five years older made it tough all along the line.' And he explained how Renata would have been required to pioneer her way through life with no mentor or peers to support her, and he was too young to be a real 'partner in crime'.

'That's probably why, when she was ten, she started keeping a notebook,' he said.

'What, a diary, you mean?'

'Not really a diary,' he said. 'It was more a book where she gathered her thoughts and tried to make sense of the world.'

'That sounds very advanced for ten.'

'Yes, but she was no ordinary child,' he said. 'You only need to read a few pages to see that. In fact, if everyone could just read a few pages, we'd all be a lot closer to understanding what God is and what it needs from humanity.' And looking into my eyes, he added: 'Making that understanding happen is sort of a mission for me.'

'I see. And do you still have it – the notebook?'

Nodding, Gian Paolo said Renata had given him the whole manuscript just before she died.

'I see,' I said. 'So you read it when you were what – thirteen?'

'Yes, but I'd read bits long before then,' he said. 'And I remember reading it all the way through in the holidays just before starting secondary school,' and he went on to explain how Renata was always adding bits to the book and changing passages, and the version she gave him before she died had so many extra pages sellotaped in, it was quite different to the one he'd read previously. He then offered to make me a photocopy of the book so I could see what life was like for Renata having to think all her original thoughts with no one to share them with.

Making another note on my pad, I said I'd like very much to see the book and would be grateful if he could remember to make a photocopy for our next session.

'Yes, of course,' he said. 'Then you'll see what truly amazing wisdom her feelings gave her. And how incredibly alone she felt.'

He then looked towards the window and added: 'I guess I'm kind of lucky I had Renny so I never really knew what it was to feel alone.'

'Yes,' I said. 'And did life become more difficult for you after Renata died?'

'You can say that again!' he said. 'I just feel so isolated now, even with Renny's book.'

'And the isolation is because you're the only person in the world who has "new feelings"?'

'Not exactly,' he said, then explained he was sure there were others like Renata and him scattered round the globe. 'The real difficulty is knowing I can't speak about what I feel without people thinking I'm crazy,' he continued. 'In fact, you're the first stranger I've ever talked to about it.'

Nodding, I started to make a further note on my pad when the thumping sound of something heavy hitting the floor above made me look up. Gian Paolo was standing, staring at me wildly, his lips trembling. The room then suddenly strobed half a dozen times from total darkness to blinding white light and Gian Paolo said: 'You've already made up your mind I'm insane, haven't you!'

Blinking to clear my vision, I tried to think how to reply. I was then seized by an overwhelming pity that twisted my heart so painfully, it left me croaky as I said: 'I don't think anything yet, Gian Paolo. It's much too early.' I then asked him to sit down and try to relax before adding: 'If you had an awful day yesterday, you really need to concentrate on recovering from that before anything else.'

After pacing up and down a while and shaking his head, he re-seated himself and said. 'I suppose you're right. I shouldn't blame you for anything.' He then sat back in his seat and added: 'Yesterday did shake me up though.'

Massaging the spot on my forehead where a small pain was developing, I said: 'If it's any consolation, I had a pretty disastrous day myself.'

Settling back into the sofa, he said he had noticed I looked tired when he came in. 'It made me almost reach out to you,' he said. 'But I remembered just in time.' He then gave a half smile and added: 'What happened? Nothing too awful I hope.'

While I regained my composure, I told him about the protestors at the conference venue and how the train bombs had made my journey home hellish. I then found myself telling him – despite my intention to say nothing – how I'd seen the train bombers and experienced death-anxiety similar to a condemned prisoner walking to his execution.

Although part of my mind was screaming to keep quiet, I couldn't help asking if any of the people he'd reached out to in his life had ever subsequently experienced uncanny insights into other people's feelings.

As the question left my lips, I blamed my disturbed night for having asked it, but, nonetheless, found I was holding my breath while I waited for an answer.

His brow furrowing, he said: 'Now you mention it, there have been one or two instances,' and he told me how one of his lecturers was a man called Doctor Okocha, who he described as a brilliant thinker specialising in Continental philosophy – particularly Heidegger, Sartre and Nietzsche. Gian Paolo then said he had grown close to Okocha since the first year of university and hadn't been able to stop himself reaching out to him quite a few times.

'I know it's given him funny visions,' he continued, 'because a couple of times I've caught him rubbing his eyes and shaking his head.' Gian Paolo then told me he'd asked Dr Okocha what the matter was once when they were having tea in the college coffee bar and the lecturer said he'd just imagined seeing a large globe floating across the room, opening a black hole in its underside and dropping out dark blobs.

'But you say he also experienced other people's feelings?' I said.

'Yes,' Gian Paolo said, and he explained how Doctor Okocha had told him a couple of years ago about feeling guilty for not having acted to prevent the suicide of one of his students who had become depressed. When Gian Paolo asked how he could possibly blame himself when the person in question had done such a brilliant job of keeping up a front of jolliness to everyone, Doctor Okocha said the student had been in a tutorial with him on the day she took her overdose and he'd felt a wave of awful hopelessness as he looked at her and imagined a figure preparing to swan-dive into an abyss.

Gian Paolo thought at the time it sounded like a basic 'there' experience and resolved to watch out for anything else Doctor Okocha might say. But months passed without him volunteering anything so Gian Paolo wrote off the contact with the suicide student as a one-off.

Then, last year, Doctor Okocha had told him how he'd been having tea with a male student a few weeks previously when a feeling of passionate yearning had suddenly filled him and the student's body had momentarily appeared to be naked, sporting a powerful erection.

According to Gian Paolo, it was only because he had been gossiping at the time with Okocha about how that particular student was rumoured to be madly in love with the lecturer that he mentioned the experience. Gian Paolo then said: 'I remember being quite relieved to hear Dr Okocha had made some sort of "there" connection because of something other than death.'

'Oh? Why do you say that?' I said.

'What – about death?'

'Yes.'

'Because my first experience of "there" with Renata was when her friend Sue died,' Gian Paolo said. 'And then there was the suicide student – plus, the only other time someone I'd reached out to told me about a "there" experience was a girl whose sister had been expecting a baby but it died twenty-five weeks into the pregnancy.'

'I see. So there's death again.'

'Yes,' Gian Paolo said, then he told me the girl in question was a highly gifted languages student he used to talk to in the college gym. Her name was Sara and she had left university a couple of years ago after graduating but, just before she went, she told him about a visit she'd made to her sister to offer emotional support on the loss of her baby. The tragedy had come to light when the sister had been for a scan and it had shown the baby was dead in the womb.

According to Gian Paolo, Sara had visited expecting to find her sister grief-stricken, but when she sat down and put an arm round her, all she picked up from her crying was a vivid feeling of guilt.

Sara had also told Gian Paolo how, during the visit, she experienced a sudden vision where the Old Bailey statue of justice appeared standing life-size behind her sister and that, once she'd recovered from the shock of the image, she somehow became convinced her sister's sobs really were more about guilt than sorrow. So she asked her sister if she felt the baby's death had been her fault in some way.

To Sara's amazement, her sister confessed she hadn't wanted the baby because she'd become full of doubts early in the pregnancy about whether she really wanted her husband to be the father of her children and be tied to him for life.

Apparently she'd married him when they were barely out of their teenage years and, the further the pregnancy had progressed, the more decided she'd become it would be a big mistake to settle with him – in fact, she'd ended up wishing she'd had a termination.

A problem with oxygen supply to the foetus had made the wish come true, and then, although the sister was relieved, she also felt incredibly guilty and selfish.

When Gian Paolo finished telling me the story, he yawned and asked if I thought Sara's and Doctor Okocha's experiences mirrored my one with the bombers.

Feeling disconcerted, I said: 'Yes, they have some common elements. But let's leave that now. You still haven't told me why you had such an awful time yesterday.'

'God, no! I'd forgotten,' Gian Paolo said, then, checking his watch, he added: 'Have we still got time?'

'Of course. Tell me everything,' I said.

Shifting his position and crossing his legs, he told me how he'd been to see the band because when he was feeling 'lovey', going to a concert was the best way not only to look at, but actually make physical contact with, people and talk to them.

He then described how, on Monday night, he'd been dancing and chatting with people at the concert when the 'lovey' feeling started working itself to a crescendo. In line with the usual pattern, the people he was 'lovey' towards became happier and energised because they felt somewhere inside them a fellow human was truly appreciating the miracle of their existence.

'It's at this point I usually get weary,' he continued, then he explained how in the small hours of Tuesday morning, after the concert, he didn't feel tired at all, but highly invigorated, as if he was moving to another level of 'lovey'.

He then described how he started to feel like he was being driven by an irresistible urge to spell out to the whole planet precisely how much he was in love with it and how ready he was to act as a channel to bring as much creative, living force into the world as he could.

Then he told me he left the concert venue and walked round Cambridge looking at the stars and, after walking for ages, he found himself out of town on one of the meadowy hills that buffer the developed land from the farm fields.

The moon was low in the sky, shining with such intense light it was too bright to look at for long. The glow it gave the landscape gave him the feeling he was walking in a magic world and he felt wonderfully elated as he made his way onto a roughly beaten track running through wild grass at the top of a ridge.

The air was warm, even though the sky was perfectly clear, making the stars look like an illustration in an astronomy book. He then told me he remembered gazing up at the Plough just as a helicopter began flying overhead, filling the night with its engine drone and blade chugging.

Then, when the chugging was gone and only a faint drone remained, Gian Paolo's gaze was caught by a flock of flapping silhouettes spiralling across the moon and he remembered wondering whether the creatures were bats or starlings.

The helicopter still droning far away, he then moved under a tree and took off all his clothes. According to Gian Paolo, the cool, bristling texture of the grass under his feet and breath of night-time air on his body made him feel so alive and in touch with the universe, he just stood there for ages looking at the stars, his spirit drifting for what seemed an eternity.

Eventually, he became satiated with the sky and returned his attention to the moon and the vast blue-grey patches on its surface but its brightness forced him to look away again.

Then, as he continued to describe his night on the hill and how his mind had tried to soak up everything the stars could tell him, I became so fixed on the odd mix of self-aggrandising spirituality and masturbatory eroticism of his story, I forgot to apply any psychoanalytical interpretation to what he was saying. So, when he suddenly hid his face in his hands and started to cry, my first thought was to comfort him with an arm round the shoulders and I rose from my seat.

Fortunately, my years of analysis enabled me to check my reaction quickly and I sat back down before he even noticed I'd moved and I said: 'This is a safe environment, Gian Paolo. Take as much time as you like.'

Uncovering his face, Gian Paolo tried to smile through watery eyes and said: 'I know I'm just being silly. But sometimes I can't bear how so much love and creativity just comes up against dumb brutishness.'

'Yes, the world can be a harsh place,' I said, trying to avoid sounding weary. 'But what happened exactly? Was it something sexual?'

'God no! Far from it,' he said and drew up his legs so he could hug himself into a ball. He then quietly rocked for a while with his chin on his knees and, feeling it was down to me to break the silence, I was on the point of prompting him again to explain what had taken place when my gaze was suddenly arrested by a naked man sitting in the far corner with his head slumped back against the wall, his eyes closed.

The suddenness of the vision sent a shock through me, chilling my skin. Then the naked man disappeared leaving me fighting to control my breathing as Gian Paolo said: 'I don't know why I didn't hear them, but two policemen suddenly came out from behind the tree and seized my arms.

'I was so shocked; I couldn't speak when they asked who I was and what I was doing.'

Beginning to weep again, he added: 'I'd just been feeling more connected with the universe than ever in my whole life then I had two morons grabbing me and making me ashamed of my nakedness. It's too much.' He then hid his face again and sobbed freely.

The abandon in his crying was like that of an early school-years child and I wondered if it held a clue to the aetiology of his illness since it had been around this period he had first 'shared' himself with Renata.

After waiting a minute, I tried to bring him out of his sobbing by asking how on Earth the police had found him in such a remote place at that time of night.

Wiping his eyes with his shirtsleeves, he said: 'What?', his face puzzled, as if he was seeing me for the first time.

'I asked how the policemen found you under your tree,' I said.

Giving his eyes a final rub, he recounted how the police told him to put on his underpants, then handcuffed him, picked up the rest of his clothes and took him to a police car parked at the bottom of the hill.

'When they started questioning me at the police station, I could tell they thought I was a burglar,' he said. Then he explained they'd chased a housebreaker onto the hill earlier that night and tried to track him down using the thermal-imaging camera in their helicopter, and they thought Gian Paolo was him.

'But when I could give them every detail of the gig and they saw I had nothing in my pockets,' he continued, 'they started to think I was just a spaced-out student and switched to asking me about drugs.'

He then told me how the police just kept asking him over and over who he was and where he lived, then they left him sitting in a reception room – in just his pants – while the sergeant telephoned a prosecutor for advice on whether Gian Paolo could be charged with indecent exposure.

The thought of being in court for a sexual offence had made Gian Paolo's whole insides shrivel, he told me, but he could tell from the phone conversation the sergeant was unable to make the charge since no other person had been present on the hill and he caught the disappointment in the sergeant's eyes when he glanced up.

He then noticed the sergeant's gaze stray to his body, which made him scared he was in danger of sexual abuse; and this fear seemed close to realisation when the sergeant had him locked up in a cell without any clothes at all for what he said would just be a few minutes but actually ended up being ten hours, during which he repeatedly peered in through the cell's spy-window.

'Every time he looked in, his face looked really red and I could hear a kind of jig-jig rattling of his keys,' he said. 'And it just went on all night.'

Looking away, I managed to hide my smile at his failure to see the sergeant had obviously been using him as material for a prolonged masturbation session. 'But still,' I said. 'Ten hours is an awfully long time!'

'I know. It was gone two in the afternoon when I got out and I hadn't slept a wink,' Gian Paolo said. 'The blankets were just so filthy.'

'But are they allowed to hold you so long when they can't charge you?' I said.

Gian Paolo shrugged.

'Perhaps you should get advice about making a complaint,' I said. 'Especially if you think the sergeant had some sort of sexual motive.'

Sighing, Gian Paolo said: 'I think I'd sooner just forget about it. It's not worth the fuss.'

'But you seem so upset,' I said. 'Perhaps you'd feel better if you at least had an apology.'

'From the police?' Gian Paolo said with a half-smile. 'That'll be the day.' Then uncurling and putting his feet back on the floor, he added: 'Besides, it's not the sergeant that upset me. It's the shock of being grabbed when I was so deep in meditation.'

'Yes,' I said. 'What was the meditation about?'

'Well,' he said. 'It was like I was really connected, you know. Like I was receiving guidance no one's ever had before.'

'I see,' I said. 'And what sort of guidance were you getting?'

Gian Paolo smiled again and said he knew it sounded funny, but he truly felt the universe had been showing him how the distance to the moon and stars was immaterial to a spirit. How space was completely transcended by thought: that if a mind filled itself with thoughts of a particular place, then that location became immediately close at hand, even if it was millions of miles away.

'It's like if you think intimately about someone for a while, they become the most immediate person in your life,' he said, 'and it doesn't matter if they're on the other side of the world.'

He then suggested if a person was standing on a crowded train, squeezed in by dozens of commuters while thinking about a particular individual, as far as the person's spirit was concerned, that somebody was here and now and the whole crowd was nowhere. 'Well, the same thing applies to God and the universe,' he continued. 'It can simultaneously be in billions of parts at once, simply by having concern for those parts.'

'I see,' I said. 'But isn't it accepted that God is everywhere?'

'No, I don't think it is,' he said. 'I think accepted wisdom says God is all-powerful and everywhere purely in terms of the world and humanity.' He then explained how in his meditation on the hill he'd sought guidance on whether all life, love, truth and beauty were concentrated in Man's little corner of creation or whether they existed elsewhere. Because, if they only came into material existence through Man, then God's sole concern in the whole of creation was Earth – which would mean it was severely limiting its omnipresence for some reason.

'And what was the outcome of your meditation?' I said.

'That's the problem,' he said, and he told me he'd just reached the point where he'd formed an understanding material life was present beyond the Milky Way when the police grabbed him.

'It was so frustrating because I felt I truly understood how the existence of life was actually quite banal,' he continued, then he said the natural corollary to this understanding was whether any other forms of life were capable of bringing love, truth and beauty into physical existence. But the police had pounced before he could really think about it.

'I see,' I said. 'That must have been quite a shock.'

'You're telling me!' he said and let out a deep sigh.

Checking my watch, I realised time was running out and I should probably turn the discussion away from police sergeants and meditations, and back to his family. I had a strong hunch that if I could find out more about his development as a boy, I'd find evidence of a sexual relationship between him and Renata that was the root of his problems and probably even accounted for the naked 'meditation' under the tree.

'Okay, Gian Paolo,' I said. 'I think we should forget yesterday for now and talk more about your upbringing.'

Gian Paolo crossed his legs and said: 'Okay. Which bit?'

Drawing a line on my pad, I said: 'I think we can put aside your father for now and concentrate on life at home.' I then asked what family life had been like.

'In what way exactly?'

'Generally,' I said. 'I mean, did you have a close relationship with your mother? Or perhaps she was too busy to spend much time with you?'

Gian Paolo gave a small shrug and said he thought she'd had a hell of a job to bring up three children on her own, and it wasn't made any easier by her having no qualifications or education beyond the basics.

'So it was a struggle?' I said.

'Oh yes!' he said. 'She found it very difficult to manage three of us. We were left pretty much to run wild.' He then said he thought she'd viewed all her children as being so clever and gifted they'd somehow grow into millionaire geniuses if she just put food in one end and wiped the other. According to Gian Paolo, her master plan had been that her children would keep her in luxury once they were rich – and, in Aldo's case, she'd struck lucky.

'But that's pure fluke,' he continued. 'She had no concept intelligence was only part of being a success,' and he explained how, although all the children had unusually high IQs, they had still been just empty-headed kids who needed training and wise guidance.

'But she must have been incredibly busy trying to run the home,' I said, and I suggested perhaps he couldn't blame her too much for failing to educate him in the way he thought he should have been, especially since she was young herself and probably unable to pass on much wisdom.

Gian Paolo laughed and said: 'You can say that again. The only wisdom she ever shared was on sex.'

'Really?' I said. 'What sort of wisdom?'

'Well, I think when she was about 30, she suddenly discovered sex could be fun,' he said. Then he explained how, at that time, she'd had a string of boyfriends who would come to pick her up for evenings out while Renata was left to look after him and Aldo.

'Some took one look at our crappy council house and never came back,' he said, adding others lasted a few weeks by trying to take an interest in the family, bringing the children chocolate and sweets.

'I can't believe your home was that bad, Gian Paolo,' I said. 'I seem to remember nineties social housing was actually pretty decent.'

Giving another shrug, Gian Paolo said he supposed their 1950s-built family house hadn't been too bad, even though the kitchen walls were just painted-over brick with no plaster and the bedroom air vents were crudely-cut holes with rusty grills open to the elements. But his family didn't make the best of the house, with its carpetless stairs and kitchen lino that was so grimy and tattered, bits of it used to stick to their feet when they walked round without slippers.

According to Gian Paolo, poor Alice didn't have much time or energy for housework and the place was usually a mess. The top of the fridge had a permanent layer of fluffy dust while the net curtain over the kitchen window was blackened where their three cats went in and out. The corners of their second-hand three-piece suite were ripped to shreds by the cats sharpening their claws, and every other tile round the fireplace was broken or missing.

'But you had heating and enough to eat?' I said.

'Oh yes. We had real gas fires you lit with a match,' he said. 'And we were fine until we started going to other people's houses.' He then explained that, like most kids, they didn't really take any notice of their home décor, but when they saw what school friends had, they started to realise they didn't live the same way.

'And what did your friends have exactly?' I said.

'Carpets on their stairs – and carpets everywhere else; fitting right up to the walls,' he said. 'And baths that didn't have a ring of rust around the plug, and central heating, and toilets with a lever instead of a rusty chain.'

'I see,' I said. 'But tell me about the sexual wisdom Alice passed on. When did that start?'

Gian Paolo stroked his chin and said the first incident he could recall was when he was about eight or nine and Alice was clearing junk from a bedroom cupboard and found a box with about fifty condoms in it. When she opened it, Aldo saw inside and asked what was in the little packets.

'I think she was embarrassed at first and said they were "French letters",' he said, 'which made me and Aldo laugh, because the packets were so small.' He then told how she'd rushed downstairs, promising she would be back in a moment.

Then, when she returned, she was carrying a rolling pin, which she tucked between her thighs, saying it represented a man's penis.

Seeming to enjoy the memory, Gian Paolo said he and Aldo looked at the size of the rolling pin, then at one another, and whispered simultaneously: 'blimey!'. Gian Paolo then explained Alice had tried to put one of the condoms on the rolling pin, but it was too thick and the condom split. She'd then tried with a couple more before accepting the rolling pin was perhaps oversized and she'd be better off explaining how condoms worked without the demonstration.

Grinning broadly, he said: 'I don't know why she was suddenly so candid,' then he told me her explanation included details of how their father bought condoms in big batches because he used one almost every night and that, although he might have performed sex frequently, it was just for a very short while and Gian Paolo and Aldo should do things differently when they grew up.

'And did she explain "differently"?' I said.

'Yes. She said we should take our time and give the woman loads of pleasure before having penetrative sex.'

'I see,' I said. 'And weren't you and Aldo a little young for that kind of advice?'

'I can't speak for Aldo, but I know I was,' he said. Then he explained all he'd really understood from what she said was he was supposed to develop a penis the size of a rolling pin and go on a mission to satisfy womankind!

Gian Paolo then let out a laugh and added: 'It was bizarre, looking back. But I think the truth is, she was so enthusiastic about what she was discovering, she couldn't help passing it on.'

'I see,' I said, then asked if there was anything he could remember from before that time that might have served to eroticise him so he at least understood some of what his mother was saying. 'Say doctors-and-nurses games with your sister?' I suggested.

Suddenly frowning, he said: 'What are you saying – that I was sexually-knowing too early because of Renata's and my special feelings?'

'I'm not saying anything,' I said. 'I'm asking if you had any other sex education before that given by your mother – which I think we both agree was a little premature.'

'Well, no, not in the formal sense,' he said.

'But perhaps informally, say in the form of games?'

Gian Paolo gave a sigh and said: 'Doesn't everybody have some kind of doctors-and-nurses games when they're children?'

'Pretty much,' I said. 'But we're only interested in you at the moment.' I then asked what was the earliest sexual experience he could remember.

Looking skyward, he said: 'I suppose I was quite precocious.' He then explained the first time he'd masturbated to orgasm was long before he was anywhere near puberty. It had come about when he had been playing with himself in the bath one day and wondered what would happen if he didn't stop and just let the pleasure keep building and building. Then, having found the confidence to let go, he discovered orgasm and managed to overcome the shock it gave him to keep on discovering it several times a day for weeks after that.

'I think the first time I realised there was a limit to pleasure,' he continued, 'was when I had to masturbate so hard one day to climax I actually got a sore on my penis.'

'And was your mother still bathing you at this stage?'

Sucking his lip a moment, he said: 'I can't really remember to be honest. I think if I went away and thought about it, I might be able to recall, but it's hard to put things from so long ago in order.'

I agreed and said it was only when we mapped memories onto major life events that we could draw up any sort of history. But if he thought about his first day at school – when he would have been four and a half – could he recall if it was before or after that he took part in games with his sister?

'I'd say it was after that.' Then, frowning with concentration, he added: 'Yes, it was definitely after that, but probably not much more than a year or two.'

'So you would have been somewhere around six?' I said.

Shifting in his seat, he said: 'It's like I say, I can't be too precise, but it probably is somewhere round there.'

'And what form did the games take?'

'Well, it was probably only once,' he continued, 'but the time I remember is when she got into a kind of show-me-yours-and-I'll-show-you-mine situation with me and Aldo.' He then said he thought the game must have been before his serious masturbation phase because he could remember her being much more interested in Aldo than him because he could make his erection wiggle.

'Every time he did it, she laughed her head off and I know if I'd been able to do it, I would have, just to make Renny laugh,' he said.

'And you think that may have been the only occasion Renata joined in such a game?' I said.

'It's the only one I can recall,' he said. 'But it's like I say, it's hard to remember.'

Checking my watch again, I said: 'Okay, I think we can call it a day for now.' Then I suggested we make an appointment for next week but, in between, he must find time every day to sit down in a darkened room with just a candle for light. Then he should put on some unobtrusive music – maybe jazz or a classical piece – and let it play at low volume over and over while he concentrated on the candle flame and allowed his thoughts to come in any order they liked.

'The point is to let your mind float and see what comes to the surface,' I said.

His face serious, he asked if he should keep a note of any thoughts relating to his childhood sexual experiences, or whether I was interested in other areas too.

'It's up to you if you want to make notes or not,' I said, then added he was a highly intelligent young man who could no doubt do a good job of capturing anything significant on paper. But the object of the exercise was to relax and not be afraid of his own thoughts. 'It's about overcoming the anxiety certain ideas or memories may be causing you,' I said.

* * *

After I'd arranged with the unit's receptionist for Gian Paolo to come back for a session on Wednesday of the following week and said goodbye to him, I returned to my office and picked up a voicemail on my desk phone. It was from a detective based at a nearby police station who wanted to make an appointment to interview me as soon as possible as part of the investigation into the bombing of the two trains the previous day.

Impressed with the promptness of the response to my call of yesterday, I rang straight back and agreed for the detective to come to my home at six o'clock that evening. I then opened up the document on my computer with Gian Paolo's case notes and typed: 'Events recalled relatively easily by Gian Paolo suggest he experienced his first orgasm long before puberty and plausibly between the ages of six and seven, at the time he originally experienced "there" with Renata.

'The details he provided of a childish sexual experimentation game with Renata are consistent with the everyday exploration games children play, but I believe it's probable he indulged in other experiments with his sister which are more inadmissible to consciousness and, consequently, beyond easy recollection.

'To begin the process of uncovering these memories, I've directed Gian Paolo to carry out regular free-thought exercises before our next session. I'm concerned, however, his high intelligence has enabled him to realise I'm probing the area of his and Renata's probable incest. He actually asked directly whether he should record memories of childish sex games with her and, although I tried to mask my interest in this precise area, I think he still has suspicions.

'If he is consciously aware my priority interest is what happened between him and Renata during the "there" experience when he was rising seven – and she rising twelve – it's likely the repression of the memory will be all the greater.'

I then recorded some ideas about why Gian Paolo might have wanted to be naked when he was meditating on the hill and what his inability to spot the police sergeant's use of him to masturbate might signify, after which I closed down his case notes document and went to my weekly planning meeting with the unit's deputy director.

The rest of the day passed without me being able to stop my mind frequently drifting to the idea I might be guilty of disrespecting Renata's memory by casting her as an emotionally disturbed child who had embarked on a sexual relationship with her favourite brother to try to prevent him leaving, in the same way she would have felt her father had done. But I managed to dismiss the idea as just one of those nagging doubts.

By five o'clock, I felt tired and was glad to have the interview with the detective as an excuse for leaving early.

After dropping into my deputy's office to say goodnight, I took a lift down to the basement car park and walked through the subterranean gloom to where my Audi was parked.

As I approached, I pressed my sonic key and watched with satisfaction as the driver door clicked open and the indicator lights flashed, warming the Audi's dark corner with soft orange and fleetingly revealing the car's sleek chassis.

Once behind the wheel, I settled into the low-slung seat and wrapped my fingers round the wheel's familiar, hard-leather sheath. Then, with my whole body relaxing, I turned the key and brought the powerful engine to life with its usual understated growl. An irresistible impulse then rose in me to rev the engine and I dabbed my toe on the gas pedal, enjoying each dab's deep bass note.

Flicking through the radio stations, I couldn't find one playing anything I liked so I took out a London Philharmonic recording of Dvorak's *New World Symphony* from the compartment by the gear stick and inserted it into the CD player. The orchestra launched straight into a thrilling *da-da da da da – dum da dudda dum*, and I pulled off, guiding the car out from its tight space against a pillar and along the dimly-lit driveway to a ramp with a swing barrier.

By the time I reached the dual carriageway leading to Cambridge, the London Philharmonic was thumping its kettle drums behind dramatically staccato strings while a host of violins washed over the sound, like vast waves breaking on rocks.

Seventy, eighty, eighty-eight miles an hour, and the Audi's engine remained at soft purr while I shot up the outside lane, checking my mirrors for anything that looked like a police car.

Within thirteen minutes of leaving my desk, I was coming off a roundabout onto the turning to the suburb containing my house and reduced my speed to thirty. Although the slow movement of the *New World Symphony* was relatively quiet, I turned down the CD volume and steered the car round a left-hand turn, onto a sloping road that rose up to the development of newly built houses where I lived.

At a point around two hundred metres up the slope, a perfectly bald young woman, wearing a brightly patterned dress and thick belt, dashed from the pavement into the road and bounced off the Audi's bonnet, landing somewhere to the rear of the car.

Slamming on the brakes, I made a screeching skid and came to a stop near the kerb. I then flung open the driver's door and

– making sure the handbrake was on – I hurried out of the Audi and back down the roadway. I could see the whole road down to the corner I'd just turned, but there was no sign of the young woman.

Quickly scanning the grass-verged pavements, I told myself she couldn't have gone far. Then I saw her: she was standing by a hood-style phone booth with the phone's receiver to her ear. When our eyes met, she hung up and put a hand to her ear as if she was signalling I should listen for something. Then she vanished.

Trembling all over, I made my way down the hill to the booth to look for some sign the woman really had been there and, picking up the receiver, I felt a scalding heat that made me drop it instantly. I then dabbed cautiously at the receiver's black plastic with my fingertips and discovered it was, in fact, a perfectly normal temperature.

Telling myself to calm down, I turned round and began walking back up to the car, noticing as I did so several faces had appeared in the windows of nearby houses.

When I was within fifty metres of the Audi, which still had its engine running, I saw a white-haired old lady peeking out between the living room curtains of the house directly in line with where the young woman had dashed from the pavement.

Filled with a sudden need to make sense of what had happened, I turned up the old lady's path and made my way to her doorstep. The hallway beyond the front door's glass panels looked dark and, as I pressed the doorbell and heard its chimes ring round the gloomy interior, I began to formulate questions to ask when the old lady opened.

But a minute passed with no sign of movement in the murky hall so I rang again. Then, after another minute of stillness, a thin man with a white rat clinging to his shoulder appeared from the gap running between the old lady's house and the one next door, and said: 'No point ringing that, my dear. She don't open to no one she don't know. Not even if they're a meals-on-wheels lady. If she don't know 'em, she just leaves 'em standin'. Like you are!'

The smoothness of the short hair across the bony head of the rat reminded me of the perfectly bald young woman and it took a conscious effort for me to stop looking at the rat's skull and focus on the man's unshaven face.

'Would she open to you?' I said.

The man let out an aggressive sounding laugh and said: 'What was it spooked you? A cat? Squirrel?'

'Excuse me?' I said.

'I don't blame you worryin' about a lovely car like that. Must've cost a few bob!' he said.

Controlling my voice as best I could, I asked if he'd seen what had happened just before I hit my brakes. 'I mean,' I said, 'were you looking out the window by any chance?'

'No, my dear. I just had a nosey when I heard the squeal,' he said. 'I was expecting a thud as well, but it sounds like you missed whatever ran out.'

My gaze straying back to the rat, which was scrambling to improve its grip on the shoulder strap of the man's grubby vest, I said: 'So you didn't hear anything hit the car then?'

'Why, have you got a dent in her?' he said.

'I don't know, I haven't looked yet.'

'Ah, well! You'd better check it now,' he said. 'Expensive car like that. Your insurance will want witnesses.'

'Yes, I suppose so,' I said and, taking out a business card from my jacket pocket, I handed it to the man – watched by rat eyes – and added: 'Do you think you could give this to the old lady and ask her to call if she saw what ran in front of me.'

Reading the card, the man gave another aggressive laugh and said: 'Psychiatrist, is it? I don't think she'll be wantin' anythin' to do with your clan, even if she did see somethin'. '

'Oh?' I said.

'No, not psychiatrists! Not her!'

A powerful desire to be home suddenly seized me and I suggested he could perhaps ask her what she saw on my behalf then give me a call with any information she gave him. 'I'd be most grateful,' I said.

Pocketing the card then adjusting his trousers round the crotch, the man leered at my bust, making my stomach turn, and said: 'I'll see what I can do, my dear.' And, with his hand still on his groin, he added: 'I'm pretty good at sticking my big oar in when I wants to.'

* * *

When I reached home, I had only twenty-five minutes before the detective was due to arrive and decided the pasta convenience meal I'd planned for dinner would need to wait until the interview was over.

Having gone upstairs to change out of my suit into lounging trousers and flip-flops, I went back down to the kitchen-diner and fed Sebastian before fixing myself a strong gin and tonic. Then, as I carried the drink to the living room and settled on the sofa, the memory of the bald woman returned and I took a large gulp of gin, willing my nerves to steady.

Leaning my head back, I allowed my thoughts to drift a while and soon found an image came to mind of Gian Paolo's eyes as they'd looked during our first session together. I could picture their deep blueness incredibly clearly and the thoughts behind them suddenly seemed perfectly readable. He was weighing me up: trying to gauge if I was suitable for something important he wanted to do.

Smiling at my own thoughts, I took another large sip of gin and told myself shock was making me fanciful and I should know better than to think I could tell what someone was thinking from their eyes. Of course, I could make a guess at someone's feelings by studying their face and body language, but everyday thoughts were impossible to read without verbal clues.

And then I remembered what Gian Paolo had said after the first session when I'd been setting up his next appointment: 'It's not an accident that it's you I've come to see.'

The words seemed worryingly foreboding, and I wondered if they had something to do with the mission he'd set himself to get humanity to change its relationship with God but I told myself not to think about that now and just relax, so I picked up a magazine and began flicking through its glossy fashion photos.

Sebastian came and rubbed himself against my legs meanwhile and, looking down at him, I said: 'Come on then, cutie pie,' and patted my lap. He jumped up and almost instantly arched his back, swearing at the empty space beside me while his claws dug through my trousers.

Glancing at the space then back to him, I said: 'What is it? What's the matter?' and tried to stroke his back. He turned quickly in a tight circle, growling, his fur on end.

Lifting him rudely to the floor and standing up, I said: 'Silly cat! What the hell's the matter?' Then, brushing his hairs from my trouser legs, I took another sip from my drink before placing it on the telephone table and beginning an agitated walk up and down between the window overlooking the street and the room's chimney breast.

As I walked, I saw Sebastian make his way to the kitchen-diner with his tail held low and scanned the sofa for clues as to what he might have been growling at. Then, after several minutes' pacing, during which I only paused to sip my drink, I saw a dark saloon car go slowly past the house before reversing back up the roadway and parking outside my gate. A large man with a round face and birthmark on one cheek then stepped out of the car and approached my front door.

Checking my watch, I thought how typical it was of a policeman to lack the manners that would have made him stay in his car and wait ten minutes for the appointed interview time in case his earliness was inconvenient.

As the doorbell sounded, I drained my drink then went into the kitchen-diner so I could put the empty glass by the sink. I then made my way up the hallway to the front door and saw how the policeman's round face suddenly pulled back from one of the glass panels when he saw me coming.

When I opened the door, he held up his identity card close to my face and said: 'Professor Small? I think you're expecting me?'

Guiding his hand back so I could read the name on the card, I said: 'Yes. Good evening, Detective Connard. Won't you come in.' I then guided him up the hallway, into the living room and offered him a drink.

'A cup of tea would be lovely. Thanks very much indeed,' he said and I went to the kitchen-diner to put the kettle on while he sat in an armchair and unpacked papers and a pen from his briefcase.

When I returned with his tea, he gave his thanks then invited me to take a seat on the sofa. So I plopped down and, placing my now refreshed gin and tonic on the coffee table, I said: 'I'm not sure I can really be of much help apart from confirming what I already said on the phone.'

Detective Connard smiled with just his mouth and said he had a few routine questions to put to me which were now part of a standard procedure for terrorism cases. 'Everyone who rings in is personally interviewed as soon as possible,' he said, 'so the incident team can build up a picture before the trail goes cold.'

Taking a sip from my drink, I said: 'Fine. Ask whatever you like.'

His pen poised over his paper, Connard said: 'Can I start by asking how you came to be in the attack area on Tuesday morning?'

'Well,' I said. 'I'd taken the 7:56 fast train from Cambridge and I arrived a little before five to nine.'

'And you're sure of the time?'

'Yes,' I said. 'I remember checking my watch with the platform clock as I got off.'

Connard made a note and said: 'Is that something you're in the habit of doing or was time particularly precious that morning?'

'No, it wasn't precious,' I said. 'In fact, I had over an hour to kill before the conference.'

'And once you got off the train, you left the station straightaway,' he said, 'without going into any shops or making any calls?'

'Yes, I went straight out,' I said. 'I remember I was going down to the underground taxi rank but when I saw what a beautiful morning it was, I decided to walk.'

Making another note, Connard said: 'And what route did you take?'

After thinking a moment, I recounted how I'd gone across the station forecourt onto the main road and turned left, then crossed over a side street about two hundred metres up before taking the next turning, which was the one containing the venue.

Connard pulled out a map of the station area from the papers on his ample knee and, tracing my route with his pen, he said: 'And where was it exactly you encountered the men you think were the bombers?'

I explained I'd just crossed the first side road and walked past a coffee shop when I saw them walking towards me. They were wearing rucksacks and sweating heavily under the arms and I said I supposed that had made them stand out.

Fixing his eyes on mine, Connard said the rucksacks must have made them stand out an awful lot for me not only to notice them among the crowds but for their faces actually to stay in my mind long enough to recognise their photos hours later on television. 'Are you sure the men you saw weren't just two different Arabs who looked like the ones in the photos?' he said.

'Yes, I'm sure it's the same two,' I said. 'I stopped when I saw them and watched them pass right by me. Their faces made a strong impression.'

Raising his eyebrows, he said: 'You actually stopped and watched them pass?'

'Yes.'

'I see,' he said. 'And did anyone else find their appearance so extraordinary they came to a halt?'

'Well, no, but it wasn't just the rucksacks,' I said, and explained how when I first saw them, I experienced an odd glitch with my vision that made me stop to rub my eyes. 'Then,' I continued, 'when the men were passing me, I felt… well… it's hard to explain!'

Connard urged me to go on, saying: 'You mustn't hold anything back. I have to be confident I have a one hundred per cent reliable account of what you saw.'

'Well…' I began again, then, letting out a brief laugh, I picked up my drink and said: 'I don't really know. It was such a strange thing.'

Blinking with concentration, Connard said: 'A kind of premonition perhaps?'

'Goodness, no! I don't believe in premonitions,' I said. 'No, it was more a kind of… well, a kind of feeling there was something odd about them.'

Making another note, Connard fixed me with his eyes once more and asked if I was sure that was all and whether I hadn't seen or heard something I didn't want to tell him.

'No. It's like I say, there was just something odd about them.'

'So odd it stopped you in your tracks?' he said.

'No,' I said. 'I stopped to rub my eyes because of my vision problem.'

Chewing the inside of his cheek, he scribbled something else on his paper then looked back up and said: 'You know it could be very serious if you chose to withhold something.'

A hint of exasperation rising in me, I said: 'I'm not withholding anything. If I wanted to do that, why would I bother ringing in the first place?'

Tilting his head, Connard said people often called in to feed the police misinformation about terror attacks – to try to throw them off the scent. 'Sometimes calls come from people who've actually been involved,' he said.

Starting to feel the effects of the gin on an empty stomach, I allowed myself a hearty laugh and said: 'I hope you're not implying I'm in some way connected with terrorism!'

Connard looked nettled and, pulling out another paper from the pile on his knee, he said: 'Well, professor, who knows?' Then he explained he had it on record my father – Martin Arthur Friedrich – had been a member of the Nazi party.

My exasperation rising several notches, I said: 'Excuse me! What in heaven's name has that got to do with anything?'

'Well, it could have some bearing,' he said. 'And I have to use all the information at my disposal in these cases.'

'Do you really!' I said. 'Well, let me tell you, I find it very wrong you've been snooping into some dusty old file just because I've had the decency to try to help.'

'It's like I say, professor,' he said. 'There are new procedures for terror cases. We have to check all the possibilities.'

'And you think it's possible I might be a Nazi and have teamed up with Islamic extremists to attack London?' I then huffed in annoyance and added: 'It's absurd! Really absurd!'

The faintest of smiles pulling at his mouth, Connard suggested it may well suit the agenda of a far-right group to have Islam and the West fall into deeper conflict so a neo-fascist party could step in and save the day with some extreme military solution. 'Not that I'm saying at this stage the men were definitely Muslim extremists, you understand,' he said.

Having caught his faint smile, I told myself he was goading me and I should avoid taking the bait, and said: 'I think you've been watching too much television, detective. The little neo-fascists knocking round today have nothing to do with the 1930s Nazis.' I then suggested the jumped-up little men who led today's far-right groups were just intellectually limited opportunists who desperately needed to compensate for their personal inadequacies by attaining some sort of power.

'But isn't that exactly what Hitler was?' Connard said.

I disagreed and told him he was falling into the trap of seeing Hitler the way he was popularly portrayed, but, in truth, he was a very bright man – and talented artist – who also possessed genuine visionary and leadership qualities and an almost superhuman strength of will.

'You sound quite an admirer, professor,' he said.

'That is also absurd, detective,' I said, and explained no one could admire a man who was responsible for the unspeakable horrors of the Holocaust, but there were plenty of young men in the 1930s who – like my father – were attracted to Nazi ideology because Hitler was a strong leader and seemed like he could deliver on his promise of a better world.

'A better world, or one without Jews?' said Connard, and I caught a note of anger in his voice.

'I'm afraid your history education is lacking again,' I said, then explained National Socialism didn't start with anti-Semitism but was actually based on the vision of a brave new world where strong, intelligent people ruled with the aim of ridding the planet of chaos and deprivation. Of course, Hitler believed the strong rulers must be Aryans and that led to the madness of his policies, but his underlying purpose was genuinely well intentioned. 'It's just his tactics were primitive,' I said.

'Primitive?' Connard said.

'Yes. I mean take the Bundeskinder programme as an example,' I said. 'What we know about genetics today shows it really was laughable to try to breed people like racehorses.'

'I see,' Connard said. 'But didn't the children from that programme actually turn out pretty well?'

Sitting back with my drink, I said no one really knew since all the children just disappeared – absorbed into normal society, and the one or two cases where people think someone who later rose to prominence might have been a Bundeskind didn't suggest they were anything very special. 'One is thought to have become a pop singer!' I said.

Then, taking another sip of gin, I explained science today could engineer people to have blonde hair and blue eyes easily and even give them a nil possibility of Downs syndrome and probably, in a few years, no chance of developing a variety of other diseases either. 'But the idea generations of healthy Aryans would somehow produce a better world just has no empirical basis,' I said.

'Anyway,' I continued, 'the thing is, my father – like many other young men of his generation – believed in the vision of a strong German people, leading the world to a brighter future, and signed up to National Socialism.'

I then explained how, as soon as my father saw what Nazism meant in reality – in terms of the death camps and crazy human-engineering experiments – he recanted every Nazi ideal he'd ever signed up to.

'When I was born nine years after the war,' I said, 'he brought me up to respect human life as sacred and always exercise my own moral judgement.' I then said how my father also told me he thought the French had got it right in the eighteenth century with a strand of moral philosophy he referred to as 'the code of *sensibilité*'.

'Sonnsy-biltay?' said Connard, sitting upright.

'*Sensibilité*,' I said. 'It was based on the idea a person should have *une âme sensible* – a sensitive soul – so they would make decisions based not just on reason and logic, but what *felt* humanly right.'

'And you think that's where the Nazis went wrong?' Connard said.

'God, yes! Don't you?'

Pausing a moment, Connard said he'd always thought the Nazi master plan had been doomed to failure because it stemmed from a megalomaniac madness rather than because it was built on too much reason.

'Well, you're misguided again, detective,' I said. 'The Nazis' ideological grounding was highly rational.' And I went on to explain many Nazis were extremely well read and took the philosopher Nietzsche at his word when he said there were no moral absolutes and if Man only had the courage of his convictions to pursue an act to the very end, then it would become morally right, even if the whole world saw it as wrong to begin with. 'And Hitler, with his faith in the will's supremacy, certainly believed that rationale,' I said.

'So you're saying Hitler should have been more sensitive,' Connard said.

I laughed out loud again, enjoying the muzzy gin feeling and said: 'I'm not sure that's quite what I'm driving at.' Then, seeing Connard's nettled look return, I quickly explained my point was the Nazi leadership should have taken note of the fact their soldiers were being physically sick with disgust as they carried out the leadership's orders and that should have brought about a realisation the 'final solution' was profoundly at odds with everything decent, healthy and human.

Poising his pen above the papers on his knee once more, Connard said: 'So your father stopped being a Nazi after the war?'

Sighing, I said: 'I thought I'd just explained, detective. My father was never a Nazi.' And I reiterated how he was simply a young man who believed in the fine words and ambitious ideals of the government of his day and gladly fought for his country in the belief that what he was doing would lead to a better world. 'As soon as he saw where Nazi thinking was really leading Germany, he ran from it in horror,' I said.

'And,' said Connard, 'that's when he decided French philosophy was actually better than Germany's – which must have been quite a concession for a German!'

Smiling at what I guessed from his tone was a joke, I said: 'Yes. My father used to say "the French understand morality better than anyone, they just lack the backbone to practise it".'

* * *

When Connard had finished his questions, I saw him to his car then quickly prepared my pasta dinner, which I ate at the table in the kitchen-diner. In order to dilute the alcohol in my system, I drank two large glasses of water with the meal then took a third up to bed with me.

As I sat propped against my pillows, with teeth brushed and make-up removed – and Sebastian nuzzling my hands with a wet nose – I felt a sudden urge for company and dialled Michael Servo's number from the bedside phone. His familiar answerphone message came on, informing callers he wasn't home, and I'd just begun leaving a message when he picked up and said: 'Yes, hello, Joy. I'm here – just screening.'

As we chatted, I found myself doing most of the talking and telling him about how I'd seen the suicide bombers yesterday and contacted the police, but was now regretting saying anything because of the bad taste I'd been left with from the interview with the detective.

I then told Michael all about the Gian Paolo Friedrich case and how I'd been experiencing odd visions ever since he'd come for his session on Monday morning, then I admitted

77

I was starting to wonder whether Gian Paolo's 'there' experience could possibly be real and if I'd been through something analogous with the suicide bombers.

'Goodness! It sounds like you're having quite a time of it,' Michael said.

'I know. I feel so on edge,' I said. 'When I got home this evening, I had two G and Ts before I'd even eaten anything.'

Michael laughed and said: 'Only two! Dreadful!' Then he suggested if I was seriously stressed, I should come with him and his partner Mo to Paris that weekend. 'We've booked a suite at the Georges Cinq,' he said. 'It looks fabulous on the website.' He then told me he and Mo had also booked tickets for the ten o'clock train to Paris Gare du Nord for the Saturday morning. 'So we should be nicely in time for lunch on the Champs-Élysées,' he said.

'Oh Michael! It does sound tempting,' I said. 'And I really could do with taking my mind off things. But it's probably too late to book a ticket for Saturday isn't it?'

'Nonsense!' he said, and explained there were always spaces in the train's first-class section on a Saturday and I shouldn't worry about a hotel since even if the Georges Cinq didn't have a room free, I could always stay in their suite. 'I'm sure there'll be a canapé-convertible in le salon,' he said.

'Canapé-convertible?' I said.

'A sofa bed, dear!' he said. 'Really! You must brush up on your français if you're coming.'

Smiling, I said his suite sounded very grand, but I didn't want to butt in on him and Mo if they'd planned a special occasion and wanted to be alone.

'Don't worry about that, my dear,' he said. 'We just booked it on a whim to celebrate Mo's promotion.'

'Promotion? Oh Michael!' I said. 'That's fantastic news. What's the job?'

'Speechwriter to the environment secretary.'

'No!'

'Yes. He's very excited about it,' Michael said. 'But he can give you all the details himself when we see you.' He then suggested I go online and book a first-class ticket for the 10 a.m. fast train and let him know if I couldn't find a hotel room for Saturday and Sunday night so he could speak to the Georges Cinq about a canapé-convertible.

'You're staying two nights then?' I said.

'Yes, we've booked to come back Monday afternoon, on the three-thirty,' he said.

Making a snap decision, I said: 'Okay. I'll clear my Monday meetings and book the day off then get back to you when I'm set.' I then said goodbye, hurried to my study and powered up the laptop so I could buy a ticket to Paris and look forward to forgetting about the last three days' stresses.

Come Fly with Me

Three days later and Michael, his partner Mo and I were strolling in Saturday afternoon sunshine on the Champs-Élysées, looking for a restaurant for lunch.

My strange experiences with Gian Paolo Friedrich and the annoying conversation with the detective seemed far away as we strolled past cafés with black-waistcoated waiters hurrying to and fro between the café interiors and pavement seating, clearing glasses and dressing tables.

Tempting as several places looked, we'd enjoyed an unusually large breakfast on the train into Paris, so none of us particularly had an appetite and we decided we would just keep walking until we felt genuinely hungry.

Turning up a side street past a tabac where a long queue of Parisians was spilling out onto the pavement to buy tickets for La Loterie, we headed south with the sun on our faces, admiring the wrought ironwork railings fronting the little balconies of the apartment blocks.

Pausing to look at the stonework façade of one nineteenth-century building, Michael said: 'Isn't that beautiful. It's very similar to the porticoes of our hotel.' And, smiling at Mo, he added: 'It must have taken some hairy-armed workman a week to carve one block.'

Mo and I added our admiration to Michael's and he said: 'It's a shame you couldn't get in at the Georges Cinq, Joy – it really is fabulous.'

'No, I'm fine, really,' I said. 'My place is incredibly comfortable – and so pretty.'

Patting my hand, Michael said: 'Well, as long as you've got everything you need, my dear.' Then we carried on up the street, drinking in the beauty of old sandy walls with their colourful shop-front canopies and blue-enamelled plaques, showing the street names and arrondissement number.

As we neared a busy crossroads, I looked up at some carvings under the eaves of a six-storey building when my eye was suddenly caught by a football-sized blob of dark fur, flashing past the building's balconies in a twisting fall. I managed to discern the blob had frantically scrambling legs just as it hit heavily against the green-cross sign of a chemist shop and was deflected into a somersaulting arc towards the pavement, where it landed like a wet rag.

'Oh my God! I think it's a cat,' I said turning to Michael and Mo and gesturing to the opposite pavement. Mo immediately nipped through a gap in the traffic to reach the other pavement while Michael said: 'What is it? What's the matter?'

'I think a cat has just fallen from one of those balconies,' I said, pointing across the road.

Watching Mo take up a squatting position beside the cat, Michael said: 'Well, I shouldn't think it's survived that – not unless it really does have nine lives!'

Steering Michael across the road by his arm, I said: 'It gave the chemist sign an almighty thump – poor thing!'

Arrived alongside Mo, I could see the cat's body was shuddering in spasm and a small pool of blood had collected beneath the horrendous abdominal wound that had left its hindquarters almost severed from the rest of the body. Mo was pressing his hand over the face of the animal and, looking up at us, he said: 'It should only take a few seconds. His breathing's already very weak.'

Realising Mo was suffocating the cat, I said: 'Are you sure we shouldn't get it to a vet? Perhaps something can be done.'

Mo pulled a sympathetic face and said: 'I saw his eyes, Joy. He's in a terrible state. It would be wrong to prolong it.'

Squatting beside Mo and examining the gaping wound in the cat's abdomen, Michael said: 'He's right, Joy. And there probably isn't a vet for miles. You know what the French are like for animal welfare!'

Feeling my stomach turn, I looked away and said: 'I suppose so. But it seems wrong to put a cat to sleep without telling the owner.' I then looked up to see if I could work out which balcony the cat had fallen from. Pedestrians continued to pass by, meanwhile, with only the merest of glances at Mo with his shaven head bent over the cat's broken body.

Then, after a few seconds of scanning balconies, I returned my gaze to the scene of the little tragedy and said to Michael: 'Are you sure it's not hurting him – you prodding like that.'

'No. He can't feel a thing below the thoracic area: the whole lower body's paralysed. If he's feeling pain, it's in the front limbs, which I would say both have fractures.'

Taking a closer look at the cat, whose convulsive trembling had now stopped, I said: 'How can you be so sure about the pain?'

Michael rose from his squat and, taking out a tissue to wipe his hands, he said: 'When you've cut up as many mice as I have, my dear, you just get to know.' We both then watched the cat come to perfect stillness and, a moment later, Mo turned to look up at us, his hazel eyes watery behind his spectacles. 'I think he's gone now,' he said. He then turned back and, keeping his hand pressed to the cat's face, he added: 'I'll just make sure though.'

I was on the point of saying it was very cruel of the cat's owner to have allowed such an accident to happen when a thin, young woman with cropped, bleach-blonde hair emerged from the building's heavy street door and, spotting the cat, said: 'Minou! Minou! Qu'est-ce que t'as fait cette fois?'

Noticing her approach, Mo removed his hand and said to Michael: 'Don't tell her about the pain thing. Just say we kept it company while it died.'

Michael nodded and, turning to the woman, he explained in French the cat had sustained terrible injuries from its fall and hadn't survived long after hitting the pavement.

Looking flushed, the woman approached the cat and bent down as if she was going to pick it up, then, noticing the blood and gaping wound, she stopped, turned back to Michael and asked if much time had passed since the fall. Michael said only one or two minutes and the woman began a gabbling explanation about how the cat had developed a habit when it first came to live with her six months ago of walking on the balcony handrail of her fifth-floor apartment and she feared one day it would fall off so she'd been living since Christmas without opening any windows. But today a friend had come to visit and – because it was a warm afternoon – he had unlocked the windows without her knowing and it was only a few seconds ago she'd realised the cat was gone and, seeing the window open, she'd guessed what had happened.

Michael smiled consolingly and asked if she had anything she could wrap the cat up in – to make it ready for burial.

The woman looked puzzled and said: ' "L'enterrement"?'

Turning to me with a look of uncertainty, Michael said: 'Enterrement is right for burial, isn't it?'

I confirmed it was then suggested to the woman she would probably want to conduct some sort of little funeral rite for the cat since it had been her pet for the last six months. The suggestion made the woman smile and, as she wiped her palms against the thighs of her lightweight dress I saw the black triangle of her pubic hair and outline of her breasts and realised she was completely naked under the garment – apart from her open-toed sandals and a silver crucifix on a neck chain.

The woman then asked if we would mind watching over the body while she went back upstairs to fetch an old bed sheet. As she spoke, I noticed thick droplets of perspiration coating the skin above the undone buttons of her dress front and, breathing in the fresh-pheromone scent of her body, it suddenly occurred to me she'd probably been having sex when the cat had fallen.

Glancing up to one of the fifth-floor balconies, I saw a bare-chested man leaning out and looking down at us, and, pointing towards him, I asked the woman if that was her balcony. She followed my point and confirmed the leaning man was her friend. Then her face becoming serious, she said she did not have a garden like English people so would not be burying the cat, but she would wrap it up carefully in a sheet before putting it in the bin then light a candle for its soul in church.

Eyeing her crucifix, I said, if she was Catholic, she would understand animals didn't have souls, but a little prayer for the poor creature could do no harm.

To stop a silence developing, Michael said the cat had died quickly from its fall and a shock-induced paralysis had prevented it feeling anything beyond very minor pain, generated by multiple fractures in the anterior limbs.

The woman smiled weakly at Michael and said: 'You are docteur of maid-san?'

Exchanging a quick glance with me, Michael replied: 'Doctor yes, but not medicine. I'm a geneticist.'

The woman pulled a puzzled face so Michael translated what he'd said.

'Ah! Yes. I yunderrz-tand.' She then glanced down at the cat and added: 'Sank you for ev'ry-fing. I am 'appee my minou 'ave you to 'elp 'eem die.' Michael smiled sympathetically again and, suddenly looking tearful, the girl spun round, ran back through the building's street door and hurried up to her fifth-floor apartment.

When she reappeared two minutes later, she was carrying a loosely folded bed sheet and a two-litre bottle of water. She then placed the bottle beside the cat and performed sizing-up motions with the sheet to work out how best to wrap it.

Spotting her difficulty, Mo gently took the sheet from her and swept the cat up in one swift movement. He then rolled up the dangling sheet ends to form a bundle and said to the woman: 'Where would you like me to put it?'

Holding the street door open, the woman beckoned Mo into a small courtyard with a rack of pigeon holes for post on one side and a line of wheelie bins on the other. She then lifted the lid of one of the bins, saw it was full, and opened the one next to it. Then she gestured to the interior and said the cat could go in.

Mo drew near and, looking wistful, he said: 'Did he have a name – your cat?'

Tilting her head, the woman said: 'Excuse me?'

'A name. Did the cat have a name?' Mo said and raised the bundle towards her.

'Oh yez. Za name,' said the woman, ''Eez name whazz Berthe.''

Laying the bundle in the bin, Mo said: 'Berthe is a nice name. But isn't it for a girl?'

'Yez, 'ee whazz a femelle.'

Mo broke into a smile and watched the woman close the lid before following her back out onto the pavement, where she removed the top from the water bottle and tipped it over the pool of blood. She then used the sole of her sandal to try to wipe away the bloody liquid and succeeded only in making the pavement look like a road-accident scene.

After we'd said our goodbyes and shook hands with the young woman, we took the next turning right and headed west for a few blocks until we came to a five-street junction with cafés on four of its corners. The pavement area of the furthest café was bathed in sunshine so we made our way across the busy junction and took a table under the front section of the green awning bearing the café's name: Café Anglais.

As we settled into our wicker seats, Mo said: 'I have to say I've got even less appetite now.'

'Yes, I know what you mean,' I said. 'The sight of blood certainly hits you in the stomach, even if it is just an animal's.'

Scanning round for a waiter, Michael said: 'I don't know, I feel quite peckish.' Then he said he could make do with a few peanuts, as long as the café had a claret with plenty of body to fill the gap. 'Maybe a Châteauneuf-du-Pape,' he said.

Looking at the carte des vins, Mo said: 'Yes, I could do with a drink. We can eat later.'

'Yes, perhaps the plan should be we have a few drinks and nibbles here then go back to the hotels,' said Michael. 'Then we can freshen up properly for dinner.'

I agreed with Michael's plan as a muscular young waiter with a wispy beard arrived to take our order: Châteauneuf-du-Pape, peanuts, bread and olives. The waiter then returned to the café's interior with Michael watching his rear while Mo examined his fingernails and said: 'It's a shame really, she seemed quite a sweet little thing.'

Turning to Mo, Michael said: 'Don't tell me you took a shine to the trollop with no underwear?'

Mo gave a brief laugh and said: 'Not the woman – the cat.'

Slipping off a mule so I could massage the ball of my foot, I said: 'Yes, I heard her say it was "a femelle"! – which was a bit confusing after she'd been calling it "he" all the time.'

'Yes. She said its name was Berthe, which I knew was a girl's name because of Flaubert's novel, *Madame Bovary*,' Mo said. 'Madame Bovary calls her daughter Berthe.'

'Flaubert?' said Michael. 'I thought you read English literature at college.'

'I did. It's just we were taught you couldn't possibly study nineteenth-century English writing without reading *Madame Bovary*,' said Mo.

Rearranging the ashtray and cruet on the aluminium tabletop, Michael said: 'Well, I hope Flaubert's Berthe ended better than the cat!'

Mo shook his head and said: ''Fraid not. She was an even more unfortunate soul than the kitty.'

Laying a hand on Mo's forearm, Michael said: 'For goodness' sake, don't start about cat souls or Joy'll tell you off, like the trollop!'

Removing my other mule, I said: 'I didn't tell her off, Michael. I simply reminded her, as a Catholic, she couldn't pray for a cat's soul because it doesn't have one.'

Mo took a hanky from his pocket and polished the lenses of his spectacles, saying it was interesting I said that since it reminded him of a newspaper interview he'd once read with a Catholic cardinal who was speaking out against abortion and euthanasia but said in the same article he'd had his dog put down because it was old and suffering. 'It struck me as a funny kind of double standard,' Mo said.

Continuing to massage the ache in my foot, I said I could see his point then explained it was, however, only right for a human being – as the steward of creation – to take the decision to put an animal without an immortal soul to sleep when it was perpetually suffering. A human being, on the other hand, does have a soul and, therefore, the capacity to have Jesus in his or her heart: so it can only be God who decides when that life should end.

Toying with the carte des vins, Mo said: 'Yes, it makes perfect sense put like that.'

Slipping my foot back into its mule, I said: 'Perfect sense, but you don't agree one bit!'

Raising his hand, Michael said: 'Hold on! Friends should never do religion or politics!'

'Come, Michael,' I said. 'We're sophisticated people. I know Mo is a Buddhist.' I then added just because we believed different things, we could still respect each other's point of view. 'And I'm curious to know what Buddhists say about mercy killing after the cat thing.'

'Yes, you were very impressive, sweetness – even more butch than usual,' Michael said, twinkling at Mo. 'But, as an atheist, I'm never too comfortable with religious explanations for why people do things.'

'Well, perhaps you can make an exception here,' I said and – my eye caught momentarily by a passing group of Americans – I explained I was keen to research a little more about different religions to help me with the religious mania element of the Gian Paolo Friedrich case.

Throwing me a stern look, Michael said: 'Oh, Joy! I thought you were going to forget all about that – the strange hallucinations and everything.'

'I didn't say I'd had hallucinations,' I said, folding my arms. 'What I actually said was I experienced fleeting visions, and maybe an imagined auditory perception. But I'm fine now.' I then urged Mo to explain the Buddhist thinking on euthanasia, saying what he could tell me now might save me ploughing through too many textbooks next week.

After a quick glance at Michael, Mo said: 'Well, I don't know if you're aware, but Buddhist thinking is very fragmented, so I can only really tell you what I believe.'

I smiled and said: 'Don't worry. I won't hold you accountable. I'm just looking for a starting point.'

Noticing the waiter approaching our table with a tray, Mo said if he was to try to explain what happened with the cat, he'd say the Buddhist view was that, although all life is precious, human beings have a duty to show kindness to animals.

'I see,' I said, 'so you believe animals have souls but you have the right to put them to sleep if it's a question of mercy.'

'Well, not exactly,' Mo said and, leaning back while the waiter half-filled our glasses with Châteauneuf-du-Pape, he added: 'You see, we don't believe anything has a soul as such – just a ray of life.' He then went on to explain the Buddhist discussion group he belonged to saw life as being something that had existed since the beginning of time – that couldn't be created or destroyed. Everlastingly everywhere, it simply chose at certain moments to make itself manifest on Earth.

'Think of it like the sun,' he said. 'It's continually out there shining, but it's only when there's a break in the clouds we get a sunbeam.'

Warming to his explanation, he then said this view meant all living things were interconnected because, like the sunbeams, we were all rays from the same source and, breaking off a moment to glance again at Michael – who was now asking the waiter about gay bars in the quartier – he continued by suggesting I could understand what that interconnectivity meant if I thought about the exact nature of what it was that looks out through my eyes – the thing I thought of as being my self, or 'I'.

'Now, Buddhists realise what looks out through your eyes is in fact the same perfectly clear and eternal consciousness that looks out of my eyes and those of every other human being that ever lived,' he continued. 'An eternal, universal consciousness.'

'That could be true, but I think you're placing too much emphasis on consciousness,' I said. 'To my mind, consciousness is simply what Freud said: "a kind of sensory organ that perceives data arising from elsewhere".'

Mo smiled and said that might hold water in psychiatry circles, but the consciousness, or *I*, we were talking about wasn't simply a sensory organ but actually what I – and everybody else – thought of as their individual self.

Sitting back in my chair with a slightly giddy feeling, I said: 'Well, it's an interesting idea, but I don't see why it puts you so at odds with the cardinal and the sanctity of human life.'

Mo looked thoughtful and said he supposed it was because the idea of God as universal consciousness rather than a paternalistic deity ruling from a throne meant individuals were entirely free to make judgements about abortion or their own death.

'Hang on!' I said, then argued his idea of a source we all sprang from still meant there was some kind of entity greater than Man and that must therefore be better placed to make life and death decisions.

Taking another glance at Michael, who was now paying the waiter, including a hefty tip, Mo said: 'You've got me there, Joy. I can't answer. But I can definitely take it up with my discussion group.' He then took another sip of his wine and fell into silence, cradling his glass in his palm.

As the waiter gave his thanks and walked away, Michael turned to Mo and me and said: 'Well, I'm glad you two have come up for air. I was beginning to wonder if I should order absinthe and a chessboard!'

I smiled and said: 'Shouldn't we be on the Left Bank for that?'

Michael nodded at one of the turnings and said: 'Now you mention it, I'm pretty sure if we headed down there we could be across the river in a few minutes.'

Sitting back with an olive, I said: 'Please, Michael, I'm joking. No more walking; this is a perfectly nice spot.'

'Yes,' said Michael, 'and according to the waiter, there's a lively gay scene just round the corner; so, if we feel like partying later...'

'Really, Michael!' I said. 'I don't know where you get the energy.'

Popping a ball of bread into his mouth, Mo said: 'I'm sure if we had a little nap before dinner we could all recharge our batteries.'

91

Mo turned out to be right and, after a superb dinner at a tucked-away restaurant near the Bois de Boulogne, we went to a club and ended up drinking until the small hours. The Sunday then drifted by in similar fashion with the three of us waking on Monday with real hangovers, but we still managed to fit in some designer-label shopping before catching the mid-afternoon train back to London.

By Monday night, the excitement of the trip and exertion of the journey home had left me nicely weary and I slept so soundly back in my own bed that I woke fully rested next morning, ready for the return to work.

After catching up on emails in my office, I worked more on the critique I'd begun the previous week of lengthy proposals Department of Health officials had drafted concerning a five-year national training programme for psychotherapists. Then, as I began to write conclusions for the critique, I realised I needed to research further into Europe-wide best training practice, so I minimised the document on my PC and opened the web browser.

But instead of entering 'psychotherapy training' in the search, I found myself searching for information on world religions and soon landed on a useful summary paper giving a brief explanation of every known religion – including one with six million adherents called Bahá'í, which I'd never heard of before.

As I read more of the paper, I saw its explanation of Buddhism largely accorded with what Mo had told me during our Café Anglais discussion. I then scanned the other religions before printing off a hard copy to take home, to read in bed, after which I searched the medical sites in my favourites list for documents on other countries' approaches to psychotherapy training.

It wasn't until the next morning, however, I was able to put the finishing touches to the critique and circulate it to my deputy and team leaders for comment. Then, as soon as I'd sent the circulating email, I headed up the corridor to my deputy's office to give her a brief outline of the counter-proposals I'd made – to see whether or not she'd support them – but she wasn't at her desk.

Disappointed at not being able to talk things through there and then, I decided I needed a coffee and had just started making my way to the lifts down to the staff canteen, when I was suddenly stopped in my tracks by an extraordinary sound:

'*Love me tender, love me true…*'

Drifting up the corridor from the psychiatric unit's reception was a voice of such perfect beauty it held me frozen mid-stride while a thick, liquid feeling poured out of a hole at the very centre of me.

'*All my dreams fulfil. For my darling, I love you…*'

As the song continued, I unfroze and found myself able to walk on, but only in the direction of the voice.

Turning right up the reception corridor, my mind formed an image of a choir of Elvis Presleys singing to the accompaniment of a note-perfect orchestra.

'*And I always will. Love me tender…*'

I then found the more I listened, the more euphoric I felt: the heart-bursting sorrow I'd so often experienced on hearing music since Brian's death was now as unimaginable to me as frostbite to a sunbather.

Walking now in synchronisation with the slow beat of '*Love me long, take me to your heart…*', I felt an ever-growing elation that made me want to strut like the 1950s film stars I'd seen as a girl, puffing out their cigarette smoke with a toss of the head.

My heart swelling with joy at the confident power flooding through me, I came to a pair of swing doors dividing the corridor from the reception area and, deciding against simply walking through the pinned-open door, I crept up to the closed one and peered through its window.

A tall, dark man with broad shoulders was standing before the reception's vending machine, a large brown envelope tucked under one arm while he counted a line of coins in his palm. He then ran his fingertip over the machine's buttons, whistling *Love me tender* as he did so.

Burning with excitement, I stepped slowly through the doors, craning my neck to see the man's face, which, from my position behind the window, had been hidden by a hanging tress of jet black hair and wide sideburn, shaped to a point on his cheek.

At my approach, the man looked up from the buttons and smiled with a curled-lip grin that showed off his cheekbones and straight nose so perfectly, he suddenly seemed impossibly handsome. The eyes then twinkled with the playful confidence of someone who understands how beautiful they are and enjoys being admired.

'Elvis?' I said, holding my breath.

'Excuse me?' said the man and, suddenly, his body shrank into the slight form of Gian Paolo and the hanging hair became curly and swept back from the forehead.

'Oh! Gian Paolo,' I said, 'it's you.'

Glancing at the wall clock, he said: 'Yes, professor. Who else?' then, without waiting for an answer, he added: 'I know I'm a bit early, but I was just so keen to get here.'

All my elation gone, I said: 'You must be: there're still forty minutes before your appointment.'

'Yes,' he said. 'Sorry if I'm clogging up your reception, but there's something I just love about being here,' he said. Then smiling at me again, he added: 'I guess it's because I feel so much easier when I come – like I know everything's going to be all right.'

Re-establishing my equilibrium, I said: 'Well, I'm glad you feel less anxious here. But I don't think you should see our sessions as the answer to quite all of your problems.'

Looking me in the eye, Gian Paolo said: 'I don't know, professor. I think you can do more for me than you imagine.' Then he held out the brown envelope and added: 'Here's the copy of Renata's notebook I promised.'

I accepted the envelope then invited him to make himself comfortable before making my way back to my office where, despite being desperate for a coffee, I sat down, pulled the notebook from the envelope and read its title page: *The Booble.*

I could see from my PC screen, meanwhile, that an email marked urgent had arrived from a senior Home Office official – which I knew was inviting me to take part in a seminar on psychiatric problems in young offenders – but my desire to read the notebook was so great, I swivelled away from the computer and turned over the top page of the manuscript. The second sheet was filled with verses under the heading: *Why God is Silent.*

Picking up the phone, I dialled Addeel Chowderey and said: 'I know it's a terrible cheek, Addeel, but are any of the chaps in your office going to the canteen in the next few minutes who could get me a cup of coffee?'

Addeel gave a short laugh and said: 'Sure, professor. You have it white, no sugar, don't you?'

'That's right,' I said. 'I wouldn't ask, but I have a session with a patient in about half an hour and there's something I really need to read before I see him.'

'No problem. I'll see you in ten,' Addeel said and hung up.

I then read:

Why God is silent
And lo, there lived a beekeeper in the country
Whose care for his bees was renowned far and wide
Because of the unstinting kindness that characterised it
And the unrivalled sweetness of the honey it produced.

Such was the beekeeper's love for his bees
He would sit for hours watching their comings and goings
Fascinated by their twirling-dance rituals
As they buzzed together in their busy, contented world.

And, by means the beekeeper was wise to, the bees felt his love
And learned to trust his benign presence so completely
He was able to do without all protective clothing;
And even the newborn bees recognised him as their benefactor.

After a lifetime watching the bees
The beekeeper came to understand the language of their dances:
'Turn right through ninety degrees; fly for this amount of time;
A tall tree marks where to turn left.'

And understanding their language increased his love
And he began to wish he could tell the bees of his sentiments
By saying how there was such a thing as everlasting God
And this was creating all living creatures and the universe

And could produce miraculous beauty and other wonders
While also being the love that flowed through Man;
And this Godly love was flowing through the beekeeper now
Into the beloved bees, uniting him and them in divine oneness

Thereby proving they, like he, were parts of a perfection
Lying on the other side of material existence. But he knew
The size and beauty of these ideas was too great to express
In the bees' language. So he remained silent.

After reading the verses a second time, I left my chair and went to look out of the window at the grassy expanse over the road from the hospital. Light clouds were casting soft shadows, turning the grass into a patchwork of greenish greys and I could see a male figure in the distance throwing a ball for a dog, which was bounding round with its tail wagging.

A musical knock then sounded and Addeel Chowderey entered, carrying two of the canteen's ribbed-paper coffee cups.

Taking my purse from my bag, I said: 'Addeel, you're a lifesaver!', then gave him the money for both coffees, despite his attempts to refuse it. I then said: 'While you're doing favours, can I ask another?'

'Of course, professor,' he said. 'How can I help?'

'Would you tell me what religion you are?'

'Hindu,' he said, then quickly added he was, however, not particularly religious. 'My mother's the spiritual one,' he said. 'I'm more about trying to make my way in the world.'

Removing the lid from my coffee, I asked if his mother's spirituality meant he'd been brought up with correct Hindu teaching.

'Sure,' he said. 'I can tell you plenty about it if you want.'

Perching on my desk, I took a sip of coffee and said: 'Great! What I'm actually trying to find out is whether you believe God has ever spoken audibly to Man.'

Addeel looked surprised and said: 'You mean spoken out from a cloud or something?'

'Yes – that sort of thing.'

Pouting, he said: 'I'm not really sure, but I do know the Vedas…'

'The Vedas?' I said, cutting in.

'Yeah – the Vedas: our Bible or Koran, you know,' he said, then explained the Vedas had been written by scholars taught the truth directly by God, but he was unsure if that meant He'd actually spoken to them. 'Why do you ask?' he said.

'Oh, it was just something I read.' I said and explained a text had made me think about a bit in the Bible where God literally tells Jesus's disciples out loud that Jesus is His son and they should listen to him. I then readjusted my position on the desk and said I thought if no other religions claimed God had actually spoken out loud, then perhaps the Bible story was simply meant to be an allegory.

'Allegory?' said Addeel.

'Well, perhaps not allegory,' I said. 'More a symbolic storytelling – like when the wise men follow the star to Bethlehem.'

Looking surprised again, Addeel said: 'You mean the frankincense and myrrh stuff isn't true?'

'Oh, yes,' I said. 'It's just the guiding star isn't.' Then I reflected a moment and added: 'At least I don't think it is. It gets a bit confusing!'

'I know what you mean, professor,' Addeel said. 'Sometimes you can know loads but when it comes to the real nitty-gritty, you have to ask a holy man.'

'Yes, I suppose so,' I said.

Toying with the lid on his cup, Addeel said: 'If you like, I could ask my mother about God speaking out loud. If she doesn't know, she'll know someone who does.'

'Oh no! It's really not that important,' I said, and glanced at my screen to see if any emails had arrived since we'd been talking.

'If it's any help,' Addeel continued, 'I know what my dad would say.'

'Really?' I said, glancing at the wall clock.

'Yes. He'd say God's voice is actually speaking to us now, in all the literature of the world,' Addeel said, then explained he knew that sounded a bit weird but he understood what his father meant since he felt the same about his music.

'Really? I didn't know you were a musician,' I said.

'I'm not. I'm a deejay,' he said. Then he told me he loved music more than anything in the world and if he could make a living out of deejaying, he'd give up his job tomorrow. 'No disrespect to the hospital,' he said. Then, looking wistful, he suggested music spoke to the soul and our emotions. 'What most people don't get,' he continued, 'is our feelings are the most important part of us.'

Sipping my coffee, I smiled and said: 'That's a very romantic point of view.'

Looking a little hurt, he said: 'I don't mean just love and romantic stuff, but real, deep feelings.' He then suggested compassion was merely a feeling but, without it, there could be no civilisation.

Taking another glance at my emails, I said I could see his point.

'Yes,' he said, 'but do you get the importance of emotion itself?' Then, breaking into a smile, he added: 'But what am I saying? You're a psychiatrist!' He then turned away and said: 'Anyway, I mustn't take up any more of your time.'

'Not at all,' I said. 'I really appreciate you telling me about the Vedas. It's very good of you.'

Opening the door in preparation to leave, he suddenly turned back and said: 'And it's good of you to talk to me like I'm a real person – not just some IT dummy.' He then raised his cup, thanked me for the coffee and left the room.

Reseating myself, I picked up the photocopy of Renata's notebook again and, as I flicked through the pages, my eye took in a couple of lines from a piece entitled *The Lord's Prayer (God's Pyjamas)* and the beginning of another text headed *Man's Oh-So-Vain Vanity*.

The lines intrigued me and I felt a real urge to read on, but my computer's clock showed only twenty minutes remained before my session with Gian Paolo was due to begin, so I put the photocopied pages aside and opened the urgent Home Office email. As I'd thought, it was inviting me to take part in an event at their London offices, but instead of a seminar, it was to be a question-and-answer session where I'd be one of a panel of experts fielding policy officials' questions on young offender issues.

My diary showed I was free on the event date so I blocked off the whole day then replied to the Home Office, accepting the invitation. I then emailed Michael Servo to tell him I'd be in London three weeks from Friday, at the Home Office, and suggested he and I meet up in town that evening for dinner, at a restaurant of his choosing.

Once the email was sent, I brought up Gian Paolo Friedrich's case notes so I could refresh my memory of our last session together and, after reading how I'd asked him to carry out free-thought sessions before today's appointment, I picked up my notepad and pen, and headed for the analysis room.

When Gian Paolo entered a few minutes later and took his seat on the adjacent sofa, I noticed how fresh he looked and said: 'You look very well, Gian Paolo. Been getting plenty of rest?'

He confirmed he had, then explained how since he'd started the free-thought sessions – staring at a candle while he allowed his thoughts to flow randomly – he was becoming much better at relaxing and, now, when he woke in the night, he was able to fall back to sleep almost immediately.

'I didn't know you were having trouble sleeping,' I said, making a note.

'It's not all the time,' he said, then told me how he'd developed a habit in recent months of waking in the night then tossing and turning for hours before going back to sleep. 'Of course,' he added, 'when the alarm goes off, I'm dead to the world!'

'I see,' I said. 'But the free-thought exercises have helped?'

'They seem to,' he said. 'I slept at least eight hours every night last week.'

'Good,' I said. 'And have you been dreaming much?'

'Loads.'

'Really?' I said. 'Did you take any notes?'

Sitting forward quickly, he said: 'No. Was I supposed to?'

I replied I hadn't asked him to, but it might be a good idea from now on if he kept a dream diary.

He said he'd make sure he did in future then told me, if it was any help, he could clearly recollect his dream of last night, which had been centred on an incident from early adolescence when he'd cut through the tips of his toes with a rotary lawnmower while cutting the grass at home.

I asked him to tell me more and he explained the dream had begun with him arriving at hospital with his mother, Alice, and sitting with his leg over the arm of a chair in an examination room. The male doctor that came in to treat him didn't speak or look at him, but simply removed the crude bandage Renata had wrapped round his bleeding foot.

Then, he was alone with the doctor and, as the bandage came off, they both could see the toes had healed perfectly. The doctor then said: 'The young think they've got all the answers,' before dissolving away and leaving Gian Paolo grown up and alone with Alice, and wearing a doctor's white coat.

In the next piece of the dream Gian Paolo could recall, he was pushing at a door and, after he'd managed to shove it open, he found himself in the office of the hospital's chief executive. He was lying face-down on his desk with his arms stretched out at right angles and his long brown hair straggling over the collar of his white coat. His secretary, who was wearing a nun's habit, was sitting cross-legged in an armchair, looking on.

Gian Paolo approached the desk and turned the man's face to one side so he could shave off his beard with a foamy depilatory cream, then he mutilated the man's hands with the rotary lawnmower. As he was carrying out the mutilation, Gian Paolo was thinking to himself the man was a fraud who was just pretending he could heal people but anyone with knowledge of science would know that was just a fairy tale.

The secretary then uncrossed her legs and started to remove her nun's habit but Gian Paolo hurried from the office before she could reveal her body to him. He then ran panting along a dark corridor while the secretary chased after him, except she was no longer a woman but an unknown man with a sword. Gian Paolo had then woken up.

As he finished describing the dream, Gian Paolo noticed I was smiling and said: 'Is something funny?'

'Are you sure that's a real dream, Gian Paolo?' I said.

'Yes,' he said. 'Why?'

Suspicious he'd invented the dream, I said: 'If you've read as much Freud as you say, surely you can see it's so textbook, it's virtually a cliché.'

Sitting back with his eyes fixed on mine, he said nothing, but the anger in his look strengthened my belief in the dream's inauthenticity and I wondered why he should want to lie to me. I then said: 'If you were to have a wild stab at interpretation, what would you say?'

Looking out the window with a shrug, he said: 'Oedipus complex?'

Nodding, I said: 'I'd say so.' Then, deciding I wouldn't waste any more time on the dream, I said I thought it would be best if I left it to him to note down the latent thoughts behind the dream's manifest content when he got home. 'So long as you're happy you know enough about how to do that,' I said.

Gian Paolo confirmed he was and I said: 'I think we can use our time more usefully now if you tell me a bit more about your father – and why exactly you can't break out of your disastrous relationship.'

Still looking angry, he crossed his legs and said: 'Okay, but just staying with the Oedipus thing a minute, I think it's worth noting I would have felt as a three-year-old I'd pretty much achieved my oedipal wish.' He then explained that, with his father leaving the family home at that time, and him being Alice's favourite child, it was highly probable he would have thought on some level he'd succeeded in doing away with Claudio and taking possession of Alice.

He then suggested that might explain why he'd grown up believing there was no beneficent father figure out there, watching over him.

'Are we talking about life here or religious beliefs?' I said.

'Both.'

'I see,' I said. 'But as you were growing up, you did have contact with your father, so you knew you hadn't completely done away with him.'

Gian Paolo said that was true, but he'd always felt his father was a kind of stranger who didn't have any real connection with him. He then went on to tell me when he'd reached adolescence, he found himself unable to address his father as 'dad' and had been calling him Claudio ever since.

He then added: 'I don't know why, but even now, if I try to say dad, it just sticks in my throat.'

'Perhaps you think he doesn't deserve the title,' I suggested.

'That's for sure!' he said. 'But I think it's more to do with feeling I've already killed "daddy" off – it's just the unconnected stranger left.'

I asked why he couldn't overcome that feeling and work now at building a relationship with Claudio.

He reflected a moment and said: 'Maybe because I don't want to shed any tears when he does actually die. Like I'm practising him being dead as a kind of self-defence mechanism.'

'Interesting,' I said. 'But why would you fear the loss of someone you feel so little connection with?'

'Perhaps because of the pain from when he went away the first time.'

Making a note on my pad, I was about to ask him to give illustrations of exactly what made his relationship with Claudio so bad when I felt a touch on my arm. Looking down, I saw with a start a curly-haired boy of three was now sitting right beside me. Gian Paolo's hand then flicked out at high speed and clamped shut round something near my face, after which he unfurled his fist to reveal a crumpled bluebottle, saying: 'Don't worry, professor. It's only a fly.'

My skin tingling, I brushed at my arm where I'd felt the touch and saw the space next to me was now empty. 'But it felt just like a hand – a child's hand,' I said.

Gian Paolo looked concerned and said: 'Did you just see something?'

'See what?' I said.

'I don't know,' he said. 'Whatever made you jump.'

Wiping my palms, I said: 'Well, just for a moment...' Then, restrained by an inner voice, I stammered: 'Oh, it's ridiculous – it was nothing.'

His concerned look intensifying, Gian Paolo said: 'Please, professor. If you saw something, tell me.'

The need to release the shock in my system wrestled with the inner voice and, after a few moments' hesitation I said: 'Well, I thought I saw a curly-haired little boy – sitting right there.'

Sitting back, Gian Paolo looked pensive and said: 'Interesting,' then asked if I'd ever seen anything else in our sessions together.

The question made my chest thud but I gave what I thought was a casual laugh and said: 'I don't think we should get into what I think I might or might not have seen. We're meant to be talking about you.'

'But you have seen things?' he said.

'Like I say, Gian Paolo,' I said, 'I don't think it's a good use of our time to discuss it.' I then told him we needed to focus on him and his family, and why he felt compelled so much of the time to think about metaphysics.

Running his fingers through the hair at his temples, he said I may well be right but if I'd been having some sort of 'there' experiences since we met – like the experience with the suicide bombers – it showed a pattern we shouldn't ignore.

'A pattern?' I said.

'Yes,' he said. 'A pattern in the type of people who respond to me reaching out to them.'

I tried to laugh casually again and said: 'I don't think we should go too far down that route, Gian Paolo.'

Rising from his seat, he began pacing and said: 'But don't you see? There're three people I know who've had "there"-type experiences – all with one very distinct thing in common.' He then leant on the table and added: 'You, Doctor Okocha and Sara – the languages student – you all have exceptionally high IQs.'

Keen to avoid being sucked into the cosmology for his delusions, I said: 'Really, Gian Paolo, I think I have to insist we park this discussion. It's not helpful at this stage.'

Pushing away from the table and resuming pacing, he said: 'But don't you see how obvious it is? People see all sorts of strange visions when I'm around them, but the only people ever to see something when I've not been there are you, Okocha and Sara.' He then came to a stop and suggested that was because our advanced intelligence included the seeds of 'new feelings' and him reaching out to us had somehow activated them.

Recognising the typically psychotic behaviour of someone seeking to make their madness shared by those around them, I gestured to the adjacent sofa and said with a note of sternness: 'Please, Gian Paolo, sit down!'

Heaving a deep sigh, he retook his place and sat with his elbows on his thighs, his hands dangling between his knees.

As I turned to a fresh page on my notepad, I wondered whether I should start prescribing drugs for him but almost immediately dismissed the idea as I realised he wasn't over-anxious or depressed and there was no real sign of schizophrenia at this stage.

My search for classifiable symptoms wasn't helped either by the letter I'd received from his head of faculty in response to my request for him to have his exams deferred. It stated Gian Paolo had not only been exhibiting no signs of abnormal behaviour at university but had, in fact, been achieving unprecedentedly high marks for all his work – past and present.

Glancing up, I saw Gian Paolo was deep in thought, tapping his thumbs together, and I took the opportunity to note down the areas I wanted to probe in the remainder of the session: Claudio's stance towards Gian Paolo; and the depth of Gian Paolo's resentment of Claudio. I then said: 'So, can you give me some specific examples of disastrous moments with your father? Or is disastrous actually a piece of hyperbole?'

Gian Paolo looked up and said: 'I don't do hyperbole.' He then explained how the latest situation in the long line of disastrous situations with his father was based on the fact he now viewed Gian Paolo as a smartass bookworm who thought he had all the answers because his eloquence always carried sway in any debate between them.

According to Gian Paolo, these constant debating defeats were making Claudio vengeful to the point where he was now actively hoping his son would fail in some way and learn life wasn't as easy as he thought. That way Gian Paolo would see Claudio wasn't the abject failure he believed him to be but someone who'd simply been faced with difficult situations in life and taken a few wrong turns, like everybody else.

Biting his thumbnail, Gian Paolo added: 'So now we're locked in this antagonism with him just praying I'll fall on my arse, while I get more and more pissed off he won't admit his mistakes.' He then suggested all he wanted to hear from Claudio was: 'I'm sorry I wasn't there for you.' 'So I'd pretty much call that a disaster, wouldn't you?' Gian Paolo concluded.

'I see,' I said. 'And have you tried talking frankly to him about your relationship?'

Gian Paolo gave a mirthless laugh and said he'd never in his life been able to enjoy an honest conversation with Claudio since Claudio's first instinct was always to say what he judged other people wanted to hear rather than the truth.

'It's just flannel all the time,' Gian Paulo continued. Then he described an incident from twelve months before, when Claudio had visited the elder son, Aldo, at his office. One of Aldo's employees had been introduced to Claudio and, aware he was her boss's father, she'd asked conversationally if Aldo had shown signs as a child he was going to be such a super-entrepreneur.

In recounting the incident, Claudio had said he didn't know if he should say Aldo's commercial brilliance was a complete surprise to him or to admit Aldo had shown his exceptional talent for making deals as early as infant school, swapping footballer cards for profit in the playground.

Gian Paolo had asked Claudio why he simply didn't answer Aldo's employee's question with the truth. But Claudio dismissed the idea, arguing he couldn't bear going to his hotshot son's office then saying something to make Aldo look bad to his staff.

Gian Paolo argued in turn it was impossible to know how someone would react to a particular piece of information, so it was best just to respond to them in good faith and allow them to make up their own mind.

'But suppose I say the wrong thing?' Claudio insisted.

Exasperated, Gian Paolo replied there wasn't a 'wrong thing' as such, then suggested the worst faux pas would be to alienate someone through a half-baked attempt to control their opinions.

Gian Paolo then concluded by saying if Claudio continued only ever to say what he thought would somehow manage other people's perceptions, he'd so completely lose sight of the truth he'd end up buried in his own bullshit.

'I remember the anger in his eyes when I said that,' Gian Paolo said. Then he told me it was the closest Claudio had come to losing his temper since he'd re-established contact with him.

'But he took it on the chin,' Gian Paolo continued, 'and just came back with, "The young think they've got all the answers".'

'Ah! Like your dream.' I said.

A trace of crossness back in his eyes, Gian Paolo said: 'I thought you didn't believe my dream.'

'I didn't say that,' I said. 'What I suggested was it was a very minimally disguised dream about oedipal conflict which I was surprised you hadn't seen through yourself.' I then shifted in my seat and added: 'I also think if the dream includes a direct quote from your father that rather supports that view.'

Gian Paolo tossed his head and returned to tapping his thumbs.

'Anyway,' I said. 'I'd like to forget the dream and talk more about why you find it so difficult to forgive your father. After all, he was very young when his marriage to Alice failed.' Then, unsure whether Gian Paolo was listening to me as he continued fiddling with his thumbs, I added more loudly: 'Isn't it a bit harsh not to allow him a few mistakes.'

'I understand how young he was, and I do allow his mistakes,' said Gian Paolo. 'The problem is it's hard to forgive someone who doesn't ask forgiveness; who just keeps telling you it wasn't their fault and they didn't do anything anyone else wouldn't have done.'

'Perhaps,' I suggested, 'you need to make him feel he's a bit forgiven already – then he'll be confident enough to ask your full forgiveness.'

'You think I don't know that!' said Gian Paolo, then added if Claudio wasn't so full of 'bullshit and flannel', they would have had a talk ages ago, when they were first back in contact.

'I see,' I said. 'But if you know that's the situation, do you not think you could find some diplomatic way of instigating a dialogue?'

'It's like I say,' Gian Paolo continued. 'It's very difficult.' Then he told me how every time he visited his father – and his second wife, Alana – the three of them invariably ended up sitting round after lunch with Claudio in the middle, drawing them into conversation about himself and why he's the way he is.

'It's become an almost unbreakable pattern,' Gian Paolo said.

'I see,' I said. 'And what sort of things does he say exactly?'

Inhaling deeply, Gian Paolo said: 'Oh, I don't know. Just random stuff.' He then recounted a conversation where Claudio had said how, when he was a younger man, he used to go to the offices of his bookmaking firm on a Sunday morning then go down to the firm's betting shop on the ground floor and sit at the counter for hours, working out odds for the coming week's races.

'I remember him telling me,' Gian Paolo continued, 'how when he was on his way to the office, he'd see people through the windows of their houses and think, "Look at those suckers wasting time while I'm getting ahead". And I just thought, "You fool! Can't you see they're having lives: spending time with their families".'

The vehemence Gian Paolo spoke with showed again his resentment over what he felt was his father's neglect of him, and I used the moment to test the depth of his anger by saying: 'I must say, Gian Paolo, you really should look a little harder for an opportunity to talk with your dad. And if he does start flannelling, you must manage the situation by letting him know you think he's not being honest. Otherwise you have to accept some of the blame for the way things are.'

Expecting an angry reaction, I was surprised when he simply gave a rueful smile and said: 'It's such a joke. He's meant to be the adult, but I have to make all the running.' He then looked me in the eye and added: 'Do you not think he should learn everything isn't always about him; that the world wasn't created to be his audience.' And shaking his head, he exclaimed with a sigh to the ceiling: 'God!'

A silence then fell while Gian Paolo recommenced his thumb tapping. Then the rueful smile returned and he added: 'You know, I often think he and Alice should have stuck it out.'

'Oh?'

'They're so two of a kind: like big kids – always needing someone grown-up to manage them,' he said. Then he told me he was fully aware he was acting like all children from broken homes in rationalising why his parents should reunite, but in the case of Claudio and Alice, he suggested they really were a perfect match.

'And do they also match in the sense Alice should be seeking your forgiveness?' I said.

Gian Paolo laughed and said: 'No! She is what she is. A silly eight-year-old in a grown-up body.' He then explained she and Claudio matched because of the way she also bumbled along in her own fantasy world, desperate for everyone to be her audience – even though she had nothing to perform for them.

'That sounds a bit harsh,' I said. 'She is your mother after all.'

Sighing, Gian Paolo said: 'I suppose so, but she's just so incompetent. She's no idea about anything beyond her own little world.'

Writing 'Alice' as a new heading on my pad, I said: 'I see. And can you explain what you mean exactly by incompetent – maybe with examples?'

Gian Paolo thought a moment and said: 'Take her thirtieth birthday.' He then told how Alice had suddenly decided as the family was eating dinner that she would mark her birthday by taking Renata, Aldo and Gian Paolo to a funfair in town. So they quickly finished eating then walked the three quarters of a mile from their suburban council estate to the local underground station to catch a train to what Alice thought was the closest stop to the fair.

But she'd set off with no map or proper information and the four of them ended up wandering round in town for what seemed like hours. Then, with the August sun all but gone,

Renata – who was twelve at the time – decided to take charge and ask passers-by where the fair was.

After drawing a few blanks, she came across an old lady who directed them to a bus stop, where they waited nearly an hour for an old double-decker that took them just five hundred metres up the road.

By the time they reached the park where the funfair was situated, the night was advanced and Alice was starting to worry about missing the last train home. But they continued on nonetheless and reached the area by the park's lake where all the attractions were located. They then took a ride on a carousel, the tickets for which were so expensive, Alice was left with only enough money for one more attraction.

'I can remember her walking around,' Gian Paolo said, 'with her finger to her lips, frowning, like she always does when she's anxious, and I just thought "let's go home".' He then explained how Aldo had laughed his head off as soon he realised how distraught Alice was because there was nothing he found funnier than her being forced to admit she didn't know what she was doing.

'That's a very interesting reaction,' I said.

'Yes, I suppose so,' he said. 'But it's standard practice with Aldo.' Gian Paolo then explained Aldo was always trying to point out how useless she was as a parent, to avoid him shouldering all the blame for his 'bad boy' behaviour.

'And Alice used to tell Aldo he was a bad boy?' I said.

'Oh yes! Aldo was always in the wrong,' Gian Paolo said. Then, sitting back, he added: 'I don't know where it started exactly, but I can't remember a time when Alice wasn't nagging him to stop being difficult. They were always arguing about something.'

'What sort of things?' I said.

'Oh, you know,' he said. 'Everything and nothing. Take your plate to the kitchen. Don't drink from the tap. Get to bed. That sort of thing.'

'And these turned into major rows?' I said.

'Yes,' he said. 'I think Aldo felt if he could make her really mad, he'd get all her attention.' He then explained since Aldo was the 'bad boy', he probably thought rowing was the only way he could connect emotionally with Alice.

'So there was competition for attention between you and Aldo?' I said.

'No, the battle was between Renata and Aldo,' Gian Paolo said quickly. He then described the fierceness of the rivalry between his brother and sister and suggested it was largely due to there having been no father to give Aldo attention at an age when he was seriously in need of a male role model.

'So that's another wrong to your father's account,' I said.

Gian Paolo leant forward and said: 'Look. I'm not blaming Claudio for everything. It's just when a father jumps ship, you get problems functional families would never even imagine.'

Checking my watch against the wall clock, I said: 'Okay. That's useful background, but I think we should get back to you now.' I then glanced at the note I'd made on my pad from our first session and said: 'Why don't you tell me more about the last of the "new feelings" you and Renata experienced. "Floaty", I think you called it.'

'Ah! floaty,' Gian Paolo said. Then, sitting upright, he fixed his eyes on mine once more and, after several seconds' silence, a smile began to form on his lips.

Uncomfortable under his gaze, I said: 'You're smiling, Gian Paolo. May I ask why?'

'Because it's just struck me,' he said. 'Apart from when I talk about new feelings, you can't actually find anything in what I say that says I'm nuts – not in your professional judgement anyway. In fact, all your ideas about incest and guilt complexes are just textbook theory. And if I'm sane, you're completely wrong about everything.'

Holding his gaze, I waited for him to elaborate, but another silence started to develop so I said: 'You make it sound like I want you to be unwell.'

Buffing his nails, he said: 'Maybe you do. Maybe you need to diagnose some illness so you don't have to admit you're wrong and that I'm actually as sane as you are and the feelings I've been talking about are real.'

'Is that really what you think?' I said.

'Yes, now I think about it,' he said, and sat back once again, his arms folded.

'Okay,' I said. 'Let me say, first, your case is complex and I wouldn't expect to make a diagnosis after three sessions. Second, it's you who came to me for help – I assume because you genuinely believe you have a problem.'

'How do you know I'm not making up my problem?' said Gian Paolo.

'Why would you do that?'

'I might have reasons,' he said. Then, crossing his legs, he added: 'But let's not worry about that now. Let's talk about floaty.'

Concerned Gian Paolo's denial of his condition signalled an advancement of his psychotic state, I suggested we agree to fix his next appointment for the day after tomorrow and schedule him in for twice-weekly sessions for the foreseeable future.

'Fine with me,' he said, then he went on to explain floaty was probably akin to what people experience when they talk about astral flight. In his case, however, the flight was more a physical sensation, like he was some kind of data-gathering apparatus fixed to the front of a probe that could travel galaxies in minutes.

'Sometimes,' he continued, 'as I approach a sun, I can actually feel an unbelievably intense heat on my skin, then my stomach churns with the rush of being thrown out a million kilometres into space by one of the sun's arms.'

The outlandishly fantastic nature of floaty compared with the 'new feelings' Gian Paolo had previously described added to my fear his psychosis was deepening and I wondered whether I'd made a mistake in prescribing free-thought sessions.

'What's the matter, professor? You look worried,' he said.

'Nothing,' I said and, repositioning the notepad on my knee, I added: 'I was just wondering if you weren't spending too much time alone at the moment.'

He gave a shrug and I continued: 'When we've got your appointments set up in the diary, I'll get you an access card for a drop-in centre. There's one quite near the university.'

Gian Paolo gave a puzzled look and said: 'Sorry, I don't know what a drop-in centre is,' so I explained it was somewhere he could go any time, without an appointment, and get support from qualified counsellors. 'They can help if you ever feel isolated or frightened,' I said.

'I see,' Gian Paolo said. 'Thanks very much.' He then uncrossed his legs and said he was aware floaty sounded weird put into words but he might be able to communicate it better if I partnered him in a game he and Renata used to play as children.

'It probably won't work,' he said, 'but it's worth a go.' He then moved to sit at the front edge of his sofa and, holding out his hands, he bid me take hold of them.

Surreptitiously checking my radio-frequency 'panic button' hadn't dropped out of my pocket, I asked him to explain exactly what he was intending to do.

'It's quite simple really,' he said. 'We just hold hands and look into each other's eyes. Then I try to feel floaty and you see if anything happens.'

The indications he'd given in the last few minutes that his psychosis was advancing were still turning in my mind and I decided to be doubly cautious about physical contact with him, so I excused myself and left the room, promising I'd be back in a moment. I then went to my deputy director's office and asked her to use the video-monitoring facility available from her PC to observe the remainder of my session with Gian Paolo. That way, if I was unable to reach the panic button, she could raise the alarm.

As she activated the monitoring software, a framed rectangle of blackness flickered onto her screen which a second later gave way to four live images of the consultation room. The main image showed the room's water-play area while Gian Paolo was visible sitting on the sofa in the centre one of the three smaller images running down the frame's right side.

Clicking on the view featuring Gian Paolo, causing it to become the main image, my deputy and I watched as he looked round the room for a few moments, after which he rose, crossed to the play-equipment shelves and picked out a curly-haired doll.

Watching him as he moved into the bottom one of the smaller views, we saw him waggle the doll's arms and stroke his thumb over its face. I then explained to my deputy I'd left the room because Gian Paolo had asked to play a game where he and I would hold hands and, although I was taller, I was concerned he was strong enough to overpower me if he chose to.

'Do you think he might?' she asked.

'Not really. He's very gentle,' I said. 'But his psychosis seems to be deepening, so you never know.'

'Really? What are his symptoms?' she said.

I glanced at the screen then explained he was delusional and thought he was bringing 'new feelings' into the world: emotions no one had ever experienced before. I also told her the feelings themselves were quite plausible if one accepted he was the Homo superior.

'Oh God! Not another superior sociopath,' she said. 'I can't stand it!' She then enlarged the PC image of Gian Paolo by the shelf unit and said her prison work threw up so many psychotics who thought their hideous crimes somehow made them super-men, she'd just about had it with delusions of grandeur.

I replied that, although Gian Paolo had constructed a fantasy world where he was superior to others, he was unlike criminal psychotics in that he displayed none of their intimidating arrogance or desire to elevate himself. 'It's quite surprising really,' I said, 'given he has pretty good grounds for arrogance.'

'Such as?' said my deputy.

'Well,' I said, 'he's a Cambridge post-grad and his tutors seem to think he's actually quite brilliant.'

'Oo-er!' she said. 'The more complicated the machine, the more difficult to fix!'

I agreed it was a complex case and said it was likely to become more so when I started probing him on what he'd originally stated was his problem: an obsessive compulsion to think constantly about metaphysics.

Sitting back in her chair, my deputy said: 'Ah! Give me religious mania to sicko supermen any day!'

As she spoke, I noticed Gian Paolo move before one of the windows flanking the sink unit and stand with his arms out at right angles, his head slightly on one side. I then took hold of the PC's mouse and enlarged the view with him in it.

My deputy let out a short laugh and said: 'Oh God! He thinks he's Jesus! Religious mania and delusions of grandeur then!' She leant closer to the screen and added: 'Unless he's just playing aeroplanes!'

Concerned Gian Paolo's crucifix pose was another signal his illness was deepening, I borrowed my deputy's desk phone and arranged for two nurses to be on standby to help me in the next fifteen minutes if a problem arose, then I returned to the consultation room.

When I entered and retook my seat, Gian Paolo switched his gaze from the window to me and said: 'All set then?' He then came back to his sofa and sat on the edge once more, his hands held out, and said: 'I was just feeling floaty then, so now's probably a really good time to try.'

My heart racing, I looked into his eyes and took hold of his hands. Their extreme coldness made me withdraw instantly with a gasp. 'Your hands are frozen, Gian Paolo,' I said. 'What's happened?'

He gave a short laugh and said: 'Yes, funny isn't it. I often get physical changes when I've been floaty.'

Gingerly exploring the backs of his hands with my fingertips, I felt the chill once more and wondered if he'd been washing under the cold tap to play some kind of trick on me, so I reached up to his cheek to check its temperature. Incredibly, it was even colder than the hands, although the day outside was sunny and twenty-five degrees.

Resolving to review the video of the session as soon as it was over, I cautiously took hold of his hands and looked into his eyes once more.

'Relax, professor. It's just a bit of fun really,' he said.

We then settled into position and, as we gazed at one another, I realised what an unusually beautiful young man Gian Paolo was, with his dark curls and flawless, olive skin.

Smiling he said: 'That's no good, professor. You've got to stop thinking. That's the way Renny and I used to do it.'

'But it was different with Renata, wasn't it?' I said. 'I mean, she was able to feel floaty independently of you, no?' I said.

'True. But I think you have the seeds of new feelings if you just try,' he said. 'Shush now, and look into my eyes.'

I did as he asked, trying to relax and, after a minute's silence had passed without incident, he said: 'Now close your eyes.'

No sooner had I obeyed than a picture formed in my mind that seemed as real as if my eyes were open. It comprised the massively curving horizon of a sandy-coloured planet, luminescent against the velvet blackness of space. I was also aware of an ear-clogging silence like that on a high cliff top, when the sea is too far below to hear.

As I focused on the image, the planet's surface loomed bigger and I felt as if I was gently gliding towards it through cold water. I could then make out hills and craters on the planet's surface and I suddenly realised, the more detail I could see, the faster the ground seemed to be passing beneath me.

Moment by moment, the gentle gliding was transforming into a feeling I was bulleting along at an unimaginable rate and, just as I started to feel panicked by the speed, I shot over the curve of the planet and out into nothingness, my stomach dropping like a parachutist's.

The sensation caused my eyes to blink open and I was met by Gian Paolo's expressionless face, his gaze fixed on a point somewhere above my head. I then tried to free my hands from his cold grip but they were stuck.

Pulling harder, I said: 'That's enough, Gian Paolo! That's enough! Let me go!'

Expression returning to his eyes, he complied and said: 'Sorry. I didn't want to drop you.'

A surge of anger rising in me, I said: 'Drop me! Who in God's name do you think you are? Peter Pan!'

His hands flopping into his lap, he threw me a hurt look.

Fighting to control my anger, I said: 'Look. I don't know what you just did there, but I don't like it! Really I don't.'

'Sorry,' he said again.

'I mean, if you want me to help you, you can't go round playing silly tricks in these sessions.'

'Tricks?'

'Yes,' I said. 'Hypnosis, subliminal suggestion, or whatever the hell that was.'

The hint of a smile on his lips, he sat back and said: 'So you did see something?'

Feeling my anger rise a notch, I told him I had no intention of playing along with his silly game by letting him know its effects. I then ended the session and accompanied him back to reception where I directed the receptionist to diarise twice-weekly appointments for him over the next six weeks and arrange for a drop-in centre pass to be posted to him.

After bidding him goodbye until the day after next, I made my way back to my deputy's office, my knees like jelly. My deputy was at her desk, her head bent over a dossier.

'Did you watch?' I said.

She confirmed she had and that, having seen nothing alarming, she'd released the two nurses standing by to help.

I thanked her then returned to my office, where I rang Addeel Chowderey and asked him to make the video of the session available as soon as possible. I then sank back in my chair and picked up the photocopy of Renata's notebook, my fingers trembling.

After several seconds' fumbling with the manuscript, I lay it on my lap then pressed my hands together to steady them, but a memory of the sandy-coloured planet came back and made my whole body shudder.

Hurriedly sitting forward, I opened my desk's bottom drawer and dropped the notebook in before kicking it shut with a bang. I then placed my palms on the desk and tried some controlled breathing while I collected my thoughts: how had Gian Paolo's hands and face become so cold? How had he made me see the planet? If he'd hypnotised me, wouldn't my deputy have noticed?

After several minutes' deep breathing, the phone rang and Addeel told me the video was ready, so I navigated my way to it on a shared drive and clicked it into life. The part of the session I wanted to see most was the minute or so during which I would have been walking back from my deputy's office and Gian Paolo had made his hands and face go cold.

Fast-forwarding to the spot where Gian Paolo had adopted his crucifix position, I watched for several minutes without seeing him do anything to chill his hands before I came back in the room, so I rewound to see if I'd missed something from earlier and landed on the section where I'd suggested he seemed to blame his father for a lot of things and he'd replied: 'It's just when a father jumps ship, you get problems functional families would never even imagine.'

Chiding myself for not having asked what sort of problems he was referring to, I made a note on my pad to probe him on what he meant at our next session, then returned to the beginning of the video file. Logic told me if I watched every second closely, I couldn't fail to spot how he'd played the 'floaty' trick on me.

LONDON'S CALLING

Even after two hours' scrutinising the video of the 'floaty game' session with Gian Paolo, I found nothing to explain how his hands had turned so cold or what he'd done to hypnotise me into imagining the sandy planet.

Then, at our next session, two days later, I was tempted to quiz him on what he knew about hypnotism but decided I didn't want him thinking his suggested-image trick had impressed me so I focused instead on talking about Renata and how her ideas on metaphysics might have influenced him.

Although he readily admitted her influence had been great, he seemed to have many ideas of his own and, as we continued discussing his insights during the next three weeks' sessions, I felt a number of my religious beliefs sorely challenged. It also became apparent the beliefs he and Renata held in common about God and the universe were all covered in her notebook.

When the Friday arrived for me to attend the Home Office question-and-answer event, discussing young offender issues, the upset I'd felt over the floaty game was just a memory and I decided to take Renata's notebook with me to read on the train.

As I boarded the 9.02 a.m. London service at Cambridge station, I recalled the train bombs of the previous month and prayed nothing similar would happen on this trip. I then settled into my first-class seat and, after removing the lid from the coffee I'd just bought at the station kiosk, I took out Renata's manuscript from my case and found the page headed *Man's Oh-So-Vain Vanity*. I then read:

In the beginning was God
The immeasurable, immortal, unfathomable spirit
And, driven by its immeasurably creative nature, the spirit sought
To branch out from spiritual being and make itself material

So it big-banged the universe into existence
And, after fourteen billion years, the bang is still banging
Into an expanding universe, proving that, to an immortal,
Fourteen billion years is but a finger-click

The real challenge for the spirit was to interfuse itself
With the matter of its big bang:
Making particles, molecules and cells
Vessels for itself

So it clustered some matter into a cell
That could somehow hold life within its compass
And the life gave point to the matter-cluster,
Launching God's first attempt at materiality: the microbe

Four-and-a-half billion years of matter-clustering on Earth
Saw Man arrive, encompassing consciousness within his cells
And this consciousness was a tap through which
Love, truth, beauty and creativity could flow

But the cosmic miracle of an aesthetic consciousness on Earth
Spawned a vanity in the matter that was Man.
For the man thought love, truth, beauty and creativity
Were his own exclusive properties

So he ignored that he was simply a tap
And looked to ensure his little matter-cluster –
Which he saw first and foremost as being himself –
Would be an eternal fixture in creation

As I thought about the idea of Man's consciousness being a tap, the train lurched forward and began trundling its way out of the station. My eye was then caught by a patch of blue among the fluffy clouds out of the window and I recalled what Mo Parrell had said in Paris about life being ever-present, awaiting opportunities to appear on Earth.

The memory made me smile and I read on:

Man's first move, and possibly greatest vanity,
Was to anthropomorphise God by making it man: Jesus.
And although Jesus was only a partner in a trinity
He had a kingly father who priests say actually has a face

And a Holy Spirit whose express purpose is to descend on Man.
So, with the manlike duo of father and son firmly at the helm
And the junior partner of Holy Spirit at Man's exclusive disposal
Man's anthropomorphisation of God was complete and, consequently,
    step one in Man's bid for immortality

The next move was for Man to put himself beyond obsolescence
By claiming, cogent as evolutionary theory might be,
It only applied to animals and plants since God
Had placed Man above evolution, by creating him in His own image

And though 150 million years of dinosaurs suggested
Man's little thousand centuries was insufficient evidence
Of his placement beyond evolution,
Still Man had a means of dealing with the doubts

It involved him and his oh-so-vain vanity
Turning his back on the scientifically obvious
And guaranteeing his speck-in-the-universe material self
Could live eternally because

A Man-resembling God said so.

When I'd reread the verses enough times to glean all the meaning I was going to, I lay the notebook on the table with my empty coffee cup and noted with surprise the train was slowing in preparation to join the London rail network. Checking my watch, I realised I'd been reading almost an hour.

I rubbed my eyes and analysed what the verses were making me feel: annoyance at what was a deliberate, if enigmatic, attack on Christian doctrine; discomfort at not quite being able to grasp the subtext on Man's relationship with God; admiration for the depth of thought shown by a girl who would have been no more than eighteen when she wrote the verses.

As the train continued through the built-up landscape of north London, past a modern-looking football stadium, I stowed the notebook back in my case and took out the paper I'd been emailed two days previously, explaining the question-and-answer format of the Home Office event and who would be my fellow panellists.

I then spent another half hour reading papers before the train arrived at London's main northern terminus and came to a stop. I saw from the platform's clock the service was one minute behind its 10.18 arrival time, but I still had more than an hour and a half before the Home Office event so I unhurriedly packed my papers back in the case before descending. I then made my way through the ticket barrier at the end of the platform and headed for the taxi rank in the terminus's basement.

In passing the steps down to the underground station, it occurred to me how much cheaper it would be to take a tube to the central London headquarters of the Home Office, but my loathing of crowds and a dim fear over the security of tubes were enough to keep me heading for the taxis.

In the underground car park, there were cabs continually arriving in ones and twos through an arched entrance and replenishing a line of noisy vehicles picking up customers with suitcases, rucksacks and shopping bags. Glancing along the customer queue, I wondered whether I would spend less time on my feet if went back for a tube, but when I saw how quickly the line was moving, I took my place and soon found myself hiring a cab covered with a garish advertisement for an airline.

Sitting back in the plastic-scented interior, I watched through the window as we left the station through another archway and joined the busy road beyond. I then sat in one queue of traffic after another, all the way to the other side of central London, idly watching the passers-by, most of whom seemed to be tourists or young mothers.

When I finally arrived at the Home Office building, I made sure I obtained a receipt from the taxi driver so I'd be able to claim back the ludicrously high fare he'd just charged me. I then made my way through the building's main entrance and joined a queue of some half a dozen people lined up before a swanky reception desk staffed by three women in navy blue blazers.

After waiting several minutes for my turn to approach, I felt pleased when one of the women switched her gaze away from her PC screen and greeted me with a broad smile. Then, once I'd identified myself, she quickly found my name on a list of expected visitors and said she would call someone to come and fetch me presently.

Next, she gave me a security pass on a lanyard and invited me to take a seat on one of the plush settees in a carpeted area on the other side of the lobby. I thanked her and, as I crossed the space, I eyed several spots before opting for a settee at the carpeted area's far end. I then settled into a corner seat that allowed me to watch an LCD screen showing a corporate video and keep in view both the main entrance and a revolving door that led out to a paved precinct at the side of the building.

The video included dynamic music and voice-overs by a couple who sounded warmly sincere as they listed the Home Office's successes in improving people's lives. The statements of success fitted neatly with sequences of high definition images, showing Home Office-commissioned workers delivering services to citizens of all races, ages and backgrounds.

As the video was looping round for the third time, I noticed a slightly-built young man in a stylish suit come through the Perspex-protected turnstiles that barred the lobby from the rest of the building. I then continued to watch as he approached several of the people sitting on the plush settees and, after receiving a nod from a tall man, he shook hands with him. The pair then headed towards where I was sitting, the tall man struggling to pull his overnight case as its wheels caught in the carpet's soft pile.

Making eye contact with me, the young man – who I could now see was, in fact, at least forty – came up to my corner seat and said: 'Professor Small?'

I confirmed I was and he introduced himself as Damien Cleary from the Home Office's internal communications team. He then introduced me to the tall man and, as we shook hands, I learnt he was one of my fellow panellists and the chief executive of a charitable organisation providing counselling to drug addicts.

After a brief conversation about our journeys, the tall man and I were led to one side of the line of turnstiles where a security guard pressed a card against an electronic reader so the chief executive and I could pass through to the lifts beyond.

Damien Cleary then used his own card to come through the turnstile and, after pressing the lift call button, he explained he was taking us to the Director of Communications' office on the fourth floor where we would be able to freshen up and enjoy tea and biscuits before going to the conference room where the event was being staged. He then started to tell us about how keen officials had been to book a place at the event when he was suddenly stopped by a ground-shaking bang, followed by a rumble then a crashing of glass.

There followed two long seconds of perfect silence during which I made a guess the noise had come from an axle snapping on a lorry, causing its heavy load to spill onto the road outside. The silence then ended with the distant shout of a man, closely followed by a woman's scream.

Looking back through the turnstiles, I saw clouds of black smoke were billowing into the lobby and noticed the receptionist who'd greeted me was now out of her seat and mouthing 'Oh my God! Oh my God!' as she stared at the precinct entrance.

A chill gripping me, I turned to Damien Cleary and said: 'It must be a bomb!'

'Christ!' he said. Then, after a quick glance at the frantic people now rushing the turnstiles, he took my arm and, guiding me firmly towards a corridor, he said: 'Come on. There's a shelter up here.'

As the chief executive and I were hurried along the corridor, I looked back at the crowd clamouring round the turnstiles and said: 'Hang on. Shouldn't we do something for those people?'

'No,' Damien Cleary said. 'Let security take care of it,' and he explained it was possible there was a bomber among them, working as part of a planned attack.

My mind racing, I allowed myself to be escorted with the chief executive to a door with two signs – one saying 'Bomb Shelter Area 5'; the other bearing the silhouette graphic for a men's toilet.

Pushing the door open, Damien Cleary ushered us inside and said: 'We should be okay in here.' He then turned to an official by the washbasins, who was picking up his briefcase in preparation to leave and, raising a flat hand, said we all needed to stay where we were since it was likely we were under attack from terrorists.

The official immediately looked fearful and said we would be safer if we evacuated the building but Damien Cleary shook his head, saying the guidance for attacks was for everybody to stay in the bomb-shelter areas, away from glass.

The scared-looking official seemed about to press his argument when a second huge bang made the toilet's four cubicle doors rattle on their hinges, then another rumble rang out.

We all fell silent while the smell of brick dust and burning began to permeate the toilet. The silence then deepened as we became lost in our own fears and would probably have lasted indefinitely if the unexpected flush of a toilet hadn't brought us out of ourselves.

One of the doors then clicked loudly and a bald man with a big stomach emerged from the furthest cubicle and crossed to the washbasins, pushing up his sleeves in preparation to wash his hands. Then, catching sight of the four of us in the mirror, he stopped short and, holding our reflected gazes, he said: 'Is something wrong?'

'Didn't you hear the bangs?' Damien Cleary said.

'Yes. A couple of right thumps, weren't they,' said the bald man, turning on a tap.

'We think it's a bomb attack,' I said.

The bald man looked into the mirror version of my eyes as he washed and said: 'I see. I was wondering what you were doing in the gents.'

Tucking his briefcase tightly under one arm, the scared official said he wasn't going to wait around and moved towards the door, but Damien Cleary stepped into his path and protested it was too dangerous. 'At least until we know what the situation is,' he said.

His face contorted by panic, the official said: 'How come you know so much about it?'

Damien Cleary explained he worked in internal communications and had once rewritten a poorly drafted security notice for the office's intranet, detailing the guidance for a terrorist attack, and he could remember what the advice was.

The scared official looked at each of us in turn, his face tense, then, as the staccato cracks of distant machine-gun fire suddenly broke out, he spun on his heel and said: 'You hear that? We'll be shot like rats in a barrel.' He then reached for the door's handle but was immediately driven back as the door banged inwards and half-a-dozen people in white overalls swept inside.

A small man in a dark suit then entered and, speaking loudly to the backs of the new arrivals, said: 'Just stay here a minute will you, while I find out what's going on.'

The overalled group – who I guessed were canteen staff – gave no sign they'd heard him and continued to chatter, mainly in Polish, while one of them bit into a Danish pastry, watched by the plump girl next to her.

As he turned to leave, the small man was stopped by Damien Cleary, who asked him, if he was going out, to find someone in security who could tell us what we should do next.

The small man nodded and left.

'How come you didn't stop *him*?' the scared official said once the door had shut.

Damien Cleary looked as if he was about to argue back but I said: 'I think it might be better if you let this man go. He's clearly very claustrophobic.'

The wail of a siren then reached us and two distinct gunshots sounded a half-second apart.

'Hang on!' Damien Cleary said. 'That could be a sniper.'

Breaking into a half-smile, the bald man said: 'No, that's a handgun. A rifle is a much longer bang.'

'Is that so,' Damien Cleary murmured and, turning back to the scared official, he said with a sigh: 'Well, it's on your own head.'

'I'll take my chances,' the official said and, ignoring the two suited men and the middle-aged woman who'd just entered the toilet, he rushed out into the corridor.

Once he'd gone, we all shuffled towards the toilet's rear to make room for the trio just arrived and the bald man said: 'You're right about staying put until we get intelligence. We should only move if they occupy the building.' He then suggested it was unlikely the attackers were looking to do that since their objective was terror rather than occupation.

To give his opinion weight, he explained he was a deputy director of intelligence from one of the Home Office's security agencies and had previously been in the British army, serving actively in Northern Ireland, Bosnia and Afghanistan. 'So I know a rifle when I hear one,' he said. 'And a rocket launcher come to that.'

One of the suited men who'd just entered said: 'You think the attack comes from a rocket launcher then?'

'Almost certainly', said the intelligence official and a conversation started about terrorist attack methods and what was likely to be happening outside at that moment.

As the discussion turned to theories about why the attackers had targeted the Home Office, several of the canteen staff seated themselves on the floor, their backs against the tiled wall. The intelligence official meanwhile suggested the attack may have been an attempt to assassinate the Home Secretary but stopped short in his theory to listen to a volley of four or five shots.

'Now those are rifles!' he said, a finger in the air, and, leaning a shoulder against the wall, he added: 'I bet those were police marksmen taking out a terrorist.'

'Well, that's good news, isn't it?' said the chief executive.

Shrugging, the intelligence official said: 'Depends how many terrorists there are and whether they've got hostages.'

'Hostages?' said the middle-aged woman. 'You don't think they've captured a minister, do you?'

The intelligence official was about to answer when the small man returned carrying armfuls of cushions and announced he'd spoken to security staff and the advice to us was to sit tight while they were on the higher floors, compiling a list of everybody in the other bomb-shelter areas. 'Believe me, people are really jammed into some of them,' he said as he distributed cushions. 'At least you guys can sit down.'

Slipping one of the cushions under her buttocks, and those of the young man beside her, one of the canteen staff said: 'Dees are from da coffee a*rrr*ea, no?'

The small man confirmed he'd taken some of the cushions from settees near the coffee bar and, addressing all of us, said we'd probably have a bit of a wait before we were given the okay to leave the building.

Crossing to the washbasins to freshen up, I noticed my shoes pinching and, as I patted my hair into place, I realised for the first time since entering the toilet I was trembling.

Turning on a hot tap, I gained such comfort from the warm water flowing through my fingers that I spent a full two minutes washing my hands. I then dried myself on a roller-towel and gave my hair a final pat before moving to where one of the young canteen women was sitting. Smiling down at her, I said: 'Do you think I could have a share of your cushion?'

Returning my smile, the young woman shifted to make room so I thanked her and sat down as tidily as I could in the cramped space. I then started a conversation in pidgin Polish about who she was and where she came from. She seemed delighted I was trying to communicate in her language and enthusiastically tutored me on how to say words I was mispronouncing.

After a few exchanges, my Polish started to flow a little better and we managed a basic conversation about her family and the boyfriend she was living with in London. I was also able to tell her how, when I was a student, I'd backpacked my way from Warsaw to Lodz, and we discovered I had actually passed through the small town where she'd been raised.

Happy to escape the present, we shared our respective memories of Poland until our attention was caught by static suddenly hissing through speakers in the ceiling. This was followed by two doorbell notes and a woman's voice saying with excessive deliberation: 'Attention, please. Attention. The current emergency situation remains ongoing and all staff and visitors are asked to remain in their bomb-shelter areas for the time being. If your conditions are particularly cramped, you can leave your bomb-shelter area, provided you remain within sight of its entrance and away from glass. All staff and visitors are urged to ensure their names are recorded by the wardens who are now monitoring each bomb-shelter area. A further announcement will be made as soon as more developments are known about the current emergency situation. Thank you for your co-operation. If you have had trouble in clearly hearing these messages, please call building services help desk on extension three-thousand. Thank you.'

The speaker hiss then switched off and the intelligence official said: 'That sounds good. They wouldn't let us stretch our legs if the show wasn't over.'

Happy at the prospect of leaving the toilet, I smiled at my new friend, whose name was Stefania, and asked if she knew where I could buy a coffee. Jumping to her feet, she started for the door, saying the coffee would be no problem and bidding me follow her. In my keenness to comply, I tried to rise straightaway but the stiffness in my legs caused me to plop back down, my back bumping against the wall.

Noticing my difficulty, Stefania came back and pulled me to my feet with a strong arm. We then crossed together to the exit, followed by several of the other canteen workers. As I pulled the door open, Damien Cleary gave me a querying look so

I explained I was going to find a cup of coffee and asked if he wouldn't mind giving my name to a warden if one showed up.

'No problem, professor. You go ahead.' he said, his gaze drifting to the people now filing round the back of me.

Once Stefania and I were outside, we tagged along behind her fellow workers and, as they headed for a wooden door marked 'PRIVATE KITCHEN', she told me I should continue up the corridor to the restaurant and find a table near the coffee bar. She then followed the others through the doorway, calling out she would fix me a latte shortly. A large one!

Passing through double doors, I entered a modern-looking canteen with a dozen sofas in partitioned areas among the dining tables and chairs, all of which were vacant except one at the far end near the coffee bar where a white-haired man in shirtsleeves was sitting smoking a cigarette while he studied a clipboard. On seeing me, he quickly stubbed out his cigarette on a paper napkin next to where his walkie-talkie was lying.

Drawing near, I said: 'Please don't stop on my account,' and taking a seat opposite, I nodded to the napkin and added: 'Besides, that doesn't look very safe fire-wise.'

Giving the faintest of smiles, he said: 'Don't worry. There're plenty of fire engines just outside.' He then folded the napkin over several times before crushing it into a ball and squeezing it into his back pocket, just as his walkie-talkie crackled into life with someone asking where he was. Throwing me a glance, he lifted the walkie-talkie and, pressing a button, said: 'Yeah, I'm still on the ground floor. Roger.'

A static-muffled voice came back, accompanied by faint piano music: 'It's all under control down here, Peter. Have you spoken to Terry again yet? Over.'

Raising his eyebrow, the shirtsleeved man said: 'What've you got down there: bloody lounge music?'

The voice at the other end laughed and said: 'Yeah, we got some bloke doing barroom piano. But what about Terry? Over.'

The shirtsleeved man confirmed he'd spoken to someone called Terry a moment before and the situation outside was in a state of 'steady stand-off'.

'Roger, roger, Peter. I'll come back in ten,' said the voice.

'Okay,' said Peter. 'Over and out,' and he put the walkie-talkie back on the table.

Spotting Stefania come out through a door behind the coffee bar, I waved to her, then, turning back to the shirtsleeved man, Peter, I said: 'Does "steady stand-off" mean we can all go home soon?'

'Not quite,' he said. Then he told me there was still a man with a pair of scissors in a florist's shop who was holding two workers hostage and threatening to stab them if the police didn't provide him with a car to the airport and a plane to Morocco.

'I don't understand,' I said. 'How is a man with scissors keeping us all still trapped in here?'

Stroking his jaw, Peter told me the man was one of a group of three terrorists who he understood had gone into the florist's on the corner of the shopping mall next to the building at opening time that morning and handcuffed the shop's two staff to a pipe in a storeroom. The terror gang had then put up a 'closed' sign on the shop door and waited for a minister's car to arrive by the revolving-door entrance.

He then explained that, although ministers were directed by the office's security team only ever to enter or leave their cars in the building's basement car park, all of them – including the Home Secretary – were always in such a rush they frequently instructed their drivers to pick them up and drop them off by the revolving-door entrance.

Peter theorised the terrorists had become aware of this through reconnaissance and decided they could assassinate the Home Secretary or one of her ministers if they seized the florist's and used the clear view it gave them of the revolving-door entrance to launch an attack.

'And they used a rocket launcher?' I said.

His eyes narrowing, Peter said: 'That's right.'

'Oh,' I said, 'I only know because this ex-army man told me,' and I explained about the intelligence officer in the toilet.

Folding his arms, Peter gave me an odd little wink and said: 'The silly bastards didn't know how to fire it, thankfully.' He then explained he'd received information the terror gang had waited more than two hours in the closed florist's shop for one of the ministers' cars to arrive; then, as soon as a parliamentary undersecretary of state's vehicle had shown up, two of the gang had rushed out with the launcher.

To set up the weapon, one of the gang had apparently rested its shaft on the shoulder of his comrade and, while the undersecretary was leaving his car, the terrorist fired the first missile. But the man acting as gun-stand had flinched, causing the missile to fly two metres over the car.

'Funnily enough, it actually did very little structural damage,' Peter said. He then went on to tell me the blast had nonetheless shattered most of the glass at that corner of the building, causing several dozen people to suffer cuts, some of them serious. 'You see,' he said, 'that sort of blast can send glass flying well over fifty metres.'

'But what happened to the minister?' I said.

Suddenly catching sight of Stefania behind the coffee bar, Peter called out: 'Hey! Any chance of a coffee here, my dear?'

Glancing up from her coffee machine, Stefania called back: 'I do it for Joy. But I can do one for you, no problem.'

'For joy!' Peter said, shaking his head. 'They're a funny lot, these Poles.'

Smiling, I said: 'She means me. My name is Joy.'

Peter let out a small laugh and, unfolding his arms, he suggested Joy seemed a very English name for me since I was clearly not of British origin.

I explained my real name was Joey, which in Hebrew is the feminine of Joseph, but I'd quickly stopped using it after arriving from Germany thirty years ago since it made too many people think I was a man.

'So you're German are you?' Peter said. 'I could tell there was some sort of accent. Although it is very faint.'

I confirmed I was German by birth then repeated my question about the minister.

Keeping half an eye on Stefania, Peter said he'd been told by one of his security team that, after the first missile was fired, the minister and the officials with him were torn between seeking shelter in the building or just running away. But the driver was army-trained and understood immediately he needed to pull the minister from the danger zone. So he screamed at him to get back in the car. Then, without even waiting for him or the accompanying officials to close the doors, he reversed back up the roadway at top speed. The terrorists meanwhile managed to load another missile and fire it at the retreating car. 'But you need real skill to hit a moving target,' Peter said.

Then he went on to tell me how the second missile had passed through the glassless window of a ground-floor meeting room twenty metres up the building and narrowly missed several officials before exploding in a corridor and blowing a huge hole in the wall adjoining the building's reception area.

'That's where the only real casualties have been so far,' he added.

'In the corridor?' I said.

'No, by the reception turnstiles.'

'Oh my God!' I said and recalled the frantic people Damien Cleary had said we couldn't help.

'Yes, one was definitely dead,' Peter continued, 'and there's another the paramedics didn't think would make hospital.'

My earlier trembling returning, I whispered: 'How awful!'

Looking concerned, Peter said: 'Are you okay? You look very pale.'

Taking a deep breath, I said 'Yes, thanks. I'll be fine' and I straightened in my seat so I could fill my lungs. I then noticed Stefania was approaching carrying a tray with three cups and added: 'I think the shock has only just hit me.'

As Stefania put her tray down and announced: 'Coffee for everybody', Peter reached into his trouser pocket and said he would be happy to pay. But Stefania dismissed the idea and, sliding a large latte before me, she said: 'Are you okay, Joy? You look more fear out here than in toilet.'

I explained I was feeling shaky since I'd just discovered I'd only escaped death because I was lucky enough to have been collected from reception a minute or two before the missiles struck. But as I spoke, I realised Stefania was having trouble understanding me so I repeated my explanation in pidgin Polish.

Placing a comforting hand on my arm, Stefania said I should drink my coffee and not think about what might have happened. The important thing was I was safe now.

I thanked her for her kindness and took a couple of big sips of latte, fighting to control my trembling hands.

Taking a sip of his own coffee, Peter said: 'So you speak Polish?'

I replied I didn't speak it very well since I'd never formally studied it, then I introduced him and Stefania to one another. In making the introduction, I apologised if I was wrong about him being called Peter but said I'd heard the man on the other end of his walkie-talkie address him as that.

'Yes, I'm Peter all right,' he confirmed and, holding out his hand to Stefania, he said: 'I'm the central security manager.'

'Pleased to meet you,' Stefania said, shaking his hand. 'I work in restaurant.'

I quickly recapped in Polish what Peter had said about the missile attack on the minister's car and how the driver seemed to have saved the day.

Her eyes wide, Stefania turned to Peter and said: 'Oh my God! But where are bad men now?'

Wiping milk froth from his lip, Peter told her a pair of patrolling armed policemen had arrived on the scene immediately after the second missile was launched and opened fire with machine guns on the two terrorists carrying the rocket launcher. He then sat back and said: 'It's lucky they were so close.'

Nodding, Stefania said: 'And bad men with rocket were shot death?'

'One was,' Peter said. 'The other was hit but managed to get back in the florist's.'

Gasping, Stefania clapped her hands over her mouth and said: 'Oh my God! What happen for him now?'

Peter took another sip of coffee and told her reports he'd received said a number of police marksmen had arrived shortly after he'd shut himself back in the florist's. The marksmen had then taken up positions round the shopping precinct: behind benches and a large sculpture, and at the top of an escalator.

On seeing the marksmen, the wounded man opened the shop's glass door just wide enough to take two pot-shots at them with a handgun then launched into a vicious tirade about the morals of Britain and America. According to the reports, the wounded man seemed unaware the glass door he was taking cover behind offered no protection against rifle bullets.

In continuing his tirade, he became increasingly enraged and, as the blood from his wounds began to puddle round his feet and his temper worsened, the marksmen received the order to fire and shot him dead: three rifle bullets hitting him in the head simultaneously.

'Oh my God!' Stefania said again. Then, turning to me, she said: 'Who can believe thing like this happening here.'

Shaking my head, I said to Peter: 'But what about the third one? The one with the scissors?'

Checking his watch, Peter explained the last report he'd received from the head of security, Terry Soaffeyssan, was the third man was maintaining his position in the florist's back room, holding scissors at the throats of the two female workers handcuffed to a wall pipe while he tried to negotiate a car and plane for himself.

As Peter spoke, his walkie-talkie crackled into life again, this time, with a different voice asking where he was.

'I'm still on the ground floor, Terry. Over,' said Peter.

'It's all over, Pete,' came back the crackling voice. 'We can start evacuating non-essentials out the back right away. No front or mall exit yet. But the back's clear; repeat – clear at the back. Over.'

Speaking into his walkie-talkie, Peter said: 'That's great, Terry. How'd it end? Over.'

'The negotiator got close enough to grab him. Over,' said the voice.

'So we've got him in custody then? Over,' said Peter.

'Not quite,' the voice came back. 'The negotiator snatched the scissors then snapped the fucker's neck!'

Peter glanced at me with a wince and said into the walkie-talkie: 'I'm in company, Terry. Over.'

'Gotcha, Pete. Righto!' said Terry. Then he gave him instructions to tell his team and the officials acting as wardens to direct everyone on the business-continuity essentials lists to stay behind while everybody else was evacuated. 'But only out the back door. I repeat – only out the back. Over.'

Peter confirmed he understood then called his team over the walkie-talkie to discuss the detail of clearing the building while Stefania moved her chair closer to mine and asked what I planned to do next.

'Finish my coffee then call the friend I'm meant to be meeting for dinner,' I said. 'I think I'll cancel. I just want to go home.'

'Where your home?' Stefania said.

When I told her I lived in Cambridge, she said that was a long way to travel after such an experience and suggested I keep my dinner date so I could talk to someone about what I'd just been through.

Patting her hand, I said my one wish right now was to be home, relaxing.

She smiled and told me the meatballs the chef had been preparing before the missile attack were ready and it would be no trouble to bring me some.

I declined since my stomach was still in a knot from the shock of the attack but Stefania looked disappointed so I gave her a long hug, thanked her for the support she'd given me and asked how she was feeling herself.

Breaking into another smile, she told me I needn't worry since her boyfriend was Bosnian and the stories he was always telling of his childhood had accustomed her to a world of violence and bloody death.

'But you are clever woman who work for high things,' she said. 'You must not dirty your mind with brutals of life.'

Too weary to tell her of the horrors I'd come across in my work with psychologically-disturbed children, I smiled and asked her to excuse me while I called Michael at his office. I then took my phone out of my bag and made the call but there was no answer so I left a voicemail explaining I'd been caught up in the missile attack on the Home Office and would now be going straight home.

I then put the phone away and asked Stefania if she knew where there was a ladies' toilet that didn't double as a bomb-shelter area. Hearing my question, Peter leaned across the table before Stefania could reply and said my best bet was to take the west stairs up to the fourth floor – if my legs were up to it – then go into one of the ministerial offices, which were all fitted with private toilets.

'But, if anyone asks, don't say I told you,' he added, winking again.

Although my legs were tired, the need to pee gave me impetus and I soon found myself on the fourth floor before an open door with the Home Secretary's name on it. It led to a bright room with two rows of desks and floor-to-ceiling windows on one side, overlooking the street.

My breathing steadying after the stairs, I made my way through a doorway at the far end of the room and into an inner office. Then, after calling 'hello' several times and asking if anyone was there, I crossed to a workstation in one corner and noticed a small picture frame standing by the PC. It contained what I initially thought was a poem but was in fact handwritten lines saying the writer was 'not everyone' and could 'only do so much as one person'. I then picked up a larger frame containing an old cutting of a newspaper column arguing the Home Secretary was 'the principled choice' in the deputy leader election being held by her party.

My need to pee pressing, I headed for the door in the opposite corner and entered an unexpectedly large toilet with a stylish washbasin and mirror lit by a strip-light. The walls were hung with modern prints, one of which showed a sad-looking monkey with huge eyes that I couldn't stop looking at as I peed.

After washing my hands, I began to reapply my lipstick when my phone broke the peace of the toilet. It was Michael, who straightaway launched into an explanation about how he'd just come out of his weekly management meeting and hadn't heard anything about the Home Office attack, although he was navigating to a news website as we spoke. I then heard him make several noises of shock before starting a high-speed muttering which I assumed meant he was reading through a news report.

He then said: 'Well! It looks an absolute nightmare – it's amazing the casualties were only minor.'

I said his report was erroneous if it said 'minor casualties' and told him how a security man had told me one person was dead and another very unlikely to survive the journey to hospital, while several of the flying-glass injuries were serious.

'My goodness! This really is breaking news!' he said. 'And you're still on the scene?'

Retouching the line of my lipstick with a folded tissue, I explained I was actually standing at that moment in the Home Secretary's private toilet.

'No!' Michael said, sounding excited. 'You must get a picture.'

When I replied I wasn't really in the mood, he apologised for being insensitive then insisted I keep our dinner date.

'I can easily leave early and pick you up,' he said. 'You mustn't be alone.'

We then embarked on a long discussion about what I should do next which ended with me agreeing to rendezvous with him on a corner of the nearby park, immediately opposite Buckingham Palace.

'I just have to finesse a project report,' he said, 'and get it to my board director. So I can be there in fifty minutes – maybe less.'

Checking my watch, I set a time of two o'clock for him to pick me up, then I finished doing my face and made my way back down to the coffee bar, which was now crowded with people from the other bomb-shelter areas.

There was no sign of Stefania or Peter so I approached an official talking to two firefighters and asked if he knew which way I should go to evacuate the building. I also asked if he knew which direction I should take to reach Buckingham Palace. He asked to see my pass then beckoned over another official and instructed her to escort me to the building's rear exit and point me in the direction of the palace.

* * *

Outside, the sky had become completely overcast but the air was warm and I felt a surge of well-being as I headed towards the busy road leading to the rendezvous point. The nice feeling was short-lived, however, as the pinching of my shoes became so severe after fifty metres, I realised I was going to need to buy a cheap pair of flatties from the first shoe shop I came across or end up with major blisters. Continuing up the busy road, I saw Buckingham Palace was looming on the opposite side and deduced from the parade of souvenir shops, eateries and hotels I was passing that I was highly unlikely to find a shoe shop in the vicinity.

Then, as I reached the traffic lights at the junction between the palace and the park, I realised the shops and eateries had entirely given way to houses and offices, so I gave up on the shoes and crossed to the park in search of a bench where I could wait for Michael.

A short way in, I found a seat by a path bordering the park's main lake and sat down as an Italian woman at the bench's other end called out to her husband to keep Alessandro from going too near the pelican's beak.

Looking up, I saw an elegant man with thick hair wave back at her and give one of those impossibly handsome smiles Italian men produce so easily. Then he bent to say something to a boy who was among a crowd of tourists' excited children gathered round a large pelican strutting at the lake's edge.

Watching the boy as his father steered him a half-step back from the bird, I tried to picture what Gian Paolo Friedrich would have looked like at nine years old and was amazed when the lad suddenly turned round and glared straight at me. I thought at first I must be mistaken about where he was looking and glanced across to his mother, but she was busy searching for something in her handbag.

I then looked back at the boy and saw he was still glaring at me, the trace of a smile on his face. A shock then pulsed through me as his eyes suddenly became saucer-sized and floated towards me.

My flesh tightening with goose-pimples, I rubbed my eyes and told myself this couldn't be happening. I then blinked hard to reset my focus and, once my vision had cleared, I saw the boy had turned his back to me and was now reaching forward with the other children to stroke the pelican.

The shock in my system then suddenly gave way to a rush of tender feeling, as if someone had thrown a switch inside me. I then saw the boy caress the pelican's neck, causing it to shake its head with a high-speed waggle.

The children nearest the pelican withdrew to avoid its swinging beak, but the Italian boy continued stroking and, as the bird became still again, he cradled its wattle in one hand and stroked the fine feathers on its head with the other. Coos of wonder rose from the crowd as the boy continued his caresses then gave the pelican a soft kiss between the eyes.

Laughing, the boy's father whispered something that made the boy smile, then the pair turned to leave the crowd, the eyes of every child now on them. After a couple of steps, the pelican started to follow and, as it became clear the bird had become attached to the boy, the children started calling out warnings in their different languages.

Father and son turned round and, waving their arms, they tried to make the pelican understand it couldn't come with them. The bird bobbed its head twice and seemed about to turn back to the water but, as soon as the boy and father resumed walking, it went after them again, sending the children into shrieks of laughter.

A couple of metres from my bench, the boy turned round to the bird again and, raising a single finger, he told it to stop, causing it to halt instantly. He then brought his finger steadily towards the pelican's eyes and told the transfixed creature that, although he thought she was beautiful and he would love to take her home, there was no practical way they could be together so she must now go back to the water.

Along with the growing crowd, I watched in disbelief as the pelican bobbed once more then waddled back to the lake where it hopped onto the low rail separating the path from the water. It then twisted to take a final glance at the boy and, having watched him wave farewell, it launched itself with a flapping splash into the lake. The crowd burst into spontaneous applause.

Arriving by his mother, the boy gave me a sideways look then told his father they should move on quickly, before people started asking how he'd controlled the pelican. The father agreed and, taking the boy's hand, started to head up the path, but the mother stopped them and, looking stern, she asked Alessandro where he'd learnt the animal trick.

Shrugging, the boy said he hadn't learnt anything; he'd simply behaved spontaneously and that had somehow worked. Then he urged her to move on before the people still looking his way decided to come and bother them.

Rising, the mother shouldered her bag and said what Alessandro had done needed explaining. She and the boy then followed the father away from the bench while he said over his shoulder something about how he thought Alessandro had made a connection with the bird, but I couldn't understand everything since my Italian was a little rusty and the family was almost out of earshot.

As the three of them picked their way along the path, the mother's words about wanting an explanation hung in my mind and I wished I could have heard more of their conversation. The family then faded from view and I resigned myself to never knowing how the boy had made the bird obey – although I guessed it was probably no more than a fluke. I then leant back against the bench, slipped off my shoes and watched an old man at the water's edge throw bread to ducks from a crumpled carrier bag.

Wiggling my toes with pleasure, I closed my eyes and let my thoughts drift. Then, after a minute's relaxation, an image floated across my mind of the Home Secretary's office with its picture frame containing the handwritten lines. Assuming it was the Home Secretary who'd written them, what did she mean: 'I am not everyone'?

I could understand her writing about only being able 'to do so much as one person' but the idea of making a clear statement she was 'not everyone' seemed ludicrous. A bit like saying red is not blue.

Opening my eyes, I saw the old man turn his carrier bag inside out then hold it upside down over the water's edge and shake out a shower of crumbs, some of them landing on the ducks' backs. I then recalled what Mo Parrell had suggested about the interconnectivity of life and how the 'I' we think of as being our self is actually just one tiny part of a universal consciousness. So, in that sense, one could argue the Home Secretary was everyone.

But I knew applying Mo's concept was a kind of sophistry since the Home Secretary had clearly written 'I' to mean her self in a common-sense way. Spreading my toes further, I closed my eyes again and thought about Mo's idea of consciousness as observing, unalterable and common to us all. But the thought was accompanied by a pulse of anxiety, so I sat forward and tried to focus on the water, the wildlife and the strolling people.

My eye was caught by a little girl punting up the path on a scooter and the sight of her bouncing curls and rosy face gave me enough space to take a deep breath and realise if I immersed myself in work I could avoid any more overly deep thoughts for the next half hour. So I swung my briefcase onto my lap and took out some papers, deliberately avoiding Renata's notebook.

As I settled to work, a squirrel scurried up in search of food, its bushy tale snaking with quick, stuttering movements. It then took a darting sniff at my big toe and, grateful for the diversion it offered, I sat back again and watched it scamper to the next bench in a speedy, zigzagging run.

Taking out a red pen from my case, ready to annotate the business case I was going to work on, I found myself recalling what the student Lothar had told me at university all those years ago about existence fleeing into everyday objects when faced with itself.

Another twinge of panic then flickered through me and I leant forward once more and focused on the paper, resolving in the back of my mind that, as soon as I'd met up with Michael, I would buy some flat shoes, go somewhere comfortable and relax.

Dinner is served

After Michael had picked me up in his sporty red saloon, we went to the swanky shopping area containing my two favourite department stores and bought a horribly expensive pair of flat-heeled shoes for me. We then went for coffee and cake in the top-floor café of another store while Michael tried to persuade me I should stay the whole weekend with him and Mo, and be an honoured guest at the dinner party he was throwing on the Saturday night.

'I'll drop you at the station Sunday morning,' he said. 'You'll still have time to do your chores.'

I protested I had no overnight bag and didn't like leaving Sebastian for two whole days, but Michael said we could shop now for anything I'd need and Sebastian no doubt had a round of food-stops he could make among my neighbours.

I argued it was terribly spendthrift to buy a whole new set of toiletries and outfits just for one weekend.

'It's only money, my dear,' Michael said, finishing his cake. 'Besides, you'll be able to use it all again.'

A burgeoning desire not to be alone made me accept and I thanked him for being lovely enough to make the invitation and asked who was coming to Saturday's dinner party.

'Oh, it's just a couple we met at a cocktail party a few weeks back,' he said. 'He's a vicar and his partner does landscape gardening. At least, he's trying to.' Michael then explained the partner actually spent most of his time doing piecework; making up rubber clothes for a sex shop.

Finishing my coffee, I said: 'They sound intriguing!'

'Yes. I don't think they've been together very long,' Michael said. Then he told me the vicar had made him and Mo laugh so much at the cocktail party, he just couldn't resist inviting them over. 'You know how it is,' he said.

* * *

On the Saturday afternoon, when Michael and Mo went into the kitchen to start preparing the dinner, I volunteered to peel vegetables and, halfway through, suffered the disappointment of learning the main dish was to be braised hearts.

Having lost the taste for offal in my teens, I was torn between asking if I could have something else and politely being thankful for what I got. After all, Michael had been so kind in treating me to dinner the night before and Mo had been the perfect host since my arrival; it seemed ungrateful to object to a menu they'd probably put a lot of thought into.

I then told myself I used to love the liver and onions my mother cooked when I was a girl so there was no reason I couldn't eat hearts now if I just had enough wine beforehand. Besides, I was beholden to Michael after the way he'd picked me up yesterday and made our time shopping such fun. He'd entered so far into the spirit, he even ended up buying a pricey dressing gown just because it had 'M' on the pockets.

Scraping out the seeds from a pepper, I said: 'Is it too early for a glass of wine?'

Michael glanced at his chunky watch and said: 'I don't think so. Although I was about to put some champagne on ice, my dear, if you can hang on half an hour.'

Removing his washing-up gloves, Mo said: 'I'll stick a bottle in the freezer. It'll be cold in five minutes.' He then crossed to the wine rack and pulled out two bottles of champagne, one of which he wedged into the top compartment of the freezer; the other went in the fridge.

'Perhaps, my sweetness, you can find the sommelier and make sure we get our temperatures right,' Michael said. 'I do think it's a shame if champagne isn't exactly five degrees.'

* * *

By the time the vicar – whose name was Andrew – and his partner Carl arrived, the three of us were well into the second bottle of champagne and Mo had put another one in to chill. It meant my head was nicely swimming and my stomach gurgling with hunger, so I knew I'd be able to eat the hearts, provided I didn't fill up on the goat's cheese starter.

My first impression of Andrew was he looked like a rugby player, with his bull neck and dark beard, while Carl was virtually his negative image: thin and blonde with pronounced cheekbones and knobbly wrists that made him look a little malnourished.

In introducing me, Michael told them I was the country's top psychiatrist and world authority on psychological disorder resulting from somatic alteration.

'I'm not sure I know what that means,' Andrew said pecking me in greeting on both cheeks. 'But I'll have to watch it if you're going to be psychoanalysing me.' And he roared with laughter.

I smiled in the way I always do when people make that joke and said: 'I assure you I'm off duty.'

'There'd be a lot of material there if you weren't!' Carl said, pecking my cheeks in turn.

The five of us then made our way upstairs to the living room and sat in comfy seats while Michael offered Andrew and Carl champagne.

'Champagne! I say, how fantastic,' said Andrew. 'Are we celebrating? I'll drink to it whatever it is!' And he gave another roaring laugh.

Michael explained there was no particular occasion apart from me being with him and Mo for the weekend and the pair of them taking the chance to become better acquainted with some new friends.

'Oh, how sweet!' Carl said and, looking coyly at Michael, he added: 'That's *such* a nice thing to say.'

Catching the look, Andrew said to Mo: 'Is he always such a smooth talker, your other half?'

'Always!' Mo said, folding his arms. 'But I'm not sure he's my other half. Isn't that only for straights – Plato's androgyne and all that?'

'Plato's androgyne? Good God!' said Andrew. 'I can see we're at risk of high culture this evening!' And he roared again.

As Michael went back down to the kitchen to fetch drinks, Carl made small talk with me about how much he loved town houses like Michael's and Mo's and asked where I lived. When I told him I had a semi-detached new-build in Cambridge he seemed fairly uninterested so I asked about him and learnt he'd been raised by his unmarried mother on an inner-city council estate.

Overhearing us, Andrew said: 'Yes, Joy. Don't let the suave looks fool you. He's very much rough trade.' And he gave a laugh, not quite at roar level.

'Oh! So *rude!*' Carl said and, turning to me, he added: 'I wouldn't mind, but he's a total bear!'

I smiled and asked how they'd met.

Andrew explained his housekeeper had commissioned Carl to work on the vicarage garden after the church's regular gardener had died suddenly from a pulmonary embolism.

'Oh, I say!' Mo said. 'It sounds like fate!'

'Doesn't it!' Andrew said and, shifting his position in his armchair, he gestured extravagantly to Carl and added: 'Yes, when I first came across this beautiful creature, the April sun was shining, the daffodils were out and there he was, in shorts and big boots; filling a hole with multi-purpose compost!' And the roar broke out again.

Arrived with two glasses of champagne, Michael handed them to Carl and Andrew, saying: 'Your love blossomed with the compost then!'

Andrew laughed again then, taking a sip of champagne, he said: 'Yes, I'd just got off my knees in church and when I saw him I was back on them pretty damn quick, I can tell you!' and the loudest roar yet filled the room.

Carl rolled his eyes and said: 'I told you he was a bear!'

Squeezing Carl's knee, Andrew said: 'Come on, darling. It's all worship one way or another!'

'Yes, well,' Michael said, coughing. 'Dinner is just about done,' and he invited us to move to the dining room.

* * *

Halfway through the braised hearts, I realised eating was having a sobering effect on me and made a show of draining my glass in the hope Michael would top me up with more of the red wine he'd opened after the champagne ran out.

'My goodness, Joy,' Michael said, pouring me more claret, 'I don't think I've ever seen you be such a fish. You don't think it's still the shock of yesterday?'

Andrew, who was on my immediate left, asked what happened yesterday and I told him and Carl about the attack on the Home Office and how I'd been standing in the exact spot where someone had been killed and another fatally injured, a minute before the fatal missile hit.

Carl gasped with horror and said how awful the whole affair had looked on last night's TV news. Andrew grunted and said: 'The joke is, ruddy Muslims think blowing people up actually gets them into heaven. They've got more funny beliefs than the Catholics!'

Mo pointed out I was Catholic, causing Andrew to apologise immediately with a squeeze of my forearm. He then told us about his own faith, describing the time his grandmother had taken him to a football stadium just after his seventh birthday to hear a talk by a famous Christian evangelist from the US. At the rally, the evangelist had invited everyone who wanted to renounce sin and take Jesus into their lives to come onto the stage and make a public declaration.

'I wanted so much to go down,' said Andrew, 'but my grandmother wouldn't let me.' He then explained that, although he was just a little boy, he'd fought with her to make his declaration and, when she physically prevented him, he spent the next two weeks brooding about it. 'I just felt so strongly about befriending Jesus,' he said.

'Why?' said Carl. 'What possible sin could you have done at seven?'

Fiddling with his thumbs, Andrew said he was the youngest of four brothers and his father had been a busy vicar who hadn't had much time for family life. He then suggested, because he was the baby of the family, he'd sometimes fought a little too hard for attention, not realising he was actually receiving more than his fair share already. 'The truth is,' he continued, 'I could sometimes be a bit of an obnoxious brat.'

'But that's not sin,' Carl said. 'That's just families.'

'That's not how I felt,' Andrew said. 'I thought I'd gone wrong. And I knew befriending Jesus was the chance to wipe the slate clean.'

Carl shrugged and said: 'It sounds like you wanted Jesus because you'd been a naughty boy and wanted to feel better about yourself.' He then took a sip of wine and added: 'My mother never made me feel guilty about anything – which is probably why I don't want to be a Christian.'

Seeing Andrew's face sadden, I said: 'My parents never made me feel guilty either, but I'm a Christian.'

'Maybe you like the promise of eternal life rather than forgiveness,' Mo said. 'I mean, fear of death is a big deal, right?'

Recalling Renata's notebook, I said: 'Or maybe it's vanity.'

'Vanity?' Mo said, and the four of them looked at me for what seemed a long two seconds. Mo then asked what I meant.

Feeling slightly embarrassed, I said: 'Oh, it's just something I read.' Then I told them about Renata's text – *Man's Oh-So-Vain Vanity* – and how it suggested Christianity was actually the product of Man's self-love since it anthropomorphised God by making him a man, Jesus, and taught humanity was so wonderful we'd become a permanent fixture in creation, beyond evolution.

'But we are beyond evolution,' Andrew said. 'Man hasn't changed in, what… a hundred thousand years?'

Toying with his glass, Michael said one hundred thousand years was nothing in evolutionary terms and, besides, species only evolved when changes took place in the environment. 'If you give it another hundred thousand years,' he said, 'you'll probably find we do evolve because of the changes of the technological age.'

He then illustrated what he meant by saying when he went to the gym, he would check the speed and time stats on the treadmill; change channels on his headphones; watch half a dozen different video screens; and run, all at the same time. 'And that's me relaxing!' he said.

He then suggested technology and bioengineering would develop so far beyond anything we could imagine in the next million years it was ultimately bound to bring about significant evolutionary change.

'A million years!' said Carl, popping his eyes. 'You're a bit ahead of yourself aren't you!'

'I don't know,' Michael said, twinkling. 'If you think about it, a million years is only nought-point-nought-two per cent of history. Point-nought-two recurring to be precise.'

'I don't know,' Carl said, sighing theatrically. 'It must be wonderful to have such brains.'

Mo gave a little grimace then asked Andrew, who was massaging his temples, if he felt okay.

'I think that's the problem,' Andrew said. 'Wherever I go, clever people are always coming up with reasons for not believing in Jesus – I can't help being swayed.'

'Swayed?' I said. 'Not in your faith, surely?'

Leaning his chin on his hands, Andrew told us he often had serious doubts about being a clergyman and wondered whether he'd only become one to please his father. 'If I'm honest, my faith is pretty rocky,' he said.

I reminded him of his experience as a seven-year-old and protested he must have faith otherwise he could never have completed all the study necessary for his ordination.

Pouting, he said he couldn't really base his whole life on a childhood experience and the only other profoundly religious moment he'd known was in his first year at university. He then told us how he and two other students reading theology had been in his room one night and decided they'd see what happened if they prayed as hard as they could for God to reveal Himself. Then, after half an hour's intense effort, he'd broken into a chant and, spurred on by the other two, he found himself chanting a phrase over and over in an unknown language.

'I know it sounds far out,' Andrew continued, 'but I was actually speaking in tongues.'

'And do you know what you were saying?' I said.

'That's what's weird,' Andrew said. 'Although the words were gobbledegook, I knew they meant "God is great; His love is His power". But it would vary from time to time like, "God is great; His perfect love is His absolute power".'

'Fascinating,' Mo said. 'And how long did it go on for?'

'About five minutes,' Andrew said.

'And did you go into a trance?' said Mo.

Andrew looked skyward a moment and said: 'No, I don't think so. I mean, if someone had walked in, I'm sure I would have noticed.'

'And can you remember how you felt as you were chanting?' Mo said.

'Yes,' Andrew said. 'Like I'd made a connection: like I was online to God!'

Noting the intensity in his voice, I said: 'Your experience seems very powerful. I can't believe you can't draw on it to support your faith.'

'Oh, but I can,' Andrew said. 'It's just while it supports my faith in God, it makes me doubt Jesus is the only way to Him.' He then shifted in his seat and continued: 'You see, the connection I made... well, frankly, Jesus wasn't in the equation.'

'But how could you tell?' I said and suggested if he'd been in the presence of the Almighty, it would have been difficult to know whether it was God the Father or the Son.

Leaning forward, Andrew said: 'The thing is, I didn't feel like I was in the Almighty's presence.' Then, looking me in the eye, he added: 'All I felt was I was home: back where I belong.'

Mo laughed and said: 'I knew it! You're a Buddhist!'

Andrew shook his head and said he could never go for Buddhism because of the reincarnation idea. 'No,' he said. 'I need something that explains God as physically immediate: as electricity running through our veins – not some abstract system of karma points.'

'Trust you to get physical,' Carl said, but nobody laughed.

'Well,' I said, 'It sounds like your beliefs don't really fit with any religion.' I then suggested he might be interested in reading Renata's notebook.

Draining his wine, he seemed not to hear since he simply put his glass back on the table, clapped his hands and said: 'Enough of this now! Let's get back to the merrymaking – eh? Eat, drink and be merry!' And he let out a muted roar.

We all smiled and, as Michael refilled Andrew's and Carl's glasses, Mo leant close to me and said: 'I'd be very interested in the dead girl's notebook, if it's no trouble.'

* * *

Despite his severe hangover, Michael drove me to the station the next morning in time to catch the mid-morning train back to Cambridge. Although the roads were relatively quiet, it was still impossible to find a parking space – even after driving round the terminus twice – so Michael pulled up at a bus stop alongside the corner entrance and asked me to jump out quickly.

In gathering up my shopping bags and briefcase, I gave Michael a hasty kiss that landed on his mouth rather than cheek and, when I was waving him off from the pavement moments later, I found myself experiencing a tingling sensation on the lips I hadn't known since Brian's death.

Tucking my briefcase under one arm and re-shouldering my handbag, I picked up the bags of clothes and toiletries and headed for a forgotten baggage trolley I'd spotted by a wall a few metres from the entrance.

As I approached, I noticed a Mediterranean-looking man in his late twenties withdrawing a large sum of money from one of the cash machines in the wall. His hair was sticking up on one side as if he'd slept on it awkwardly and half his shirt collar was poking up from his beautifully tailored, but crumpled, suit.

Stuffing the money into his trouser pocket, he turned to watch me loading up the trolley and we smiled briefly at one another before he headed off and disappeared inside the terminus building.

Having arranged my bags securely on the trolley, I sucked in my lips to dispel the last of the tingle and, checking my watch, I made my way through the entrance and towards the ticket office, past the retail outlets lining the large concourse. As I neared one of the machines outside the ticket office, I saw the Mediterranean man bending to talk to a rough sleeper sitting on the floor by a wall.

Then, as I used the machine's touch screen to select my ticket, I saw the man take the bundle of cash from his pocket and hand several notes to the rough sleeper, who nodded his thanks as he took them. Inserting my credit card to pay for the ticket, I followed the man with my eyes as he crossed to the wall of a retail outlet, where a youth with a wispy beard was sitting with a rough piece of string wrapped round his fist, the other end of which was tied to the neck of an ill-kempt dog.

Pocketing my ticket, I watched as the man gave away more cash then, after a brief pat of the dog, he headed to the far end of the concourse where the platform gates and more retail outlets were situated. Heading that way myself, I checked the time of my train on the destination board hanging from the cavernous ceiling then guided my trolley towards a stylish-looking kiosk selling coffee.

The Mediterranean man had already joined the kiosk's queue, a couple of places in front of me, and was counting through the banknotes left in his wad. The terminus's loudspeaker system then announced my train was ready for boarding and I checked my watch again to make sure I still had time to buy a latte before making my way to the platform.

Satisfied there was no rush, I watched the man as he asked for a large hot chocolate with extra cocoa sprinkles and two chocolate-chip muffins. Then he turned round and studied the face of each of us in the queue, one after another, and announced: 'The best things in life are free, but you can keep them for the birds and bees,' and, turning back to the counter, he gave one of the women in the kiosk three banknotes and said: 'I want you to give everyone here whatever they want – and take it out of that. And if there's anything left over, I want you to keep it. And if there isn't enough, then I'll be just over there, so call me, okay?' And he gestured vaguely towards some shops.

Holding the notes up to the light, the kiosk woman nodded slowly and said: 'Okay.'

Turning back to us, the Mediterranean man said: 'Okay, of course it's okay. Everything's okay. Even okay's okay.' Then he stood silently a few moments, beaming at us all with a smile that said he was enjoying some enormous joke and bursting with anticipation for the moment the rest of us got it.

The silence then deepened and, wanting to break it before the embarrassed atmosphere became too painful, I said: 'It's very generous of you. Thanks very much.'

He clicked his heels together and said with a military nod-cum-bow: 'Not at all.'

'It was very generous of you, too, to help those poor homeless people,' I added.

Picking up the two chocolate muffins the kiosk woman had just put on the counter, he took a half-step towards me and, stuffing the cakes into his jacket pockets, he peered intently into my face, a strong waft of alcohol coming off him. Slightly unnerved, I averted my gaze and glimpsed my reflection in the kiosk's glass. Except it wasn't my reflection, but the image I'd seen in the mirror at my university digs all those years ago, when I'd suffered my first panic attack.

I blinked hard a couple of times and the reflection became the present-day me, partly obscured by the back of the Mediterranean man, who was now counting off four banknotes from his wad and offering them to me as he said he was so sorry for everything I was having to cope with. 'Treat yourself to something nice,' he said. 'Maybe a spa treatment – something like that.' And he tried to press the notes into my hand. But I held up a palm and told him to keep his money for someone more deserving.

'But you are deserving,' he said. 'Coping so bravely – with the bereavement and everything. You must have a little fun.'

My heart skipped a beat at the word 'bereavement' and, looking into his eyes, I glimpsed something incredibly familiar, but before I could work out what it was, the kiosk server called out for him to take his hot chocolate and his earlier, nonchalant expression returned. He then excused himself, stepped backwards and swept up his drink, adding: 'The offer's still open. I'll be just over there,' and he gestured again towards a cluster of retail outlets and set off.

My heartbeat recovered, I manoeuvred my trolley so it was tight against me and settled into my place in the queue, immediately behind the woman currently being served. I then glanced back and saw the man sit down by a shop wall with his legs splayed apart and, after placing his drink beside him, he took the money from his pocket and began using it to make paper aeroplanes on the floor between his knees.

When my turn came at the counter, I ordered my latte then turned back to watch the man at work, his shoulders hunched with concentration as he pressed intricate folds into the notes. He then moved onto all fours so he could bring his face closer to the work and I watched him complete several planes, all in different designs, then lay them in a neat row alongside his hot chocolate.

As I left the kiosk, I was curious to see if he would offer money to anyone else, so I decided against buying a newspaper from a nearby bookseller's and returned instead to the destination board where I could pretend to be checking train information while I stood where I could keep him in view.

During the couple of minutes I stood feigning interest in train times, the man continued making his planes, building his fleet to around a dozen, then, as a mother with two early-school-age children approached the spot next to me, I saw him rise to his knees, pick up a couple of his models and throw them dart-like towards the family.

The little boy, who was closest to the man, was struck on the shoulder by one of the planes, causing him to turn. He then burst into a broad grin as he saw the man launch another plane in his direction. 'Mummy, Mummy. Look!' the boy said in a shouted whisper, tugging his mother's arm.

The mother was reading the destination board and said: 'Hang on a minute, Barclay, I've got to see which platform we're on.'

Releasing her arm, the boy picked up one of the planes and, as he bent to collect the other, he was hit on the top of his head by a third. His hand shot spontaneously to his hair and he let out a squeal of delight then turned to his mother, but she was still busy with the board so he picked up the second and third planes and stood toying with them while he considered what to do next.

He then took another glance at his mother, who was now rifling through the little rucksack his sister was wearing and, seeming suddenly to make up his mind, he took a swordsman-like step towards the man, who was still on his knees, and fired all three planes at him in quick succession. His target returned fire, laughing, then, when the boy bent over to collect the newly thrown planes, the man took extra careful aim to hit him while he wasn't looking.

With each new hit, the boy squealed louder than ever and, as he began running around in order to dodge the attacks, he attracted his mother's attention. 'For heaven's sake, Barclay! What are you doing?' she said.

Her question coincided with Barclay making a veering run past the man and firing two more planes at him, hitting him bang in the ear and making him cry out in mock pain.

'Barclay! Stop that at once!' she said, her voice shocked. She then began to apologise to the man, suggesting it was very unlike her son to be so disrespectful and she even carried on when the man picked up the two planes Barclay had just thrown and launched them back at her.

One landed a good metre short but the other hit her square in the chest before plummeting in a tight spiral down to her feet. A long two seconds then passed while she gazed open-mouthed at the man, who was now scrambling to his feet so he could pick up more of the planes littering the floor around him.

Then, closing her mouth, she squatted down to retrieve the little plane nestling against her moccasin and, unfolding it, she realised it was a banknote and asked Barclay if he was holding any more.

The boy looked at her with adorably big eyes and said excitedly: 'It's money, isn't it! Real money!'

'Yes, it's money,' said the mother. 'Now have you got any more?'

The boy said he hadn't since he'd thrown all his planes back at the man. Then, flinging an arm around her hips as if he suddenly needed shielding, he pointed up the concourse and said: 'Look, Mummy! Look what he's doing now!'

Having collected most of the scattered planes, the Mediterranean man was now jogging up the concourse behind a group of three teenagers and, as he drew to within a couple of metres, he pelted them with his little models.

One of the two lads in the group made several feverish brushes at his hair as he felt the missiles hit, then spinning round, he caught sight of the man and said: 'Oi! Fuck off! What do you think you're doin'?'

Ignoring the question, the man went on a careering run in front of the trio and, bending at the waist as he ran, he threw a plane upwards into the face of the girl. She bent back in a reflex action as the plane veered past her cheek and ended up tangled in the tress of false plaits hanging over her shoulder.

''Ere! What are you playin' at, you fuckin' tossa!' she said and scowled at the man as his run took him arcing away from her and round the back of a cluster of retail outlets. The two lads exchanged scowls then took off after him, their trainered feet flying swiftly over the floor tiles.

In disentangling the plane from her plaits, the girl caused its folds to unravel, revealing the unmistakeable design of a banknote. She then moved quickly to where the other planes had fallen and picked them all up, unfolding them to check they too were banknotes.

'Oi, you two!' she called out as the man emerged from behind another group of shops and headed for the next cluster. 'It's only fuckin' money,' she said. 'He's chuckin' fuckin' money – the loony!'

Hearing her comment, the man twisted without breaking stride and waved in what looked like ironic acknowledgement but, within a half-second, he was brought to the floor by one of the lads slide-tackling him and the other sending a flying kick into his back.

As he skidded along on his stomach, the lads came alongside and seized him, one with his knee banging onto his back. 'It's all right,' the girl said, 'leave him alone. He's simple in the head. Look,' and approaching the group, she held out the planes and added: 'See! It's money!'

The lads studied the unravelled planes while the man got to his knees and, pulling a comic face with his tongue hanging out, he said: 'Yeah! I'm fimple in da head. That'f me: Fimple Fimon!'

The taller lad grabbed the man's jacket collar and wrapped it round his fist while he brought his face close to his ear and said: 'Well, you ain't getting it back. Understand?' and waggling the man like a rag doll, he added: 'You chuck money at people, you fuckin' lose it, you get me!' He then shoved the man, causing him to topple sideways, after which he moved to the girl and took the notes from her.

Rising to his feet, the man suddenly produced another plane from somewhere, threw it hard at the back of the tall lad's neck then took off full-speed towards the nearest exit, shouting: 'It's okay, you keep it.' Then, as he neared the way out and saw he wasn't being pursued, he called out in a sing-song voice: 'Have a nice day y'all!' And he was gone.

* * *

After stowing my carrier bags on the luggage rack in the first-class section, I stood my half-finished latte on a little table and slid into the seat behind it, dropping my handbag and briefcase onto the empty place beside me.

The train on the track immediately alongside had no lights on and I could see my reflection clearly in its windows, showing how tired my face looked, even though I'd used extra moisturiser to counter the drying effect of last night's alcohol.

Regretting not having bought a Sunday newspaper, I toyed with the idea of reading some of the papers from my case but closed my eyes instead and savoured the draining away of the ache in my feet, caused by standing so long on the concourse. The scene of the Mediterranean man pelting the youths with paper planes came to mind and I wondered why he'd moved from playing the harmless game with the little boy to putting himself in such obvious danger with the teenagers.

My first thought was he was displaying classic death-wish behaviour and I realised this was consistent with the lack of self-care he showed in having an alcohol smell on him so early in the day. His complete disregard for money also suggested self-destructiveness as did the way he treated his designer clothing: leaning on all fours on the floor and stuffing his pockets with cakes.

In thinking about the man's behaviour, I recalled how he'd peered at me in the kiosk queue and it suddenly struck me what was so familiar about his eyes: they were exactly like Gian Paolo Friedrich's. Not that they were the same colour or shape, but the expression in them so perfectly matched Gian Paolo's on the occasions I'd caught him peering at me, it gave me an eerie shudder.

Opening my eyes, I recalled what the man had said about me being bereaved and stressed, and drew a parallel with what Gian Paolo had said in our first session together, when he'd supposedly divined I was in a state of grieving over the loss of Brian.

I then mentally listed the shocks I'd experienced since that first interview: the fleeting vision of the falling patient; spotting the train bombers and the subsequent police interview; running over the phantom bald woman; Gian Paolo's hypnosis trick; my near-death experience at the Home Office.

Viewed rationally, I couldn't help but admit the Mediterranean man had been right about the stresses on me and I made a mental note to book a session with my deputy as soon as possible to talk through my anxiety levels.

I also told myself the accuracy of the Mediterranean man's comments couldn't possibly be anything other than lucky guesswork, proving Gian Paolo's assessment of my 'emotional atmosphere' in our first session together had been nothing more than a guess too.

Looking out the window across the aisle, I saw a rail employee on the platform wave at someone out of sight then I heard the familiar beeping noise signalling the doors were closing. The train then lurched into motion and I looked out of my window, hoping the view would become more interesting once we'd gone past the parked carriages on the neighbouring track. Unfortunately, they simply gave way to a high embankment wall while the view on the other side offered nothing more than a line of corrugated iron sheds, so I delved into my case and took out the photocopy of Renata's notebook.

A voice inside me warned I might be opening myself up to more upset, but I turned nonetheless to the page headed '*The Lord's Prayer (God's Pyjamas)*' and read:

Our father
(The universal spirit-ocean we're all drops of)

Who art in heaven
(Which is itself heaven)

Hallowed be thy name
(A being so far beyond nounhood can have no name but, if it did, hallowed wouldn't begin to cover it)

Thy kingdom come, thy will be done, on Earth...
(The drive of the universal spirit to exist materially will succeed because of the spirit's ultimate, if very slow-moving, omnipotence)

... as it is in heaven
(Once the spirit exists materially, Earthly heaven will do too, since the spirit's being and heaven's are the same thing [see above])

Give us this day our daily bread
(Keep the pyjamas the ocean-drops walk round in well laundered)

And forgive us our trespasses
(And learn lessons from when the pyjamas get in a knot)

As we forgive those who trespass against us
(As all the pyjamas themselves learn lessons from getting tangled with one another)

And lead us not into temptation
(Stop the pyjamas getting so hooked on pattern and fabric they forget the ocean-drop they clothe is their raison d'être)

But deliver us from evil
(Help pyjamas avoid inflicting the cruelty on one another that stems from total worship of pattern and fabric)

For the kingdom, the power and the glory are yours, now and forever
(Kingdoms, power and glory are of no interest to the spirit; they're matters solely for the vanity of pyjamas)

Amen
(That's all, for now!)

WORLD WITHOUT LOVE

When I returned to work after the weekend at Michael's and Mo's, I immediately made a one-hour appointment with my deputy to talk through my feelings and ended up sitting in a session with her for most of the morning.

It became clear as we talked, the upset I'd experienced at the Home Office had little to do with coming close to death but was actually due to the anxiety built up in me over the last few weeks being unleashed by the shock of the attack.

At the heart of the anxiety was my acute ambivalence over whether the strange happenings I'd been experiencing since first meeting Gian Paolo Friedrich were actually connected with him in some way or were simply coincidences.

In looking for evidence to support the coincidence theory, my deputy and I agreed that, although the feeling of imminent death I'd experienced on seeing the train bombers was hard to explain, my series of fleeting visions had almost certainly been caused by the unprecedented development my imagination had undergone since Brian's death, brought about by the large amount of time I now spent alone thinking about him.

This imaginative development was particularly affecting my visual centres because of the habit I'd acquired in the last two years of picturing Brian as a physical presence, accompanying me in my daily life.

My deputy and I also agreed my meeting with the Mediterranean man at the station and his almost uncanny insight into my emotional state proved how misguided it would be to believe in Gian Paolo's extraordinariness just because he'd guessed I was bereaved when we first met. 'Not unless your crazy Mediterranean man has these "new feelings" too, of course!' said my deputy.

'Well,' I said, 'Gian Paolo did say there must be others like him scattered around the globe.'

'Yes,' said my deputy. 'But what would be the chances of bumping into one – even if they did exist?'

She was right, of course: even if Gian Paolo's 'others' were a reality, they could surely only comprise a few hundred at most, so the mathematical probability of meeting one was absolutely tiny, which I found greatly comforting.

'Anyway,' said my deputy, 'what was he like – your Mediterranean man?'

'Like?' I said, still thinking about mathematics.

'Yes. Was he young, old; tall, short; fat, ugly?'

'Ah!' I said and, picturing him, I told her he was young and good looking, with thick dark hair, intelligent grey-blue eyes and lovely olive skin. 'Although he could have done with a shave,' I said. 'He had that iron-filings stubble – you know, that looks unkempt.'

My deputy made an approving sound and said: 'Rugged good looks, kind to others and money to burn!'

I smiled and told her she might be wrong about the kindness. 'I got the distinct impression he was only giving money away so he could prod at people – to see how they'd react,' I said. 'I really don't think there was anything altruistic in it at all.'

'Interesting,' my deputy said, leaning her chin on her hands. 'Perhaps he's a scientist – doing some weird kind of experiment.'

I smiled again and said he looked way too designery for a scientist. 'Much more like a creative in television or the music business,' I said. 'Something like that.'

My deputy flicked her hair coquettishly and said: 'Even better. I get enough of scientists here.' She then gave a playful arch of the eyebrow and added: 'If you know what I mean,' and we both laughed.

In bringing the session to a close, I thanked her with a hug for listening to me then went back to work feeling genuinely fortified. So it was with renewed confidence I arrived at the hospital next morning to be given an envelope that had been hand-delivered to the unit's reception desk by Gian Paolo Friedrich. It contained a handwritten note paper-clipped to some folded-over pages from a magazine. The note explained Gian Paolo had been so upset by the enclosed article he was now going into a two-day 'hibernation' where he could be alone with his own thoughts. He would, therefore, be unable to attend his session with me the following afternoon.

He ended his note saying he should be fine for our Friday appointment and suggested I read the enclosed article if I needed to understand more about how acts reported in the news were occasionally so loveless, they forced him to retreat into himself until he could reach some sort of understanding as to why they'd happened. It was, he wrote, only through such understanding he could rebuild any faith in Man's essential goodness.

Unfolding the pages, which were from a Sunday newspaper's colour magazine, I made my way back to my office and, after finding a comfortable position in my chair, I slipped off my shoes and tucked my legs up. I could peripherally see my PC screen was full of unread emails but knowing tomorrow afternoon's session with Gian Paolo was now off, I decided I had time to read the story.

It covered six pages and carried the headline 'The day terror touched the City' and an introductory paragraph which read: 'Two immigrant extremists were sentenced to a minimum of 100 years this week for attempting to bomb the London stock exchange last summer using a radio station's traffic plane. Martin Houellebecq reports from the Old Bailey.'

I then read:

The truth of the bone-chilling events that saw two men jailed this week for a string of terror offences has been drawn out piece by piece over the last eight weeks as the now-infamous 'sky-terror' trial proceeded to its seemingly inevitable conclusion.

The daily reports filling the media since the Old Bailey trial began have given a vivid picture of the plot that so nearly brought catastrophe to the City, but it wasn't until the trial's final days the full extent of the plotters' shocking ruthlessness became clear.

Diary of terror – 21 June 2009

4:25am – Algerian nationals, Basem Haniya (21) and Ismail Shihada (27), along with Somali student Ghedi Issa (20) and Iraqi-born Rahim al-Hashimi (35), park their dark-blue Mercedes van in a quiet residential close in Buckinghamshire, opposite the home of traffic-plane pilot, Ron Dell.

5:13am – Thirty-six-year-old father-of-two Dell emerges from his front door to be seized by Haniya, Shihada and al-Hashimi at gun point. He's then forced back upstairs to the master bedroom where the three terrorists tie up his wife and five- and seven-year-old daughters with brown packing tape before threatening to stab them with a 30-centimetre knife unless Dell does exactly as he's instructed.

5:22am – Leaving the knife-wielding Haniya to guard Mrs Dell and her petrified daughters, al-Hashimi and Shihada load Dell into the back of the van and hold him at gunpoint while Issa drives them to the small aerodrome containing the base of Dell's flying business. During the drive, Dell is told that, on his arrival at the aerodrome, he must advise air-traffic controllers his plane is to be flown that morning by a replacement pilot called Rudi Völlay. Dell must say the last-minute replacement is necessary because he broke his wrist in a fall late last night and will be unable to handle the flight controls. This conversation takes place in the back of the van with the three men seated round a large trolley covered with a tarpaulin that Shihada is insistent none of the group touches.

5:45am – Dell arrives at the aerodrome with his three captors, terrified his wife and children are to die a bloody death at any moment. He's met in his hangar office by Energy Radio's traffic reporter, Steve Eagles, who has no sooner remarked Dell is a little late than he's punched in the stomach by Issa and told by the pistol-toting al-Hashimi to do exactly as he's instructed or Dell's family will die. Dell is quick to confirm the situation and begs Eagles to comply.

5:50am – Using the radio apparatus in his hangar office, Dell advises air-traffic officials Rudi Völlay will be flying his plane that morning and gives them the number of Völlay's pilot's licence. When asked if Völlay is fully briefed on the security-check procedures for the flight, Dell's unsure what to answer but is given a mimed instruction by al-Hashimi to say yes. The hesitation Dell makes before replying is to prove crucial in saving lives.

5:55am – Dell gives al-Hashimi a document with detailed guidance on security-check procedures for the traffic plane's entry into central London airspace which the terrorist decides is too long and complicated for Shihada – who is to pilot the plane – to assimilate before the flight takes off. In a fit of temper, he calls Haniya at Dell's home on a mobile phone and after a brief conversation in Arabic, he hands Dell the telephone so he can hear his hysterical daughters begging their daddy to help them. Al-Hashimi then snatches the phone back causing Dell to break down in tears and swear he'll do whatever the terrorists want.

5:57am – Shihada and Issa go to the van and return six minutes later pushing the trolley from the van's rear, which has had its tarpaulin removed, revealing two Paveway II air-to-surface impact bombs which they position by the traffic plane, ready for loading.

Dell explains the strict weight limit on what the plane can carry and asks what the bombs weigh.

As each Paveway II weighs 454kg, Dell protests the plane will never get off the ground and is shouted at by al-Hashimi who says he knows the model of Dell's aircraft can carry a payload of 900kg and accuses Dell of trying to trick him. Dell quickly explains the highly sophisticated digital transmitting and computing equipment installed in the plane by the radio station weighs in excess of 550kg, which is already putting the plane's load just 50kg below the limit because the 900kg maximum must also take account of the weight of the pilot, traffic reporter and other materials on board. The two men then argue whether or not the 900kg limit should exclude the pilot's weight and it's only when Dell breaks down again in sobs al-Hashimi accepts he's telling the truth.

It doesn't stop al-Hashimi becoming furious, however, and screaming at Dell to find a way to accommodate the bombs before he phones Haniya to give him the order to execute Dell's family, starting with the younger child. Frantic, Dell proposes two options: one, strip out the plane's radio and computing equipment to reduce the current payload; two, prepare his second plane, which he uses for the flying school part of his business and which contains no heavy equipment.

When al-Hashimi insists the plane must have the apparatus necessary for Eagles to transmit his traffic information to the radio station – just like any normal day – Dell comes up with a third option: strip out as much of the computing equipment as possible from the plane - and all the parachutes, fire extinguishers and other removable fixtures - but keep the transmitting equipment and load just one bomb.

5:58am – Air-traffic official Les Greave, whose suspicions have been aroused by Dell's hesitant manner in registering the pilot change, uses an integrated security database to look up Rudi Völlay's details and finds out he's a 44-year-old German national from Düsseldorf who qualified for his pilot's licence earlier that year at a small flying school in Wyoming, USA.

Greave discusses with his supervisor why a middle-aged German would learn to fly in the US then a few months later show up in the UK working for a sole-trader flying business. The pair then speak to their terror liaison officer at MI5, Gron Korbo, who decides the situation is sufficiently suspicious to warrant an immediate check being run on Rudi Völlay using MI5's international intelligence databases. Greave is advised by Korbo to talk on the radio with Rudi Völlay in the meantime to see if he can gather any further information.

6:15am – Working under Dell's supervision, Issa and Shihada strip out as many unnecessary items as possible from the plane and load one of the Paveway IIs while al-Hashimi guards Eagles at gunpoint. Shihada then takes his place in the pilot's seat and begins familiarising himself with the controls while al-Hashimi orders Eagles to make his way on board, showing him a mobile-phone photo of Dell's packing-tape-bound family and reminding him they will die if the traffic reporter fails in any way to carry out his work as normal.

When Dell supports the order by pleading with Eagles to do as he's told 'for God's sake' al-Hashimi sneers and asks what evil-doers such as he and the traffic reporter know about God. Fearful of antagonising al-Hashimi, Dell and Eagles say nothing. But when al-Hashimi instructs Issa to board the plane too, so he can guard Eagles while Shihada is flying, Dell is forced to point out the weight-saving from the equipment they've just stripped out is only around 300kg, meaning the plane has a net increase in payload of some 150kg now the bomb is loaded. Dell then explains the payload limit advised by the manufacturer probably includes a tolerance of up to 100kg and, since the plane was already around 50kg underweight, they should be just about okay. But, if Issa flies, it means certain death for them all.

6:20am – Al-Hashimi passes his gun to Issa with an instruction for him to guard Dell and Eagles then joins Shihada in the plane's cockpit where the two men talk heatedly in Arabic for around two minutes. Al-Hashimi then emerges from the fuselage and, taking his gun back from Issa, he thrusts its barrel under Eagles' jaw and shows him the photo of Dell's wife and children once more, telling him he will die with their deaths on his conscience if he doesn't obey Shihada's every instruction once they're in the air.

Eagles confirms he'll do whatever Shihada commands but queries how he'll be able to push the 454kg bomb out of the plane and onto its target without help. Al-Hashimi smiles and says: 'Autopilot. Ismail will put on autopilot and help you.'

Knowing the aircraft has no autopilot, Dell realises the terrorists intend to crash into their target and watches in silent despair as Eagles, who he has worked with for two years, prepares to board the plane.

6:21am – MI5's Gron Korbo learns from German registry and police databases that 44-year-old Düsseldorf citizen Rudi Völlay and his eldest son died two weeks ago in a motorway pile-up while travelling in the son's car. She also learns Völlay had his rucksack stolen at Algiers airport, two days after New Year's Day, when returning from a short holiday with his wife. The rucksack's contents included his passport.

Korbo quickly makes a hotline call to a senior Ministry of Defence official requesting a rapid-response unit be scrambled immediately from Stanmore airbase to fly to the aerodrome housing Dell's flying business.

6:22am – Al-Hashimi tells Eagles at the top of the plane's boarding steps that he knows the reporter is required to make his first broadcast on the radio station at 6:40am, giving details of the traffic flow around London's orbital motorway. He also knows the radio station next requires Eagles to head into central London so he can give an initial report on the traffic situation in town, just after the station's seven o'clock news bulletin.

When Eagles confirms this is his normal routine, al-Hashimi instructs him to give the same information in his 6:40am report as he did yesterday then wait for Shihada to give him instructions after that.

The Father, the Son and the pyjama-wearing Spirit

As Eagles turns to enter the plane, al-Hashimi calls him back and waves the mobile-phone photo of the Dell family at him for a final time, telling him if he really believes in God, he won't want to face Him with the family's death on his conscience.

6:23am – Shihada taxis the plane out the hangar while talking on the radio to air-traffic controller Greave about Düsseldorf. In reply to Greave's apparently conversational questions, Shihada says he doesn't know Düsseldorf very well since he only moved there a short while ago. He then confirms his take-off time with Greave and, two minutes after leaving the hangar, the plane takes to the air.

6:26am – Greave relays the details of his conversation with 'Rudi Völlay' to Gron Korbo at MI5. He also tells Korbo the man flying the traffic plane speaks English with a foreign accent which certainly isn't German and his voice sounds like that of a man in his twenties rather than forties. Korbo asks if the flyer's accent could be Algerian and when Greave confirms it may be, the MI5 official says she's now one hundred per cent certain the man flying the plane is not Völlay but someone who has stolen his identity.

6:28am – Korbo talks over the 'Rudi Völlay situation' with her superior then phones the senior Ministry of Defence official again to brief him on the latest developments and make two further requests: first, that a fighter jet be put on standby to shoot down the traffic plane should it become necessary; second, that another rapid-response team is scrambled, this time to the Dell family home in Buckinghamshire.

Korbo's second request is the result of her educated guess Dell is complying with the terrorists because his family is being held hostage.

6:28am – Al-Hashimi comforts Issa, who has been in tears since the plane's take-off. Later testimony will reveal Issa's tears are because he feels his chance to become a martyr has been lost following the decision for him not to board the plane.

177

6:30am – The senior Ministry of Defence official phones his Permanent Secretary, disturbing him in the middle of a shower, and, after briefing him on the traffic-plane situation, he asks him to liaise with his opposite number at the Home Office so armed police officers can be sent immediately to the Dell family home.

Still drying himself with a towel, the defence ministry's Permanent Secretary is quick to grasp the situation and makes the call to his opposite number at the Home Office before leaving a mobile-phone message for one of his ministers of state, giving brief facts of the traffic-plane drama.

6:32am – A Chinook helicopter with five fully equipped commandos leaves Stanmore airbase, bound for the aerodrome where the traffic plane has taken off from seven minutes previously. Stanmore ground crews also gather to begin preparing two Nimrod jets for take-off, including loading them with live, laser-guided, air-to-air missiles.

6:38am – Having briefed a member of his ministerial team on the traffic-plane situation, the Home Office Permanent Secretary calls the head of Buckinghamshire police to request an armed unit be sent urgently to the Dell family home.

6:43am – The plane's first traffic report of the morning is broadcast via Energy Radio, after which Shihada heads the plane towards central London. He is advised over the radio by Dell that he must fly towards the Gillette tower on London's North Circular Road and, as soon as he has it in view, give air traffic control his password: 68watgft69.

Al-Hashimi becomes nervous and tells Shihada to do nothing until he's confirmed to him the password procedure is correct. He then makes Dell show him where in the safety-check procedures it mentions the Gillette tower and once he's read the paragraph in question, he queries how he can be sure the password is right since it's not written in the document.

Dell explains he's required to change the password frequently and never write it down, and that the current code, 'watgft', stands for 'Watford are the greatest football team' and the 68 prefix and 69 suffix refer to the 1968-69 season when the club was first promoted to the second tier of English football. Satisfied the password is true, al-Hashimi laughs at Englishmen's love of football and instructs Shihada to follow the procedure Dell has advised.

Greave and other air-traffic officials have been able to hear the whole conversation about the password procedure, since Dell has managed to leave the mute button un-pressed on the hangar-office transmitter.

6:50am – A team of six policemen, including three armed officers, leaves Buckinghamshire's principal police station in a marked van and, with siren wailing, heads full speed for the neighbourhood containing Dell's home.

6:50am – Happy Mrs Dell and her daughters are powerless to escape from the master bedroom, Haniya makes his way downstairs to the living room and turns on the television so he can watch the 24-hour news channel. He's expecting to see a report in the next half-hour on how London's stock exchange has been destroyed by the traffic plane.

6:51am – Al-Hashimi and Issa hear a helicopter coming in to land at the aerodrome and become suspicious.

Giving Issa the gun, al-Hashimi tells him to go outside and see who gets out of the helicopter then shoot them if they look like trouble.

As Issa makes his way to the door of the hangar, he sees a Chinook helicopter rising almost vertically from the far end of the aerodrome, from behind a one-storey brick building. He then watches the Chinook, which has military markings, climb high into the sky and turn south-eastwards in a sweeping arc.

Checking the gun is ready to fire, Issa ventures towards the brick building, looking around every few steps. When he's within fifty metres, he hears a wolf-like howl come from the runway and turns towards it, levelling his gun. He then feels a terrible thud in the centre of his back followed by the most excruciating sensation he's ever known and he collapses to the floor, unconscious.

179

One of the five commandos who made the jump a minute earlier as the Chinook hovered over long grass at the aerodrome's edge has thrown a thin-bladed knife into Issa's back, severing his spinal column.

6:51am – Greave advises Shihada over the plane radio that he must climb to eight thousand feet if he wishes to continue on his flight path into central London since the military are conducting an exercise and will have a number of helicopters in the area until 7:15am.

The court will hear later how the military exercise is a fabrication designed to drive the traffic plane to a height where it can be shot down with minimum risk to the public.

6:52am – Shihada radios Dell and al-Hashimi to ask what he should do about the instruction to fly above the military exercise.

Al-Hashimi looks nervous and tries to joke with Shihada, telling him it must be a busy day for helicopters since one's just landed at the aerodrome. He then turns to Dell and, placing a silencing hand over the radio microphone, he asks in an angry whisper what the hell's going on.

Removing al-Hashimi's hand from the mic, Dell asks Shihada if Greave gave an alert level when he notified him of the military exercise and says, if not, he must go back to the air-traffic controller and ask for one.

6:52am – Two Nimrods take off from Stanmore with live missiles.

6:53am – Shihada is advised by Greave the alert level for the military exercise is 'heightened' and he must either begin his climb immediately or change his path back towards the orbital motorway. Greave then asks Shihada to confirm he understands the alert level means the military will view him as a hostile aircraft if he fails to reach the required height. Greave also asks Shihada to confirm he understands the military has the authority to shoot him down

*if they believe he is hostile. 'But don't worry,' Greave says, 'it's just
a protocol.'*

Shihada confirms he understands the implications of the alert
level and Greave continues to reassure him, saying: 'Anyway, it's a
perfect day to get up high. And they'll be out of your way in twenty
minutes – no problem.'

Shihada reports his conversation with Greave back to Dell and
al-Hashimi who agree he should spiral up to eight thousand feet
while Eagles calls in to the radio station to say his bulletin for just
after the seven o'clock news will be a little late because of the military
exercise.

6:55am – Two of the commandos at the aerodrome strap the hands
of the unconscious Issa behind his back and, after removing the knife
from his spine and checking for a pulse, they place his living, but inert,
body in an empty hangar. One commando, who is carrying the unit's
radio equipment, then stays to guard Issa while the other moves off
to join the unit leader and another soldier, who are looking through
Dell's hangar-office window with the aid of a small periscope.

The unit leader then instructs the commando with the periscope
to maintain his watch while he takes the newly arrived soldier with
him round to the front of the hangar where the unit's fifth member is
lying on his stomach, peering round the hangar's door frame, into the
interior.

The prostrate soldier immediately briefs his comrades there
seems to be no one in the hangar apart from whoever is currently
occupying Dell's office. The three commandos then venture inside,
taking up positions in relay as they progress silently towards the
office's open door.

Arrived within earshot of al-Hashimi and Dell, the unit
leader listens for several seconds to check they're not currently in radio
communication with the plane, then he ushers the two commandos
with him to come alongside and gives the order into his radio headset
for them and the commando at the window to move in.

Before al-Hashimi and Dell can even rise from their seats, there
are three commandos in the office doorway pointing guns at them

and shouting 'keep still' while the office's window shatters and the fourth commando levels his automatic weapon at them.

After taking stock of the situation, al-Hashimi seems to come to a sudden decision and, sneering, he reaches quickly for the mobile phone in his pocket. He's instantly shot several times in the neck and chest.

As he slumps to the floor, a gurgling rattle coming from his throat, Dell jumps on him and, with one forearm rammed against his blood-covered neck, he slams his elbow three times into al-Hashimi's face, shouting: 'You f**king c*nt. You f**king, f**king c*nt.' The blows break al-Hashimi's cheekbone in two places and his nose and are the last earthly acts al-Hashimi knows.

The commandos pull Dell off al-Hashimi's now dead body then restrain him in his chair while they try to ask questions about who's flying the traffic plane and whether there are any more terrorists on the aerodrome apart from Issa. Dell's only response is to beg them frantically to save his wife and children.

6:57am – The two Nimrods fly over London's North Circular Road, climbing steadily to their flight-plan height of eight thousand feet. Hundreds of Londoners stop to look up at the jets.

6:59am – Under the orders of his unit leader, the commando guarding Issa uses his radio kit to call into the operations room at Stanmore airbase and detail the unit's success in neutralising the aerodrome terrorists. He also advises the operations room the traffic plane is carrying one Paveway II and a second bomb is now in the unit's possession.

After receiving a brief message of congratulations from the group captain and wing commander in charge of the operations room, the radio commando relays Dell's urgent request for his family to be rescued and is advised by his superiors that a team of policemen is dealing with this part of the mission and is less than ten minutes away from the Dells' home. The officers then speak to the unit leader and instruct him to keep his men onsite at the aerodrome until a police scene-of-the-crime team can get there. They also advise the unit leader the Chinook helicopter will return shortly to ferry the dead and injured terrorists to hospital and collect the second Paveway II.

The officers then resume the teleconference begun fifteen minutes previously with the Royal Air Force's air chief marshal and agree the only course of action open to them is to shoot down the traffic plane without warning since a request by air-traffic controllers for it to surrender is almost certain to cause the suicide pilot to put the aircraft into a nosedive, which will make it incredibly challenging for the Nimrods to hit and endanger civilian life on the ground.

7:04am – The air chief marshal orders the Nimrod pilots to destroy the traffic plane without warning.

7:06am – A missile from one of the Nimrods hits the traffic plane, exploding on impact. One-third of a second later, the plane's Paveway II explodes, creating a ball of fire so large emergency services phone lines are blocked by people across south-east England trying to report it. The largest piece of debris later found from the traffic plane will be a thirteen-centimetre strip of rubber from one of its tyres.

7:08am – Having turned off their van's siren three minutes previously, the team of policemen arrives in the road adjacent to the close containing the Dells' home and two of the officers remove an extendable wooden ladder from the back of the van.

The two officers and two others carrying rifles then make their way up the side passage of a house neighbouring the Dells' and climb over a fence into the Dell family's back garden where they put up the ladder as silently as possible alongside the master-bedroom window.

7:10am – Haniya hears the rattle of the ladder being extended and thinks it's beanpoles being blown by the wind in the vegetable patch of a neighbouring garden. But the rattle sounds again and he goes to the living-room window where he glimpses a rifle-carrying policeman moving in a bent-over run behind the front garden hedge.

Picking up his knife from the coffee table, Haniya races upstairs and into the master bedroom where he sees an armed officer reaching out from the top of the ladder outside, trying to open the room's window.

On seeing Haniya, the officer levels his rifle and shouts for him to drop the knife. Haniya hesitates a moment then moves to the head of the bed where Mrs Dell is sitting, bound in a cross-legged position with her wrists taped to her ankles and her mouth gagged, while her two young daughters sit terrified beside her, bound in similar fashion.

Haniya glares at her, making her cower, before scrambling across the pillows to the younger daughter and raising his knife, ready to strike. The policeman on the ladder fires at him, but the double-glazing deflects the bullet, causing it to hit Mrs Dell in the underside of her right thigh.

Haniya plunges his knife twice into the neck of the little girl, killing her instantly.

At the sound of the rifle shot, the two policemen at the front of the house smash a battering ram into the lock of the Dells' front door, bursting it open with one blow.

The officer on the ladder uses the butt of his rifle to break the bedroom window and clear a shooting hole in the glass.

Haniya manages to plunge his knife once into the neck of the second little girl before he's shot twice in the back of the shoulder by the policeman at the window.

His right shoulder blade shattered, Haniya pulls the knife from the girl's neck with his left hand and shuffles towards Mrs Dell as the policemen who've just broken down the front door burst into the room and seize him by the ankles. They then drag him face down away from Mrs Dell and keep dragging until he falls off the end of the bed.

Haniya automatically puts his hands down to break his fall and screams in pain as the drop sends an excruciating pain into the shattered shoulder, but he maintains his grip on the knife, which has put a deep, bloody slit down the bed.

Running alongside the prostrate Haniya, the unarmed policeman kicks him twice in the head then stamps the heel of his boot repeatedly onto the hand holding the knife until the weapon comes free. He then grabs the now broken left hand of Haniya, and *handcuffs it to Haniya's right ankle, making it impossible for him to stand without using the arm with the shattered shoulder.*

With Haniya secured, several officers rush to Mrs Dell and begin untying her while the rest of the police unit arrives in the bedroom, having completed its search for further terrorists.

The primeval howl of grief that escapes Mrs Dell as soon as the brown tape is removed from her mouth causes the policemen to freeze.

Ignoring the wound in her thigh, Mrs Dell climbs sobbing across the scarlet-splattered pillows and insinuates herself between her two dead children, roughly caressing the hair of them both as she lies in an ever-deepening pool of blood.

Sickened, I stopped reading a moment and took a breath before turning to the final page of the article where it reported the now twenty-one-year-old Issa was paralysed from the chest down and would spend the rest of his life in a wheelchair while Mrs Dell was in a mental hospital, suffering suicidal depression and receiving medication that kept her in a state of perpetual torpor.

Issa, meanwhile, had tried to sue the Ministry of Defence for the negligent way he'd been treated by the soldiers at the aerodrome, but his suit was, according to the magazine, likely to be unsuccessful since the trial judge had recommended anyone carrying a loaded pistol, fully intending to murder soldiers on a mission to save civilian lives, should forfeit the right to damages.

The Dell children's murderer, Haniya, was in good health despite having less than thirty per cent movement in his right arm and had even been commended by the trial judge for confirming the London stock exchange had been the terrorists' intended target, as was suggested by the papers found on al-Hashimi's body. Ron Dell was being treated for chronic alcoholism.

Glad to have reached the end, I put the magazine pages into my in-tray to remind me to ask Addeel to scan them so I could store them later in the 'Gian Paolo Friedrich' folder on my PC.

185

I then opened Gian Paolo's case notes and typed: 'While the magazine article Gian Paolo has given me as reason for missing 21 June's session is upsetting, it cannot be regarded as sufficiently trauma-inducing to drive someone into "hibernation" for forty-eight hours.

'Assuming he doesn't simply wish to miss the session so he can keep a more pressing appointment, his action suggests: (a) he's seeking to put on a show for me about how his "new feelings" include a super-sensitivity or; (b) the labyrinthine complex that enables him to keep transfiguring his incestuous childhood relationship with Renata into a virtuous act is driving him to believe he actually possesses a super-sensitivity.'

I didn't record a 'c' option about how he might genuinely have been traumatised by the article because – thanks to yesterday's session with my deputy – I was more confident than ever Gian Paolo's 'new feelings' had no basis in reality.

My confidence was also based on the reading I'd done in the two weeks immediately prior to my trip to the Home Office, which included studying more than twenty research reports documenting people's extraordinary religious, transcendental and emotional experiences.

That research showed that, although human beings are capable of extraordinary experiences – particularly under the influence of psychotropic drugs – such events are transient and would very likely lead to psychotic disorder if they became regularly repeated. It then struck me that, as I was treating Gian Paolo for psychotic disorder, I should probably accept it was possible he might regularly have extraordinary experiences.

But I quickly challenged myself on whether his treatment was for psychosis. After all, our last half-dozen sessions together had been little more than cosy chats with him talking conversationally about his childhood and religious beliefs. If it wasn't for his insistence on the reality of his 'new feelings', I would have no reason to think he needed psychiatric help at all.

Returning to the case notes, I wrote: 'There is corroboration for option (a) – his wish to convince me he is super-sensitive – since he has hinted my belief in his extraordinariness is a precondition for me being able to give him the help he needs.

'My conclusion at this stage, therefore, is that both options (a) and (b) apply: Gian Paolo wants me to believe he is different to the rest of mankind – and he genuinely believes himself to be so.

'The direction for the next phase of analysis should therefore be to pursue not only the aetiology of his delusion about his difference – and implicit superiority – but also what help he expects me to give him.'

Resolving to push him particularly hard at our Friday session on the question of the help he was expecting, I closed down the case notes then set to work on my emails.

* * *

Two days later, when Gian Paolo came into the consultation room, my initial impression was he looked greyer than any living person I'd ever seen. His walk was steady, however, and, as he took his place on a sofa by the interview table, he gave me a soulful look that pulled so painfully at my insides, I found myself holding my breath.

'So! This is it!' he said.

' "It"?' I asked, my breath still on hold.

'The moment to come clean,' he said and, crossing his legs, he added: 'I was hoping we could have had a few more sessions before this – but time's run out sooner than I thought.'

Breathing again, I asked him to explain and he said that, during his 'hibernation', he had not only been thinking about the traffic-plane tragedy but had also carried out scans of his body using his 'cyclonic' faculty. The result of that was he'd seen how the cells of his central nervous system, lungs and stomach were mutating in preparation for the spread of the cancer in his brain, which had now grown to the size of a golf ball.

'It's pretty much what happened to Renata about a fortnight before she died,' he said.

Despite the shockingness of what he was saying, I couldn't help feeling a certain excitement he'd painted himself into a corner at last by making a claim that could be scientifically substantiated.

'So you can actually see a tumour?' I said.

'Yes,' he said. 'It looks just like Australia from one angle.'

He then leant his elbows on the table, glanced fleetingly at the ceiling camera and told me he'd known definitely since late April the tumour was forming and that's what had spurred him to come to me in the first place. He then begged me not to judge him too harshly for what he was about to say, asking me to understand he'd been forced to take the action he had because there was no other way for him to approach me.

I said I was not in the judgement business and he should just talk freely. He smiled; then, sitting back, he said he was not mentally ill and never had been so any theory I'd been developing about incest and guilt trips was actually way off the mark. He then said he'd made up his metaphysics obsession purely to become my patient.

His intention all along had been to befriend me so he could persuade me and, subsequently, the geneticists I knew, to take on a project aimed at isolating the genes that made him and Renata special.

When I asked him what the point of such a project would be, he gave an intense look and said: 'To accelerate evolution.'

I smiled in turn and asked him to elaborate. 'Where do I begin?' he said, puffing his cheeks. Then he told me he believed it was 'half time' in the history of the world because our solar system had started around four and a half billion years ago and, in a similar amount of time, the sun would have burnt out, leaving Earth either a ball of icy rock or swallowed up in the sun's red-giant phase.

According to Gian Paolo, human intervention was needed now to speed up the evolutionary process so Earthly life could avoid extinction by adapting itself to survive in other solar systems, which it could then migrate to.

I suggested God had taken care of evolution so far and would no doubt take care of it in such a distant future.

Shaking his head, he said I needed to remember natural evolution was driven by changes in the environment, and each change needed to be experienced by generations of a life form before it evolved, so the only way Earthly life could adapt to planets it suddenly migrated to would be through designed interventions.

'And designed interventions means genetic engineering?' I said.

Shifting in his seat, he confirmed it did.

Aware his ideas were moving into the realms of the fantastic, I thought the discussion might nonetheless be useful in uncovering the aetiology of his 'new feelings' delusion, so I kept the conversation going by suggesting what he was proposing sounded pretty close to Hitler's dream of breeding the Homo superior.

Looking shocked, he said he wasn't seeking to develop people who could sit at the top of a new world order: he simply wished to speed up development of beings through whom more God could flow into the world.

' "More God"?' I said.

'Yes,' he said and, admitting that probably sounded strange, he told me it was actually a perfectly rational idea and he could explain.

'I'm sure you can,' I said. 'But, first, let's be clear – you're looking for me to help genetically engineer some sort of Homo superior?'

His cheeks puffing again, he said: 'Is that so wrong?', but before I could answer, he started assuring me the project would be a consultative programme where the most talented scientists worked with established ethics committees over many centuries to develop incrementally people whose only difference to naturally conceived humans would be their superior ability to bring God into the world.

'I see,' I said. 'And by superior ability, you mean their capacity to experience "new feelings".'

'Exactly, yes,' Gian Paolo said and, giving me a look that tugged at my insides once more, he added: 'But this isn't about Renata or me. It's very important you see the bigger picture here.'

Pretending to make a note on my pad so I could avoid his gaze, I said the evolutionary principle of natural selection would surely bring about the changes he was talking about if they were genuinely God's will.

'Probably, yes,' said Gian Paolo, 'but not quickly enough.'

'But it's all such a long way off, Gian Paolo,' I said. 'Perhaps science will have found a way to regenerate the sun before things go too far.'

Gian Paolo said he thought that, to achieve solar regeneration, human science and technology would need to have developed so far beyond anything we knew that Man would have to have evolved skills we couldn't even imagine now.

'I see,' I said. 'So there's your speeded-up evolution again.'

'Precisely!' he said.

A short silence followed, during which I wondered whether it was worth continuing what was becoming an increasingly bizarre discussion. But, sticking with the idea that the more room I gave him to think imaginatively, the greater the chance I might tap into the causes of his delusions, I said: 'But there is an alternative: God could always make a divine intervention with the sun – like He did with the Red Sea, for example.'

Gian Paolo's head shook again and he said God was incapable of such action. This was evident, according to him, from the fact no interventions occurred when disasters or wars threatened thousands of innocent lives, even though God, who was not only made of love, but love itself, would be compelled to intervene out of compassion.

'And what about the traffic-plane pilot?' he continued. 'How could it be God's will for two little girls to be butchered in sight of their mother?'

I pointed out the Catholic church was familiar with the argument of why a loving God should allow extreme tragedy, and the church's teaching was it was wrong to question God's will since it undermined our faith in His righteousness.

Heaving a deep sigh, Gian Paolo said under his breath: 'And you think I'm nuts!'

His remark nettled me and he must have caught a sign of my annoyance since he apologised profusely straightaway, stressing he hadn't meant to disrespect my beliefs. He then gave a placatory smile and, uncrossing his legs, asked me to consider if it didn't make more sense to look at God in terms of the bigger picture of creation. According to Gian Paolo, this showed God had only ever manipulated matter through the tiniest incremental changes over immensely long periods of time.

'There're no great waves of a wand. Just loads of barely perceptible, little changes,' he said.

'But what about the miracles?' I said.

Rubbing his darkly ringed eyes, he said wearily: 'Look, please can we just forget dogma a minute.' He then asked me to imagine a scenario where God had decided one day, out of sheer creativity, to make itself exist materially; so, fourteen billion years ago, it big-banged the universe into existence.

About nine and a half billion years into the big bang, our solar system formed and, as Homo sapiens evolved, we invented a narrative about how we were an eternal fixture in a finished universe, to make ourselves feel secure. 'The truth is,' said Gian Paolo, 'the universe is actually a work in progress.' He then suggested God itself didn't even know how creation would turn out since it was 'making it up as it went along'. 'But we'll know when it is finished,' he continued, 'because it will actually be God in material form.'

' "In material form" – like Jesus you mean?' I said.

'No. I mean the whole universe – not just one man,' said Gian Paolo. He then suggested that, in the same way God's being was brought into materiality through our minds and bodies, so the universe would become one infinitely immeasurable body giving material existence to the whole of God. 'It would be a unified body where every living creature was a blood cell, every constellation part of the skeleton and all the galaxies vital organs.'

He then said this perfection of materiality was, of course, many billions of years away and it was inevitable meanwhile that accidents happened, such as tsunamis and earthquakes.

'I'm not saying God isn't ultimately all-powerful,' he added. 'It's just it can't make an omelette without breaking eggs.'

Aware of a debate in religious circles around the mutual exclusivity of God's perfect love and omnipotence, I said: 'It's an interesting argument, Gian Paolo. But even if God doesn't have the power to intervene, it doesn't mean Man should.'

'Oh, but it does,' Gian Paolo said and went on to argue it was misguided to view God as something sitting far away in heaven while autonomous humanity carried on its business. 'Mankind is God, or at least the important aspects of it.' He then noticed my raised eyebrow and quickly added. 'You have to understand, each of us really is God, in the same way a grain of sand is the beach.'

Checking my watch, I said: 'Okay. I think we'd better leave it there for now.' I then made a note on my pad about his view of himself as being God and added: 'What I'd like to do now is take you downstairs so we can see about getting a brain scan.'

Standing up so he could reach into the front pockets of his jeans, he pulled out a polythene bag and said: 'Okay. But if you're going to get me doing chemo and all that horror, you must do something for me.' He then handed me the bag and explained it contained blood and saliva samples from him and Renata. 'You must promise,' he said, 'you'll do all you can to get a geneticist to find the bit of Renata's and my DNA that's radically different from the norm.'

Accepting the bag, I said, although I was no expert, I thought a huge amount of time and resource would be required to make that kind of analysis.

Gian Paolo looked pained and asked if it wouldn't be possible for a geneticist to fit the analysis into some existing research project.

I said I didn't think so then added: 'Besides, if there were a gene behind yours and Renata's "new feelings", your brother would have it too.'

Suddenly looking tired, Gian Paolo sat back down and, after massaging his temples a few seconds, he asked if it would make a big difference with the analysis if Aldo did have "new feelings" and provided samples.

I said again I wasn't an expert but suggested it was very likely to be easier to identify a common denominator across three subjects than two.

Gian Paolo gave a deep sigh and said the truth was, Aldo did have the ability to experience "new feelings" but had hitherto refused to give samples.

Surprised, I said: 'But when I asked if Renata was the only person you'd felt "there" with, you said yes and that it didn't work with Aldo.'

'What I actually said was it doesn't work *properly* with Aldo,' Gian Paolo said.

'I don't understand,' I said. 'So what are you saying now?'

Folding his arms, he told me Aldo was actually able to experience all the 'new feelings' he and Renata could – with the exception of 'lovey' – and he had even experienced an extra one he called 'reading'.

'Reading?'

'Yes,' said Gian Paolo and, sitting upright, he explained it allowed Aldo to gain a deep insight into another consciousness. He then told me Aldo had described the feeling as a kind of empathy where, instead of reading someone's thoughts from their face, body language or voice, he could read the quality of their spirit through eye contact at chosen moments. His choice of moments was based on what he called a 'ready-to-receive' feeling. 'A bit like when a piece of music makes you really listen,' Gian Paolo added.

'I see,' I said. 'It sounds similar to "there" don't you think?'

'I suppose so,' Gian Paolo said. 'Except it's not a two-way thing. The person being read has no idea it's happening.'

Worried by this addition to his already labyrinthine fantasy about his, and his family's, extraordinariness, I made a note on my pad and challenged him on why he'd not told me the truth about Aldo before.

'Because I wanted to keep him out of it,' he said with a sigh.

'Oh?'

Springing to his feet, he began pacing the room and said Aldo was a difficult person to deal with and had been since early childhood, probably because he'd been damaged by his love-hate relationship with their mother, Alice. She'd formed an idea early on Aldo was some kind of mini-version of Claudio and, as time went by, she developed an ever deepening habit of 'visiting the sins of the father upon the son'.

'"Just like your bloody father" was a mantra for her,' Gian Paolo said. He then told me the effect of Alice's treatment of Aldo was he'd learnt to be 'an emotional boxer': always putting up a guard in front of his own feelings while he jabbed at other people's weak spots.

'On the few occasions I tried "there" with Aldo, it was a nightmare,' Gian Paolo said. He then explained how Aldo would begin by sharing himself in the same way Renata did but as soon as his inner life was joined with Gian Paolo's, his ego would start trying to control them both.

'I'm not sure I know what that means, Gian Paolo,' I said.

Sucking his bottom lip, he said: 'It's hard to explain.' He then perched on the edge of the interview table and said: 'I suppose all I can say is, whenever I tried "there" with Aldo, then – for days afterwards – if I felt the slightest pain or anger, the feeling would sort of mushroom into these horrific torture fantasies.'

I said it was not unusual for children who'd been bullied by a parent or sibling to experience such fantasies and asked if Aldo had been a bully to him.

Gian Paolo looked thoughtful a moment and said: 'Look, now we're not in the patient-doctor relationship anymore, do you mind if we just skip my childhood.' He then told me how the samples in the bag were in hermetically sealed tubs and he had more of Renata's blood and saliva stored at home if needed.

Putting the bag in my jacket pocket, I rose, crossed to the consultation room's door and, having gestured for Gian Paolo to go ahead of me, I followed him out into the corridor and along to the lifts. We then descended to the magnetic resonance imaging section on the hospital's second floor where, thanks to a cancelled appointment, we were able to arrange a four o'clock slot for Gian Paolo to come back for a scan.

'But if I'm definitely doing it,' Gian Paolo said, 'you've got to talk to a geneticist about the samples, okay?'

I promised I would and, once we'd said goodbye, I went back to my office and emailed Michael Servo with a request for him to ring me when he had a moment. I then opened Gian

Paolo's case notes on my PC and started recording the details of our conversation, including his wish to end our doctor-patient relationship, but I was interrupted after a minute by a call from Michael.

'That was quick!' I said.

'You're in luck my dear, I'm just out from a project board,' he said.

Thanking him for ringing, I explained the deal I'd made with Gian Paolo about his brain scan and asked how much work it would take to isolate the gene he believed made him and his sister extraordinary.

'You know,' Michael said, 'I always had a feeling I'd hear more about your Gian Paolo.'

He then asked what the logic was behind Gian Paolo's self-scanning technique being part of a 'new feeling'. 'Surely that's more of a sense than a feeling,' he said. 'Like x-ray vision.'

Reluctant to enter into the detail of Gian Paolo's delusions, I said: 'I've no idea. Whatever he thinks he does is pure delusion anyway. I'm only talking about it now so I can say I've kept my promise.'

'Ah!' Michael said. 'But supposing his test proves positive and he really has scanned his Australia golf ball?'

'We'll cross that bridge when we come to it,' I said. 'The question is, is it feasible to isolate an extraordinary gene?'

Michael made a humming noise then explained each human being had around 30,000 protein-encoding genes that determined their features. Each of those genes contained a sequence of some 100,000 bits of DNA and every person's genetic program was unique, although the overwhelming majority of code was common to us all.

'So the answer is, yes, it is feasible,' he said. 'But it would be a huge amount of work.'

'What are we talking,' I said. 'Months? Years?'

'Mathematically speaking, it would be years,' he said. 'But, if a gene was absolutely extraordinary, there are guys who've spent a lifetime looking at this stuff who might spot it pretty quickly.' He then told me the director of genetic research in his company had been a leading light on the initial 'human genome' project conducted a decade ago and understood DNA coding conventions as well as anyone alive.

'The thing is,' Michael continued, 'you'd need one hell of a business case for him to look into it.'

'Thanks,' I said. 'That'll do me for now – I just wanted to be able to say I'd kept my side of the bargain.' I then finished the conversation by asking Michael his plans for the weekend and thanking him once again for the lovely dinner last Saturday and the super way he and Mo had looked after me.

'Not at all, my dear. It was lovely to have you,' Michael said. 'And don't hesitate if you need to talk more about your Gian Paolo. I'm sure there'll be more to say.'

A SPOONFUL OF SUGAR

When I arrived for work on Monday morning, my desk phone was flashing with a message left an hour previously from an extension number within the hospital. After booting up my computer and stowing my handbag in a drawer, I accessed the message and heard Gian Paolo Friedrich's magnetic resonance images were now ready but the imaging unit was unsure whether to send them to me or his GP.

Impatient to see Gian Paolo's claim about his body scanning ability disproved by the scans, I hung up the phone, made my way out of the office and went down in a lift to the second floor. I then half skipped, half power-walked along the corridors to the magnetic resonance imaging section.

After I'd identified myself to the nurse on the reception desk, she gave me the folder of Gian Paolo's images, which carried a yellow sticky label on the front marked 'urgent'. She then advised me to come back if I needed advice on arranging chemotherapy for the patient.

The mention of chemotherapy pushed my impatience to bursting point and, on the way back up in the lift, I hastily took out several images from the folder. They showed a golf-ball-sized tumour towards the back of the right side of Gian Paolo's brain. My mind racing, I hurried back to my office and, shutting the door behind me, I spread all the images on the desk. One sheet showed a side elevation of the growth: it looked like Australia.

An electric sensation pulsed through me and my fingers trembled as I sifted the rest of the images. I then sat down and tried to reason what I should do next. Clearly the tumour was life-threatening and required urgent treatment.

Deciding it was probably down to me to contact Gian Paolo about the results, I scooped the images to one side then opened the patient-records application on my PC. Gian Paolo's record held comprehensive contact details so I dialled his mobile, my fingers still trembling.

A few seconds later, the recorded voice of an overly polite woman told me twice: 'I'm sorry, the number you have dialled has not been recognised', then the line went dead. I tried again with the same result and was on the point of dialling his landline when my phone rang with what seemed unusual loudness.

It was one of the consultants from the magnetic resonance imaging section, asking if I had a moment to talk about the Gian Paolo Friedrich scans. I explained I was in the process of trying to contact him and she said it was handy I hadn't spoken to him yet since, when I did, I'd need to advise him to admit himself immediately to the cancer-care ward.

'It's as serious as that then?' I said.

The consultant confirmed it was and said there had been a slight mix-up with her receptionist who shouldn't have handed over the images without explaining the patient needed to come in for urgent treatment. She then told me she believed the type of tumour afflicting Gian Paolo belonged to one of the virulently malignant categories, although she couldn't be certain until the proper tests had been carried out. 'If it's what I think though,' she added, 'it will quite quickly be terminal.'

'What are we talking?' I said. 'A few months? Weeks?'

'More like a fortnight.'

'I see,' I said; then we talked through the process for Gian Paolo registering as an inpatient, after which I thanked her for her help and rang Gian Paolo's home number. For some reason, the line just gave an unobtainable signal, so I went up the corridor to my deputy's office and told her, in light of the seriousness of Gian Paolo's condition, I was going to drive to his home to see if I could bring him into hospital myself.

'I should easily be back by ten-thirty,' I said. 'I'll have my mobile on if you need me.' I then made my way down to the basement car park and, once inside the Audi, I entered Gian Paolo's postcode into the satnav.

Heading up the dual carriageway to Cambridge, I reasoned the only way Gian Paolo could have known about the tumour was if he'd undergone a previous magnetic resonance scan, which would need to have been arranged by his GP and I resolved to look up the GP's contact details when I was back at the hospital. I had a duty to consult with the GP about the scan results in any case.

I then thought the unthinkable: what if Gian Paolo hadn't undergone an earlier scan? But the idea made my head swim so I turned up the string quartet playing on the radio and, in the process, almost drowned out the satnav instruction for me to take the third exit at the next roundabout.

When I arrived in Gian Paolo's road, I was surprised to see it contained stylish town houses and white stone apartment buildings rather than the dusty-curtained tenements students usually rent. The parking was also surprisingly plentiful in front of his building and, as I left the Audi and made my way to the building's main entrance, I was struck by the obvious expensiveness of its wrought-iron door with its flanking ornamental trees in glazed pots.

After pressing the entry-phone button for Gian Paolo's top-floor apartment, I stood back and waited. A crow in one of the lime trees overhanging the parking area gave a loud squawk and was answered by a bird on the roof above me. Gian Paolo's voice then came over the entry phone, greeting me and inviting me up.

The apartment building had a small lift with jazz softly piping through concealed speakers and, when I emerged onto the third floor corridor, I saw Gian Paolo leaning out from his apartment's doorway. 'Nice to see you, professor,' he said. 'Although I guess this isn't such a nice call to make.'

He was dressed in an ankle-length muslin robe which the light from the room behind was shining through, clearly outlining his naked body beneath. His head was closely shaven, making him look much older and less attractive, and his eyes were even more darkly ringed than on Friday.

'What happened to your hair?' I said, struck by the contrast between his white scalp and olive face.

Giving a half-smile, he ran a palm across his cranium and said: 'I figured it would save some of the chemo mess.'

His certainty about his need for chemotherapy and apparent knowledge of why I was there disconcerted me and I found myself searching for what to say next.

Seeming to catch my uncertainty, he gestured to the bright interior behind him and said: 'Won't you come in while I get ready?'

I smiled my agreement then followed him into the room, which was spotlessly clean with laminate flooring and plush cream seating. 'My goodness,' I said, 'what a beautiful room! Your rent must be a fortune!'

'I don't pay rent; I own it,' he said. 'Aldo gave me the money.'

'My goodness!' I said. 'He must be very fond of you.'

No reply came, so I asked what the rest of the flat was like.

'Yes, come on,' he said, suddenly animated. 'I'll show you.' We then went through a glass door into a hallway with a kitchen, bathroom, box room and bedroom leading off it. The box room was an office with his computer and two high bookcases full of academic books and, as he showed me round his surprisingly large kitchen, a petite Siamese cat appeared and moved to his side.

'Hello, cutie pie,' he said, bending to tickle its head and ears. He then looked up at me and said: 'This is Shah. She's been with me since I came to Cambridge. We're very attached.' And turning back to the cat, he added: 'Aren't we, sweetie.'

Shah pushed her face against his hand and I said: 'Yes, I can see she loves you. I have a cat myself: Sebastian.'

Turning instantly towards me, Gian Paolo looked in my eyes and said: 'Don't worry, I've made arrangements for when I'm gone. My neighbour Amir is going to have her.' He then explained there was an Iranian-born medical student living in the apartment next door who he'd bequeathed the flat to. 'That way she can stay on here as long as she likes,' he said.

'You're not expecting to be here much longer yourself then?' I said.

Gian Paolo made no reply again and led me to a bedroom where a wheeled suitcase was standing beside a high wardrobe with sliding doors. 'I know what's coming,' he said. 'You see – I've packed already.'

The bedroom was all in white with a large four-poster draped with floaty muslin curtains, giving the room an Eastern look. In an alcove was a huge cushion before a low, stone-topped table dressed with a neat line of thick candles, a glass jar of incense sticks and a chrome cigarette lighter.

Nodding at the table, I asked if that was where he carried out the free-thought sessions I'd prescribed. He confirmed it was, then crossed to a chest of drawers, picked up a remote control and zapped an audio system to life, causing slow trumpet music to play out from a set of discreet ceiling speakers. 'I like to have jazz when I'm meditating,' he said and, throwing himself onto the bed, he added: 'Do you like jazz?'

He then clasped his hands behind his head and closed his eyes. Moving to perch beside him, I said: 'I'm more a classical person myself.'

Smiling contentedly, he nestled into his pillows for what I guessed he knew would be the last time, and said: 'I thought you might be.'

'Oh? Is that another part of your "new feelings"?' I said and, as I spoke, I found my eyes irresistibly drawn to the bulge of his genitals, which were semi-visible where his muslin robe was pulling taut.

'Wagner? Bach?' he said, his eyes still closed.

Unable to resist studying his body and the heavy thickness of his penis, I felt the first twinge of physical lust I'd known for years. My voice slightly choked, I said: 'Yes to Bach, not really to Wagner.'

His eyes flicking open, he suddenly sat upright, his hands moving to his lap, and said: 'Anyway, I suppose we should be talking hospitals rather than music.'

My ears burning with schoolgirl embarrassment, I kept myself in countenance by talking about his scans and the immediate need for tests and chemotherapy to begin.

His demeanour throughout the conversation was calm and, when I explained the worst case scenario was he may only live another fortnight, he grinned and said: 'I don't know. I think the worst case would be limping along six months in some hospice.'

When I suggested all life was precious and he should try to maximise the time left to him, he gave a small laugh and said: 'Nice try, professor. But I believe life goes on for ever – there's no need to cling to it on Earth.'

Surprised by his jolly tone, I said his beliefs might be useful for summoning courage to face whatever lay ahead, but a belief system that made someone cheerful about dying was probably misguided.

Adjusting his pillows, he shrugged and said he couldn't explain why he felt in such a good mood, although he did have one sorrow: 'Poor Shah,' he said. 'She's really going to miss me.'

Glancing at the Siamese – who was sitting on the rug by the bed watching us – I said I could see why he should feel strongly for an animal who wanted so much to be in his company. 'But,' I added, 'at the end of the day, it is just a cat.'

For the first time since I'd known him, he looked genuinely angry and said he'd always found it distasteful how Catholics refused to recognise animals could love. 'It's a bit like when society used to debate if women had souls,' he said.

'You're not suggesting cats have souls, surely?' I said.

'Depends what you mean by soul,' he said.

I knew I had a busy day ahead, but couldn't resist responding, given this would probably be our last discussion together. So, I said soul was the essence of a person that contained their personality, mind, emotions, will and spirit.

Pouting, Gian Paolo asked what I meant by spirit.

Finding myself on familiar ground, I said without hesitation there were two definitions: first was the uniquely different bundle of psycho-emotional characteristics all humans possessed, such as determination, courage, integrity, etcetera; second was the Holy Spirit God put into us which was our share of Jesus and gave us love, forgiveness, truth and light.

Nodding, Gian Paolo said it was an impressively precise explanation – but enough to depress anyone about dying.

'Oh, why do you say that?' I said.

'Because it sounds like you're saying a soul is a human being without a body,' he said. 'And that would mean heaven is just a load of disembodied humans hanging round with God.'

'That's a very reductive way of looking at it,' I said.

'Yes, isn't it,' he said and, leaning across to open the drawer of his bedside table, he took out a pen and paper and continued: 'But let me put a different scenario to you.' He then drew a circle with some stick figures standing on it and said it represented Man on Earth and, above it, he sketched a bearded figure on a throne, meant to portray God the Father and, on one side of

Him, he outlined Jesus and, on the other, he wrote the letters H and S, standing for Holy Spirit.

'Now,' he said, pointing at the Earth. 'You're saying there's Man down here with his soul inside him' – and he drew little circles on all the stick figures' stomachs to indicate their souls – 'and up here in heaven is God.' He then drew a dotted arrow from the 'HS' on the diagram to the men on Earth and said: 'And God's plan is to put the Holy Spirit into people who've made friends with Jesus so their souls can, at some point, come up and live with Him.'

Uncomfortable at seeing Christian doctrine represented in a management-theory diagram, I said: 'Okay, but it's very, very oversimplified.'

Nodding again, Gian Paolo said: 'I accept that, but bear with me a moment.' Then, turning over the paper, he drew a straight vertical line which he said was a divider the thickness of a cigarette paper and, to the left of it, he made a gaseous squiggle which he asked me to view as the spiritual dimension containing an infinitely vast and ever-changing God and, on the right side, he put a scattering of differently-sized circles, to represent the material universe.

'Now,' he said, tapping the left side of the diagram. 'Imagine this spiritual dimension is a realm of perfect peace, love, truth and beauty which is itself heaven and God all rolled into one. And it's this entity-transcending God that, one day, out of sheer creativity, big bangs the material universe into existence – here,' and he tapped the diagram's right side.

'Okay,' he continued, 'now let's say God – still in the spirit of sheer creativity – chooses one day to expand into materiality.' He then drew a series of little black dashes crossing the vertical line and said: 'So it pops through to the other side of the cigarette paper at different points and, so it can function in the universe, it develops little capsules to walk round in...' and quickly sketching small gingerbread-man figures, he added:

'Us!' He then filled in the little men with gaseous squiggle and concluded: 'God's pyjamas.'

In listening to him, I felt a twinge of the anxiety I'd become accustomed to in recent weeks and said: 'But isn't that squiggle their soul?'

'Not in the sense it contains their personality and emotions, no,' he said.

'In what sense then?' I said.

'In the sense it's an infinitesimally tiny and ever-changing piece of God that shines through a body for as long as that body functions,' he said.

'Isn't that sort of what I'm saying?'

Leaning back on his elbows, the paper still on his lap, he said: 'No, I don't think it is. You're saying a soul is the essence of a man which, if it perfects itself, can go and live with God. I'm saying it's God to begin with – and not actually much to do with Man.' He then developed his idea by saying the bit of God that gives rise to a human being was like electricity in a light bulb: 'It lights up the bulb while it's there. But, as soon as someone kills the light, it simply goes back to being potential on the grid.'

'I see – I think!' I said then, re-examining the 'cigarette-paper' line on the diagram, I added: 'You know, it reminds me a bit of the 1960s song by the Doors', and I quoted the lyric 'Break on through to the other side, break on through to the other side'. I then smiled at Gian Paolo and said: 'But you're way too young to remember that.' And leaning on one elbow, I added: 'The singer's idea – Jim Morrison – was, he was going to report back from the "other side" once he died. It captured a lot of people's imagination.'

Nimbly swinging round to the other side of the bed, Gian Paolo rose and headed for the chest of drawers. He then took a laptop out from the top drawer and made a few clicks on the mouse, after which he picked up the remote control and joined me back on the bed.

'The last time I went to Père-Lachaise – where Morrison's buried,' I continued, 'there were still plenty of people writing messages on his grave – and that was in the mid-nineties.'

Gian Paolo gave a big grin and said: 'That doesn't surprise me.' Then, pressing a couple of buttons on the remote, he added: 'And as for not knowing who Morrison is…'

Suddenly, the unmistakeable thunder-clap and electric piano intro of the Doors' *Riders on the Storm* piped out from the ceiling speakers and, still grinning, Gian Paolo said: 'Morrison's a god!' He then passed me the remote, said the next track should be *Break on Through* and asked me to make myself at home while he took a quick shower.

Accepting the controls with a smile, I watched Gian Paolo head for the bathroom while Jim Morrison's earnest baritone began *Riders on the Storm*. Turning up the volume, I listened to the song develop its mood of eerie foreboding and, as Morrison sang the line 'into this world we're thrown', I recalled my university days and how my theology friend, Lothar, had accused the singer of lifting the idea of Man's randomness straight from Heidegger.

Lying flat, I fell deeper under the music's spell and recalled how so many of the students I'd made friends with at university seemed to have Doors music in their record collections. Lothar's face then came to my mind and I thought how much he must have loved Heidegger to talk to me about him so often and with such passion.

When Gian Paolo returned ten minutes later, he was dressed in another lightweight muslin robe, with white under-pants clearly visible underneath, and a pair of well-worn, brown leather sandals.

'Ready when you are,' he said and, moving to the chest of drawers, he picked up the remote, silenced the Jimi Hendrix track that had just started playing and – patting the laptop – he added: 'You can have this if you like. It's got loads of good stuff on it.'

Rising, I declined the offer with thanks and said it would be a good idea if we made it back to the hospital as soon as possible since I had a board meeting at eleven. I then watched him switch off the sound system and unplug its power supply, after which he crossed to his suitcase, pulled out its extendable handle and headed for the living room, towing the case behind him.

Following a little to the rear, I watched with growing impatience as he crouched over Shah and began stroking her side while she stretched out on a sunny patch of the living-room floor. He then gently picked her up, cuddled her into his neck and told her he was going away and wouldn't see her again.

As soon as he put her down, she began crying with a tone so plaintive it pulled at my heart. 'That's a very sad sound,' I said.

'Yes, I think she understands I'm not coming back,' Gian Paolo said.

Recalling his earlier anger when he felt I'd been disrespectful to animals, I said: 'It certainly sounds that way,' and, checking my watch, I added: 'But do you mind if we step on it. I really do need to look at the papers before my meeting.'

'Of course,' he said, 'I won't be two ticks,' and he hurried off to the office, followed closely by the still pitifully crying Shah.

When he returned, he offered me one of the two envelopes he was holding and said it contained a copy of his will, detailing his wish to bequeath 2.1 million pounds to me, along with a cheque for that amount, payable to Professor Joy Small. 'I hope that's the right account name,' he said.

Taken aback, I asked how on Earth he'd come by so much money.

'Aldo gave me two and a half million a few years ago,' he said; then he explained how, shortly after Aldo had made his first billion, he'd given lump sums to Claudio, Alice and himself as a kind of payment for them not to interfere in his life. 'Once I'd set up the flat,' Gian Paolo continued, 'I didn't really have anything else to spend it on.'

'But why do you want to give it to me?' I said, thinking the gift showed how out of touch with reality he was.

Tucking the second envelope into a side pocket of his robe, he said: 'Well, I'm not giving it to *you* exactly. It's for the research.'

'Oh! I see,' I said.

'Yes,' he said and, retaking hold of the case's handle, he continued: 'You said your friend reckoned it would take one hell of a business case for his gene expert to look at Renata's and my DNA.' He then crossed to the main door and, nodding at my envelope, he added: 'Well, that's your business case.'

Feeling slightly dazzled at holding a 2.1 million pound cheque with my name in the pay line, I went with him into the hallway and, as I watched him try unsuccessfully to soothe Shah before shutting the door on her, my gaze strayed to his haunches and the white cotton pants stretching across his buttocks. We then rang the neighbouring doorbell and, when the medical student Amir opened, Gian Paolo handed over his door keys and the second envelope, then explained his kitchen cupboards were full of the food Shah liked.

In saying goodbye, Gian Paolo and Amir shook hands Roman style then, without releasing their grip, fell into a close embrace. 'Good luck, man,' Amir said, patting Gian Paolo's back. 'And don't worry, I'll look after everything here.'

On the way down in the lift, we fell silent, the lift's softly piping music the only sound between us. Then, Gian Paolo suddenly burst out laughing. 'God!' he said. 'Don't let this be the last song I hear!' The music was a big-band version of *I ain't missin' you at all*.

After making our way out of the building, we crossed to the car park and I zapped the Audi open with my key and invited Gian Paolo to stow his case in the boot.

'Do you mind giving me a hand,' he said and, nodding to his left shoulder, he added: 'I can't move my arm.'

When I asked what was wrong, he explained he'd been suffering frequent bouts of paralysis in his left side since April.

'Of course,' I said. 'I'm so sorry not to have asked before.' I then helped him lift the case into the boot and added: 'Are there any other symptoms?'

'Apart from the headaches,' he said, 'and inability to pee without running the tap for ages, not really.'

Once we were under way in the car, he fell silent again and seemed content to look out the window, his eyes fixed on some distant point. Then, a few minutes into the journey, I felt the silence was becoming heavy so I asked him about a guitar I'd seen in his bedroom. 'Is it yours,' I said: 'I mean, do you play?'

Switching his gaze away from the window he said: 'Oh, I play all right!' then he explained he'd been playing the guitar several hours a day, seven days a week, for the last dozen or so years.

'That sounds very keen,' I said. 'Music is something of a passion for you then?'

'Oh sure! My dream all through teenage was to be a pop star,' he said. 'And I did actually put out an album on Aldo's label. But it didn't sell.'

'Oh? Why was that?'

Gian Paolo pouted and said: 'I don't know for sure.' He then explained he'd taken a year out between graduating and beginning his master's degree in order to pursue a music career and had performed a number of shows in bars, clubs and college halls with the help of a fellow year-out student who was looking to become a band manager.

He then said whenever he'd sung live – performing alone with just his guitar – audiences absolutely loved it. 'They'd start joining in and swaying,' he said. 'And people in the front would be in tears, hugging each other and everything.'

At the first few shows, Gian Paolo thought the emotional audiences were just students on ecstasy, but when the crying happened at every performance, he decided the music was really touching people. 'Aldo thought so too,' Gian Paolo said. 'He came to one show where the crowd actually started chanting for me to come back when the headline act came on.'

'The problem was,' he continued, 'when I recorded the songs, they had virtually no effect at all.' He then said he'd even been bored once listening to his own track on the radio. 'I guess,' he concluded, 'the music wasn't really that good. It was just something about the performances.'

Guiding the Audi onto the roundabout at the start of the dual carriageway out of Cambridge, I said: 'Interesting. And what was Aldo's opinion of your songs?'

Giving a shrug, Gian Paolo said Aldo had never offered a view since he was only really interested in making money and, as soon as he realised the music wasn't going to sell, he stopped promoting Gian Paolo's album and advised him to go back to college.

Moving into the fast lane, I remarked how strange it was Aldo should be wholly motivated by money when Gian Paolo was so non-materialistic. I then asked if he and his brother had ever discussed why their world views were so diametrically opposed. The question made Gian Paolo grin. 'Oh yes!' he said. 'We both know where we stand on that one.'

He then explained Aldo believed we all came from a perfect place but had been thrown out into an inhospitable world where we were just left to cope as best we could.

'A bit like a baby leaving the womb,' I said.

Gian Paolo laughed loudly and said: 'You really are a Freudian, aren't you!'

I started to protest but he patted my thigh and said he was only teasing, then he explained Aldo felt the best way to cope was to make the world as comfortable as possible – and that meant making as much money as he could.

Aware of the tingle his pat had set off between my legs, I said with a slight choke: 'But what about family, and loving relationships. Aren't they what make life worth living?'

Looking suddenly sombre, Gian Paolo said: 'I guess so. But not for Aldo and me.'

I considered what he meant a moment then said: 'Because of the "new feelings"?'

He confirmed that's what he was referring to then said: 'But let's not go there now. Why don't you tell me about your life.'

Flashing the car in front to let me pass, I said I probably held the typical Catholic view: try to live a good life; become as virtuous as possible; get into heaven quickly when you die.

'Ah! Nicely straightforward! But suppose life isn't about virtuousness,' he said. 'Suppose it's actually about building.'

'Building?' I said and asked if he meant building in the sense of genetically engineering beings that could experience 'new feelings'.

'That's part of it, yes!' he said.

Tucking back into the slow lane, I said his vision seemed to assume Man could be engineered out of existence without God turning a hair.

Glancing again at the passing scenery, he said he hoped I wasn't arguing Man had some divine right to eternal existence because he was made in God's image. He then suggested, if that were so, God must be pretty violent and cruel.

'Men are only like that when they turn away from God,' I said.

'Well, they seem to have been turning away an awfully long time!' he said. Then he argued everything from the Holy Wars and Holocaust to ethnic cleansing and stonings showed Man's cruelty didn't simply stem from the malevolence of a few individuals but from rationally thought-out value systems as well.

'Take the traffic-plane thing,' he continued. 'The killers plotted in cold blood; the air force responded in cold blood; and even the judge said the poor paralysed bastard deserved what he got. I mean, for God's sake. Can't you see how hopelessly basic that makes us?'

I was about to respond when Gian Paolo suddenly shrieked at me to take a turning and clamped his fist onto the steering wheel, forcing me to veer left. My heart thumping, I glimpsed a white van half a kilometre ahead suddenly catapult off the road and down an embankment while an articulated lorry reared up in a grotesque, slow-motion twist as it ploughed into the back of another vehicle.

A half-second later, the Audi's tyres were squealing as we managed to make the turning without going too deeply into the hedge lining its off-side. I then brought our speed down from eighty to thirty and, with the car back under control, I praised him for his quickness in spotting the pile-up. Grimacing at what I guessed was a pain in his head, he said he could always be relied on to be looking further ahead than anyone else. 'That's why you need to listen to me about creation,' he said.

My heartbeat calming, I said I didn't know about creation, but he'd certainly saved the day with the crash, then, noticing a twig on the bonnet, I added: 'Although I'm not sure about the paintwork!'

Massaging both temples, he managed a faint smile and I gave his thigh a squeeze then asked how many vehicles he thought would have crashed.

'Hard to say,' he said. Then, pausing the massaging to check on the pain, he added: 'At least ten. And more than that if people weren't looking beyond the car in front.'

My hands still a little shaky, I changed down a gear to take an upcoming bend and said there must have been at least a dozen cars going too fast to stop and, although we'd probably been far enough from the collision zone to have avoided actually crashing, we would definitely have been stuck in a jam if it wasn't for him.

'No, you really saved the day,' I said. 'I'd have no chance of this meeting otherwise.' I then tapped the satnav to recalculate the route back to the hospital and glanced skyward to see where the arch of foliage covering the road ahead ended.

Reclining against his headrest, Gian Paolo closed his eyes and said softly: 'That's better: the headache's going.'

I said I was glad he felt more comfortable and assured him the hospital would be able to provide first-class pain relief when we arrived. I then saw from the satnav our new time of arrival was 10.31 a.m. and added: 'Will you be okay if I drop you with the ward sister? She'll get you settled in. Only, I really do have to prepare for my meeting.'

'No problem,' he said, settling deeper into his seat.

We then drove in silence for several minutes, he with eyes closed while I took in the beautiful effect of the sun's rays filtering through the overhanging canopy. His eyes then opened, but he seemed lost in his own thoughts so I switched on the radio at low volume, causing the flower duet from Delibes' *Lakmé* to fill the cockpit.

'Oh, I love this!' I said. 'Delibes.'

Suddenly turning to me, he said he meant what he'd told me about being able to see so far into the future, he knew where creation was headed.

Put out by the interruption, I said: 'Are you sure you shouldn't just relax?' I then overtook a pair of cyclists, struggling to make the brow of the hill, and added: 'You know, prepare yourself for the hospital and everything.'

'Look. I know it's tedious to keep having these conversations,' he said. 'But you have to understand, I really can see what lies ten, twenty, thirty million years ahead.'

Reluctantly turning off Delibes, I asked if he was seriously trying to tell me he was a prophet.

Hesitating, he said he didn't think he was a prophet, but he was able to imagine clearly what the universe would be like millions of years from now.

'The science fiction shelves are full of people who can do that,' I said.

'This is different,' he said, and told me his imaginings weren't just fantasy but a concrete vision he'd developed through his 'floaty' experiences. 'You see, I know space as a tangible reality,' he continued. 'While the rest of the world just sees pin-pricks in a black sky, I know experientially each star is a colossal mass spinning with mind-blowing force in freezing blackness.'

'But how do you know your "floaty" experiences aren't just imagination?' I said.

'Because every time I picture the future, I challenge myself on whether it's just my own make-believe,' he said. 'But a thought always persists: "follow your mind's eye; follow your mind's eye".'

'I see,' I said. 'And what exactly is it you see?'

Sucking in his lip, he murmured, 'Well...,' then he gave a half-smile and said it was difficult to put into words. He then shifted in his seat and said the best way he could describe his vision was for me to imagine our galaxy as a bright, immeasurably vast expanse where life was not only present on every planet, but in all the spaces in between.

When I challenged him on how that was physically possible, he said he didn't know exactly, but a conscious plant would develop that was able to proliferate by ingesting dark matter and converting it into particulate energies governed by laws beyond current thermodynamic theory. This plant would become as prevalent in space as bracken on a Scottish hillside and provide a bedrock for countless ecosystems, inhabited by unimaginable numbers of beautiful creatures, living in unimaginably harmonious civilisations.

'Well!' I said. 'I don't know what to say!'

Seeming not to hear me, he became increasingly animated as he described how the whole of space would be teeming with life, much of it on a conscious level as far above us as we were beyond the diplodocus. 'It's an incredibly vibrant universe packed with life, love, truth and beauty,' he said. 'You'll be able to see what it really means for God's will to be done on Earth.'

'And are there human beings in this universe?' I said.

Plopping back against his seat with a wry smile, he said: 'Man is in there – in the history books: father of the new creation.'

'Oh, come now!' I said, approaching a three-way junction with an old-fashioned, wooden signpost. 'That's definitely going too far.' Then turning right, I continued: 'It's bad enough to say there's no Heavenly Father but to say we'll actually take his place is too much, Gian Paolo.'

His smile broadening, he said he could be even 'badder' and suggest I had it in my power to become the mother of creation. 'You would be the new Mary,' he said, 'if you just got the scientists to set up my genetics project.'

Reeling from the outlandishness of his ideas, I gave a stammering explanation about how the project he was describing would require set-up of a major programme encompassing several research streams lasting many years, and that would cost at least thirty or forty million pounds.

Massaging his temples once more, he said: 'Then you'll have to go to Aldo for the money.'

Taken aback at his insistence his scheme be pursued, I pointed out it was highly unlikely his brother would agree to give me forty million pounds if I just went to him and said I needed it to make his brother's wild visions reality.

'In which case, you must persuade him to come and see me while I've still got enough brain to explain everything,' he said. Then he let out a heartfelt sigh and added: 'He is my bloody brother, after all!'

'Can't you just phone him yourself?' I said.

Shaking his head, he explained all Aldo's calls were screened by his staff and he only called back the people he specifically chose to. 'It'll be ages before he returns my call, if ever,' he added.

Leaving the shaded lane and making our way onto an A-road, I said it surely couldn't be that difficult for him to make contact with his own brother.

'You'd think!' Gian Paolo said. Then turning to me, he added: 'But then I suppose you still don't know who he is. I mean, you've not stopped yet to puzzle it out, have you.'

Although it had entered my head Aldo's billionaire status must mean he had some degree of fame, I hadn't let his actual identity become more than a vague question at the back of my mind.

His gaze on my face, Gian Paolo asked if I'd heard of the Pointless business empire.

'You mean the music and media companies?' I said.

Gian Paolo nodded. Then, in sudden realisation, I said: 'No! Not Lord Pointer! That's not Aldo! Is it?'

Gian Paolo nodded again.

'But your name isn't Pointer,' I said.

'Neither's Aldo's,' he said. 'And he's not a lord either. It's just his idea of a joke: Lord Percy Pointer! – he thinks it's hilarious.'

'Oh my goodness!' I said, feeling genuinely wowed. 'But how on Earth do I go about talking to him! He's such a recluse.'

Gian Paolo looked a little disappointed Aldo's identity was having such impact on me and, his tone slightly peaked, he said my first move should be to contact the Pointless headquarters in London and say I'm the psychiatrist treating his brother and urgently need to consult with him. 'I think there's a good chance he'll go for that,' Gian Paolo said. 'He thinks psychiatry is the funniest thing ever.'

'Well, I'm glad I'll be a figure of fun!' I said.

His gaze back out the window, Gian Paolo ignored my remark and said: 'But don't say I'm dying. He hates anything to do with suffering. Just say I'm crazy and you're treating me.'

'But if he hates suffering, won't he hate coming to a hospital?' I said.

'Don't say it's a hospital,' he said. 'Tell him it's a psychiatric clinic or something.'

Guiding the Audi onto a short stretch of dual carriageway, I said: 'But even if I do get to see him, do you really think he'll come all this way? Only, I can't really afford a whole day in London on a wild goose chase.'

His brow furrowing, Gian Paolo asked that perhaps – even if it was for just one moment – I could consider the possibility that maybe everything he'd ever told me was true: that he did possess 'new feelings'; that his genetic make-up did represent a step forward in evolution; that he could see the future. He also asked me to consider how there may never again be a moment in history when someone as rich as Aldo would have an interest in funding the vital first step in genetically reengineering creation.

'If you accept even for a nanosecond these things might be true,' he said, 'no matter how remote the possibility – don't you think that's worth a day of your time?'

And there, in a nutshell, was the source of all the anxiety I'd been experiencing since meeting Gian Paolo: I couldn't rule out the 0.0001 per cent chance he was everything he claimed to be.

Unsure what to say, I continued to drive while I thought through the enormity of the situation. My eye was then caught by the trees lining the far side of the carriageway: their foliage seemed suddenly to have transformed into a continuous line of giant faces where the leaves formed softly rounded noses, chins and eye sockets. My heart then skipped a beat as I saw that coming up in the line was a perfectly clear representation of my face as a young woman.

A panic attack looming, I rubbed my eyes, but the vision persisted so I pulled over onto a grass embankment with a slope that left the car on a forty-degree tilt.

Struggling to sit upright, Gian Paolo said: 'I don't know what you saw just then, but you should know I was reaching out to you.'

A sudden flash of anger made me snap: 'Shut up, Gian Paolo! Just shut up – for heaven's sake!' I then turned the air conditioning down and, forcing myself to breathe evenly, I added: 'I'm just very tired; that's all.' Then, in the stunned silence, I repeated: 'Very tired.'

WHAT A SWELL PARTY...

Having been granted an audience with Aldo for two days after Gian Paolo's admission to hospital, I found myself taking a taxi on the Wednesday morning from Kings Cross Station to the quiet street in the art and antiques area of Mayfair housing the Pointless empire's main offices.

As I walked back up the street from where the cab had dropped me, I was surprised by the modest appearance of the six-storey Pointless building, which had no obvious corporate branding around its entrance and was dominated on either side by solid-looking, grey stone buildings.

Drawing closer to the entrance, I spotted an unobtrusive wall plaque bearing a monochrome version of the Pointless logo and, satisfied I'd come to the right place, I entered through a narrow revolving door and into a reception area with springy flooring and soft blue uplighters.

Two casually dressed women were behind the reception desk and looked up at my approach. The nearer one, whose blouse buttons were undone to reveal a plump, toffee-coloured cleavage, greeted me in an overly warm voice and maintained an attentive look while I explained I had an eleven-thirty meeting with Lord Pointer.

After checking her PC screen, she asked me if I was carrying any identification and, once I'd shown her a couple of credit cards and my staff pass from the hospital, she escorted me to a room up the corridor where a young man with oversized biceps searched my bag and scanned me with a metal detector.

I was then invited to sit with the receptionist at a bare desk while she briefed me on how I needed to behave in Lord Pointer's presence: don't look directly at him unless invited to do so; keep my voice even and make no sudden noises; address him as Lord Pointer until he gives permission to call him Percy; don't apply perfume or create any other smells.

She then asked if I needed to go to the ladies' before seeing him and, after I'd accepted her offer and freshened up, I met with her again and followed her into a lift fitted with the softest carpet I'd ever walked on and silk wall-hangings, giving off a subtle, floral scent.

'Goodness!' I said. 'This has to be the most exotic lift I've ever seen!'

Smiling in a way that suggested she was used to such comments, the receptionist pressed the button for the fifth floor then stood with her hands lightly clasped in front of her while the doors closed. The lift then rose slowly to the first floor where it gave out a sustained piano note before opening its doors to admit two men, both of whom greeted the receptionist by name – Avinder.

One of the men then pressed the fourth-floor button and continued his conversation with the other about how certain units in the organisation were using different business models to deliver largely similar programmes and it was down to him to produce a board paper with a recommendation on whether one specific model should be adopted for all activities of a particular type.

'Interesting,' said the second man. 'What's Percy's view?'

'You know what he's like,' said the first man. 'He thinks it's all about personalities – you know, people should just choose a model that suits them. I guess what I'll actually end up doing is proposing a menu of best-practice options.'

The lift then arrived at the fourth floor and both men stepped out into a chrome and glass, open-plan space, leaving Avinder and me to smile at one another while she pressed the 'doors close' button and we continued to the fifth. Another piano note then sounded, heralding our arrival and, as I followed her out into a narrow gallery, I found myself walking on the same supremely soft carpet as in the lift.

Gesturing to a chocolate velvet sofa strewn with a dozen fluffy cushions, Avinder invited me to take a seat while she let Lord Pointer know I was there. She then disappeared through a frosted-glass door, leaving me to make a nest among the cushions and look in my bag for a mint.

The walls at the ends of the gallery contained square windows which, from my incredibly comfy spot on the sofa, appeared to look out on the quiet street at one end and some kind of courtyard at the other. The courtyard end also contained a huge tank with exotically coloured marine fish swishing gracefully to and fro and coming to the glass now and then to stare out, their mouths working rhythmically.

After a minute's mint-sucking and following the movements of a dazzlingly colourful tang, I settled further back into the cushions and felt a wave of relaxation spread through me. The comfort stopped at my feet, however, as I became aware how much my shoes were pinching.

The frosted-glass door then swung open and Avinder emerged to announce it would be a few minutes before Lord Pointer could see me.

'Would you like a coffee while you're waiting?' she said.

I replied I was fine and, as soon as she was gone, I slipped off my shoes and leant my head on the sofa's back. The ceiling was painted light blue and decorated with barely perceptible fluffy clouds and crescent moons, like you sometimes see on sunny afternoons. Throaty whale sounds were meanwhile piping out quietly from speakers fitted in the gallery's alcoves.

Pressing my toes into the carpet, I allowed my eyelids to droop and must have fallen asleep since the next thing I knew, a man's voice was calling my name and, when I opened my eyes, there in front of me was the Mediterranean man I'd seen at Kings Cross Station the Sunday before last, throwing banknote aeroplanes around. He was wearing a muslin robe similar to the one Gian Paolo wore on Monday and his feet were bare.

'You!' I said, amazed. 'Don't tell me *you* work for Lord Pointer?'

Grinning, he said: 'Sort of.' Then offering a hand to help me up from the sofa, he added: 'I am Lord Pointer. But I don't remember us meeting.'

A dizziness suddenly seized me and I had to focus hard on keeping my balance as I slipped my shoes back on.

Glancing down, he said: 'Ah, that's a shame – I thought you were going to join the barefoot tribe!' He then gestured to the frosted-glass door and said: 'Shall we go through and you can tell me where we met.'

As I moved towards the door, my legs gave way, and I was collapsing helplessly when he caught me in a reflex action then half-carried, half-dragged me back to the sofa.

'Steady as you go!' he said, sitting me down.

My legs like jelly, I tried to apologise but found I couldn't form a coherent sentence. Then, fearful I might be babbling, I forced myself to stop talking and just sit dumbly while he brought his face level with mine and said: 'You look very pale. Are you all right?'

Nodding, I took a few seconds to compose myself. Then, shuffling to the edge of the sofa and straightening my back, I took several deep breaths and told him at gabbling pace how I'd seen him at the station ten days ago and had been one of the people in the coffee-kiosk queue he'd bought a drink for. 'I think you'd been drinking at the time,' I said. 'I noticed alcohol on your breath.' I then recounted how he'd offered me money and said I should have some fun so I could overcome the bereavement I was suffering. 'I couldn't help being amazed at that. It was such an incredible guess.' I said, my breathing finally coming under control.

'Guess?' he said. 'If you've been analysing Gian Paolo, you'll know it wasn't.' He then looked into my face again and, sweeping aside the cushions next to me so he could sit down, he asked if I was feeling any better, suggesting I'd probably suffered a moment's hypoglycaemia. I agreed it was nothing serious and apologised if he'd found me heavy to carry to the sofa.

'Not at all,' he said. 'You're the lightest psychiatrist I know! Although I didn't really get the stuff about mathematics being against you.'

Realising I'd babbled more than I thought, I quickly said: 'Oh, it was nothing – just light-headedness.'

Nodding, he adjusted his robe where it was bunching underneath him and said: 'Anyway, where were we?'

I said I thought he'd just suggested I should realise he hadn't been guessing about my bereavement because I would know of his special ability to 'read' people from my sessions with his brother.

'That's right,' he said. 'Surely Gian Paolo's told you about me – how I make my money?'

My dizziness fading, I said: 'Not really; he said you could "read" people, but I don't know anything about the money.'

Spreading his arms along the sofa's back, he looked to the ceiling then told me it was his reading ability that had brought all his business success since it enabled him to tell what people had inside them: how much talent they possessed; what they cared about most; their temperament. Then, crossing his legs, he added: 'But I suppose none of that's really any help with Gian Paolo.'

Trying to recall what I'd decided on the train was the best way to handle this meeting, I said I wasn't absolutely sure how

I could help Gian Paolo if I was truthful and perhaps the best assistance Aldo could give was to tell me about the special abilities he thought he and his brother possessed – and their late sister. 'The "reading" thing might be a good place to start,' I said. 'Especially if it's brought you wealth.'

Looking into my eyes, Aldo gave a half laugh and said: 'I see. Gian Paolo's told you everything and you don't believe it.'

'Well,' I said, looking away, 'he has made some extraordinary claims – delusional ones mainly.'

Aldo smiled and said: 'Such as?'

I then gave a brief summary of the 'new feelings' Gian Paolo claimed to experience and his belief he represented the next stage in evolution. I also explained Gian Paolo's wish for me to persuade Aldo to visit him in Royston so they could talk about setting up a multimillion-pound programme to isolate their family's extraordinary DNA and use it to create genetically modified generations of human beings.

Aldo let out a roar of laughter. 'Dear old Gian Paolo! Still saving the universe!' he said, shaking his head. 'No wonder he's gone nuts!'

'These ideas are something from childhood then?' I said.

Giving a quieter laugh, Aldo said: 'Now you sound like a psychiatrist!' He then took a mobile phone from his pocket and added: 'I'll call for refreshments out here if it's easier.' Then he pressed a couple of buttons, saying: 'We really must get you some sugar!'

Laying a hand on his arm, I assured him I was fine to go inside and, rising with his help, we crossed to the frosted-glass door, which he opened for me. A small voice came from his phone meanwhile and he told whoever was on the other end he would like refreshments for two in his office now, after which he went ahead of me into an open-plan space fitted with the same carpet as the gallery and broken up by so many plants and small trees in earth beds I thought we might be in a roof garden.

Looking up to check if there was a ceiling, I saw we were under a glass canopy made up of huge rectangular panels and was just trying to work out from their frames whether they slid open when Aldo warned me to skirt a large step ladder where two men were working on an air-conditioning duct. He then led me to a space with a pair of giant, low-slung hammocks separated by a long coffee table, around which stood a loose square of expensive-looking desks fitted with state-of-the-art office equipment.

'My! This is some set-up!' I said, as a good-looking man clutching a dossier to his cashmere chest stopped to let me pass.

Aldo smiled at me over his shoulder and, suggesting I sit on one of the hammocks, he crossed to a beautifully crafted Wendy house beyond the coffee table and pulled out a thick-furred, black rabbit. He then tucked the back of its head under his chin and, as he petted its face and ears, a plump woman squeezed between two desks to the side of me, a pile of papers tucked under her arm. Spotting her approach, Aldo said: 'Professor, this is the head of my private office: Gwettay Oluke.'

The woman shook hands with me and, speaking in an African accent I found hard to understand straightaway, she said: 'You have come to talk about the brother, yes? How is his treatment progressing?'

I murmured something about only being able to discuss the case with specific individuals and she told me I should have no secrets from her. 'If something is a bother to Lord Pointer, I need to know about it,' she said, switching the papers to her bosom and folding her arms.

Taking his seat, with the rabbit, Aldo said: 'Don't mind Gwettay's busybodying, Professor. She's just trying to look after me.'

Gingerly taking my place on the hammock opposite as Gwettay placed her papers on the coffee table then moved off to her desk, I was struck by how much Aldo's mannerisms and way of cuddling the animal made him look like Gian Paolo although, facially, they were as unalike as two brothers could be. I then wriggled closer to the hammock's middle and was surprised to find it remained virtually stationary, its fabric forming a supporting basket under my buttocks.

'Please,' Aldo said, cuddling the rabbit ever closer. 'Take off your shoes. Get comfy!'

The inappropriateness of interviewing him barefoot made me hesitate, but when I looked at him with his rabbit, robe and hairy big toes, I thought what the hell and kicked off my heels. The second shoe went a bit further than I intended and tumbled into the path of a matronly-looking woman wheeling a cabin-crew trolley.

Stopping almost instantly, she scooped up the shoe and returned it, then invited me to choose a drink from the trolley, which was stocked with teas, cakes, coffee, hot and cold milk, drinking chocolate, fruits, fruit juices, confectionery and water.

Thanking her for the shoe, I tossed it under my hammock and said: 'I'd love a skinny latte, please.'

Aldo said he'd like the same and we'd both have a chocolate muffin and, once the matronly woman had placed our refreshments on the coffee table, he said to me: 'Shall we get back to special abilities then?'

Unsure if I could reach for my latte without tipping out of the hammock, I decided to sit tight and said: 'Yes, that would be good.' Then, watching him lean forward for his drink without mishap, I added: 'I think anything you can tell me about your first "special abilities" experiences would be especially useful.'

As I spoke, I noticed Gwettay look up abruptly from her desk, her eyes fixing on me for a couple of seconds before returning to the papers in front of her. 'I guess it would help to know too about your childhood relationship with Gian Paolo generally,' I said.

'Why?' Aldo said, switching the rabbit from his neck to his lap. 'So you can see if it's my fault he's crazy?'

Slightly disconcerted by his directness, I said I wasn't interested in blaming anyone for anything; I only wanted to understand Gian Paolo's condition better.

'Perhaps,' I said, 'you could tell me if your abilities made your and Gian Paolo's childhood particularly different?' Then, seeing his expression was blank, I suggested he might find it easier to start with his 'reading' ability and how it had made his fortune, then work backwards to childhood.

Having settled the rabbit, he said: 'Okay', then he took a sip from his latte and recounted how when he'd left school at sixteen, he'd gone to a central London employment agency to find a job and ended up sitting more than an hour in a queue while the agency's consultants interviewed a string of other school and college leavers about work that would suit them.

'When it came to my turn, I was lucky enough to be interviewed by the branch manager,' he said, 'and...' then he suddenly stopped speaking. Gwettay was returning and, arriving between us, she said: 'Before we get into stories about anybody's childhood, I think we need to safeguard ourselves.' She then handed me a document, asked if I had a pen and explained: 'It's an agreement not to divulge anything Percy might say to you to any third party.'

Tapping his mug with a thumbnail, Aldo told Gwettay there was no need to have brought the contract.

I agreed, saying anything Lord Pointer told me was covered under the confidentiality of the doctor-patient relationship.

'But Percy is not your patient,' she said.

I was about to explain that didn't place him outside the protection of patient-confidentiality ethics when Aldo said in a firm voice that a woman of my stature could be trusted to behave with integrity whether or not I signed a bit of paper.

Her eyebrow arching, Gwettay drew to her full five-foot nothing and said: 'Fine! But don't blame me if something gets out you don't want to.' She then turned on her heel and headed for her desk while Aldo called after her in a sing-song voice: 'Trust me; you know I'm never wrong about people!'

Picking up my latte with only a minor wobble, I said: '*Never* wrong?'

Aldo took another sip of his drink and said: 'Not about people, no.' Then he returned his latte to the table, scooped up his muffin and, swinging up his legs to lie on his side, he told me how when his turn had finally arrived to talk to the employment-agency manager, he'd bet her he could identify what work each of her previous three customers was suited to: accounts clerk; IT support; shop assistant.

Assuming Aldo had been eavesdropping on her interviews, the branch manager told him he must have misheard what she'd discussed with the third customer since she would be looking to place him in a marketing or PR role, not a shop. Aldo quickly assured her he hadn't overheard a word and insisted he was right about the third customer, saying: 'He might have come across as an ideas man, but he hasn't got a creative bone in him – just the gift of the gab.'

The branch manager had looked at Aldo through narrowed eyes and asked if he and the previous interviewees were trying to play some sort of trick on her. When he assured her all he'd done was exchange a few words with them in the queue, she came back with a challenge: if he was so clever at reading people's aptitudes, he should be able to tell her about her own skills and the work she was cut out for.

Delighted at the challenge, Aldo told her she was a 'worshipper of the money god' and should be running her own business where she would be in control of all the commercial decisions, especially about when to take risks. Her main attributes, according to Aldo, were unswerving determination, control of her emotions and an ability to focus on strategic goals no matter how much tactical detail she became involved in.

'That made her laugh out loud,' Aldo said. 'Then she asked if I was really only sixteen.'

He then explained how the branch manager, whose name was Rhianne, offered him a clerical post in the agency on the spot and said his job would be to support her with the admin side of procuring interim executives for blue-chip clients. The role he actually ended up playing had little to do with clerical work, however, and all to do with sitting in on interviews she conducted for high-value recruitments so he could give a second opinion.

After a few months' working together, Rhianne confided in him about her plan to set up her own agency, headhunting gifted executives for top management positions.

'You could come and work for me if you like,' she said. 'I'll be launching next month.'

Aldo jumped at the chance to join her – providing it was on a junior-partner basis – and the combination of his 'reading' and her understanding of the leadership behaviours candidates needed led to a high-end recruitment business with a first-year turnover of almost two million pounds. 'It was surprising how quickly we got a reputation for never putting up a duff candidate,' Aldo said.

He then told me how two years of working with Rhianne gave him enough business knowledge and cash to go out on his own. So he went into band management, signing up talent from among the groups playing the clubs and colleges on his social circuit.

The musicians he contracted to him were always gifted but he'd acquired enough business sense to know he needed to focus his development resource on grooming a few super-talented ones to win major contracts. So, he sorted the greatly gifted from the not-so-great then gave the former the time and money to develop their songs and performing skills.

According to Aldo, the strategy paid off: as each artist in development reached maturity, he was able to set up auctions for their signature among the major music labels and the contracts he subsequently negotiated meant he ended up making enough money to start his own recording company, just eighteen months after parting with Rhianne.

He then expanded the horizons of his talent spotting by travelling to the US, the West Indies and South America and, by the time he was just twenty-one, he found himself sitting at the head of a music label and artists-management business that included seven of the top-ten-selling recording acts in the world.

'I see,' I said. 'So your ability enables you to spot a genius then?'

Aldo gave a wry smile and said: 'Well, it would if such a thing existed,' and tickling the rabbit as it busied itself snuffling his thigh, he added: 'But it doesn't.'

I was about to argue his success was surely proof it did when he said: 'You see, genius isn't a person. It's God. God in a concentrated form, flowing through people – like water through a tap.' He then suggested all of us produced acts of genius throughout our whole life. 'It's just most of us have an occasional drop while the people I find have it pouring out of them,' he said.

'Interesting,' I said, 'but if genius is God, wouldn't people take more notice of it?'

'But they do,' he said. 'Why do you think the world puts "geniuses" on a pedestal?'

The matronly woman who'd served the drinks returned, wearing rubber gloves and pushing a galvanised kitchen trolley stocked with cleaning products and a huge polythene bag of straw.

Turning to the woman, Aldo asked if she would pass a second rabbit out from the Wendy house and he followed her movements as she parked her trolley and went about removing a fluffy grey ball from the house's upstairs. She then presented him with the ball before returning to the Wendy house and starting work on cleaning it out. Aldo meanwhile snuggled his face into the grey rabbit's shoulder.

I watched a moment as the woman stuffed the house's old straw into a black bin bag; then, turning back to Aldo, I saw he was now lying flat on his back, cuddling the two rabbits into his chest, his eyes closed, a blissful smile on his face.

Unsure how to restart our conversation, I asked if this was the regular time for the rabbit hutch to be cleaned.

Releasing his grip on the rabbits, he appeared not to hear me since he simply remained prostrate and smiling while the two animals moved onto his stomach and settled with their noses a few centimetres apart. So I repeated my question more loudly and felt a certain relief when he responded, saying the rabbits' house was actually cleaned out at forty-five-minute intervals throughout the working day.

When I asked if that wasn't a little excessive, he said: 'Maybe, but I can't stand the urine smell.'

'I see,' I murmured and, keen to bring his mind back to Gian Paolo, I said: 'But isn't Gian Paolo something of a genius?'

'You could say that, I suppose,' Aldo said.

'But you wouldn't say he was God would you?' I said.

'I see, of course!' he said, switching the rabbits to his thighs. 'You believe in *a* God.' He then sat fully upright and said he should have known I was the sort of person who would hold orthodox Christian beliefs.

'Oh?' I said. 'And what sort of person is that?'

Looking into my eyes, he said without waver: 'Someone who can't imagine a universe without Homo sapiens.'

Nettled, I said: 'That's a bit rich, isn't it – to suggest two billion-odd Christians have some sort of imagination deficit. Or is it you know something about God the rest of us don't?'

Smiling resignedly, he said: 'I don't want to argue with you.' He then rose, leant across the table and plonked the grey rabbit onto my lap, saying: 'Have a stroke.' Then, sitting back down, he said there was nothing unique about his understanding of 'the ultimate' since it simply aligned with Zoroastrianism, Buddhism and other strands of non-Abrahamic, Eastern thinking. He then popped his rabbit to one side on the hammock and, drawing up his knees so he could sit cross-legged, he continued: 'I guess the main point is God isn't "*a* God" with some sort of human personality.' Then, noticing the grey rabbit sniff at my hand, he said with sudden glee: 'Look, she likes you!'

Looking at the rabbit pushing at my fingers with its twitching nose, I said no one was suggesting God's personality was human.

'Okay, maybe not,' he said. 'But you do say there's "*a* God" and "He" has some sort of fatherly personality, right?'

I wanted to deny it but couldn't think how to, so I sat passively while he told me non-Abrahamic Eastern thinking understood God as a universally pervasive mind – or 'light of wisdom' – rather than a deity. 'I guess it's a bit like thinking of God as water,' he continued. 'You wouldn't dream of saying there's "*a* water", would you. It's just water.'

He then glanced up and I followed his gaze to see Gwettay and the good-looking man in the cashmere sweater approaching where we sat.

'Water has a nature, yes,' he continued, turning back to me, 'but never a personality.'

As Gwettay arrived between us, she told Aldo it was time for him to change for his one o'clock lunch at the Pointless Café and I suddenly realised I hadn't yet persuaded him to visit Gian Paolo and felt panicked our interview was about to end.

Desperate to regain his attention, I slipped my shoes on as Gwettay continued to brief him on the lunch; then I moved to her shoulder and silently willed her to hurry up while she

– seemingly unaware of my presence – listed all the Pointless-label pop stars who would be at the café: MTR; The System; Countess Creola; Wylda Warrior... Then, with Gwettay still rattling through names, Aldo suddenly looked my way and asked her to excuse him a moment.

Taking my arm, he guided me to one side and said he was very keen we continue our chat so perhaps I would consider coming to the lunch – an invitation which I accepted immediately with a squeeze of his hand. I then returned to my hammock and, as I watched him continue his conversation with Gwettay, I noticed the way he gestured and how much his mannerisms resembled Gian Paolo's. The chat then came to an end and, as Gwettay turned back to her desk, Aldo clapped the good-looking man on the shoulder and followed him to a far corner, where they both disappeared through another frosted-glass door.

His disappearance seemed to act as a cue for Gwettay: she stopped hovering by her desk, came hurriedly over to me and, bending to bring her eyes level with mine, she said: 'Professor Small, you seem a good person.'

I wasn't sure what to reply so I just smiled.

'If you are going with Percy to this lunch,' she continued, 'I would like to ask a favour.'

'Of course,' I said.

'It is a very delicate matter,' she said. Then, glancing round behind her, she told me last time Aldo had lunched with some of his artists at the café, he had drunk wine with his meal and behaved very badly. 'It's okay if he has a bottle of beer,' she continued. 'But not too much, and not wine. You understand?'

Surprised she should be having this conversation with me, I asked her to explain exactly what she expected me to do.

'Just remind him,' she said. 'Don't touch the wine. Never the wine!'

I said I wasn't sure if he would listen to me but promised I'd do my best and, after thanking me, Gwettay explained Aldo's driver, Con Dweir, would come into the café with us and could give me physical help if needed. She then returned to her desk to make a phone call, leaving me wondering what 'behaved very badly' meant and why I might need physical help.

After another mint, I saw Aldo emerge from the frosted-glass door, dressed in a designer suit and open-neck shirt, much the same as he'd worn the Sunday at the station. He and the cashmere man then came over to me and, noticing Aldo's shiny, black shoes, I said: 'You're deserting the barefoot tribe then?'

Giving a small shrug, he said: 'What can I do! I have to look the boss.'

The cashmere man then ushered Aldo and me over to a service lift and the three of us descended to a basement car park where we found Con the driver waiting for us by a gleaming, black limousine with the registration number 'P01NT'. Next to him was a large ginger man wearing a bowtie, who instantly made me think of the Billy Bunter character I'd seen in English picture books as a child.

As soon as Aldo saw the ginger man, he burst out laughing and, running up to him, he wrapped him in a huge embrace then, still chuckling, he stood back and adjusted the man's bowtie, saying: 'Perfect! You are just perfect. Probably my favourite "Percy" ever!'

The four of us then entered the limousine – leaving the cashmere man to take the lift back up – and, once we were settled, Aldo introduced the driver to me as Connor Dweir and excused himself for not being able to introduce the ginger man, who was a complete stranger to him.

As the driver manoeuvred the limousine out of the car park, he said I should call him Con, since that's what every-one knew him as, and the ginger man introduced himself in an unexpectedly high-pitched voice as Roux Alluay. Aldo then explained Roux was an actor his PR people had hired for the day to pose as Percy Pointer for any paparazzi at the café.

'We do it every time I go somewhere public,' he said. 'That's why there're so many different pictures of me in the papers.' Then glancing at Roux and giving a snigger he added: 'Or should I say pictures of different me's!'

'Ah! That's what you meant by "favourite Percy",' I said.

'Yes!' Aldo replied. 'Isn't he a beaut!'

I agreed Roux cut an imposing figure and probably matched most people's idea of what a billionaire should look like.

'I know,' Aldo said, clapping his hands. 'I can't wait till they get a load of him!' He then sat back in the deeply upholstered seat and, tittering, looked out of his black-tinted window at the busy street we were now passing along. We then turned into a lane where pedestrians were spilling off the narrow pavements and Con needed to sound his horn twice to clear our path.

Con then drove us onto one of the district's main shopping streets, where groups of tourists and other shoppers filed across the road in front of us as we sat at traffic lights. Many of the younger passers-by squinted at the limousine in an effort to see who was sitting our side of the glass and Aldo pulled back from his window, fidgeting anxiously with his thumbs.

'You really don't like the limelight do you, Aldo?' I said.

Scowling, he turned sharply to me and said I was never again to call him Aldo in public. He then sunk low in his seat, his head dropping below the level of the window, and squeezed his thumbs ever more quickly, his breathing on hold.

A tense silence then developed and, although I wanted to reassure Aldo it was impossible for the passing people to see through the tinted glass, I decided it was better to maintain the quiet and turned my attention to the classical figures carved into the top of a great arch in the junction up ahead. The limousine then moved off and, as it put distance between us and the pedestrians, Aldo pushed himself back up and exhaled deeply.

Turning back to him, I said: 'I'm sorry about the name thing. I didn't...' but before I could finish, he held up a flat hand and said it really didn't matter and we should just forget about it now, although I should understand privacy was very important to him: that's why he hired fake Percys and all his artists had confidentiality clauses in their contracts.

We then made our way along a short underpass and I took advantage of the gloom to slip off my shoes, saying: 'Is fame really as bad as all that?'

'God yes! Can you imagine anything more uncomfortable,' he said; then, after a moment's reflection, he added: 'Apart from having some kind of painful disease maybe.'

We exited the underpass, back into the full brightness of the late June sunshine, and Roux said: 'I don't know; I'd love to be famous.'

Suddenly looking jolly, Aldo slapped Roux's thigh and said: 'Of course you would,' then turning back to his window, he said in a sing-song voice: 'But not for me.'

We then moved off the underpass road and into another shopping area where I caught sight of a long queue of people, meandering along a pavement and round the corner of the next block. Most of the people seemed to be teenagers, talking animatedly and rearranging their hair with preening flicks.

As the car turned the corner, I saw how the queue continued for another sixty metres with many of the young people sitting in loose circles on the ground while others amused themselves wiggling to the music on their headphones or rough-and-tumbling in boysie displays.

'My goodness! This is some queue for a restaurant!' I said as we came abreast of the queue's head at the café entrance. 'Has all the stars' coming been advertised?'

Keeping his eyes on the paparazzi grouped by the café's entrance, which was being guarded by three bull-necked men in Pointless Café T-shirts, Aldo explained most of his artists had large fan bases that followed their every move on social media sites. He then directed Con to take us to the next block and drop him at the corner so he could walk back and enter the café through the kitchens.

'You ring Raphael please and tell him to get someone to meet our "Percy" and the professor at the door; then you drop them off – okay?' Aldo said.

Nodding, Con pressed a button on the car's hands-free phone kit and steered us round the corner of the next block, where he pulled up to let Aldo out. He then advised the person who'd answered his call that Percy would be coming in through the kitchens in a couple of minutes and they should prepare for the decoy and a special guest of Percy's to be dropped at the front in ninety seconds.

He then whizzed the limousine round the block, turned back onto the street with the queue and parked by the café entrance. A woman in a dark business suit, who'd been watching our approach from the café's steps came to the kerb, greeted Con with a nod and pulled our door open.

A gaggle of photographers quickly assembled alongside her and she exchanged a few words I couldn't hear with those nearest while she smilingly held the door open for Roux and me and gestured to the café entrance.

'I think you'd better go first,' I said to Roux, who was on the roadway side of our seat.

'No problem!' he said and he squeezed passed me, onto the pavement and into a volley of camera flashes. He then stood posing and smiling while the photographers took pictures from all sides and asked if he really was Lord Pointer and whether he'd called his stars together because he was celebrating some special occasion.

Projecting his flute-like voice as if he were pitching to a theatre audience, Roux said it had been his twenty-seventh birthday earlier that month and this was the first date he'd been able to find when so many of his artists would be in the country.

I then saw a crop-haired woman in a short skirt, who'd been with the paparazzi clustered at the entrance, come over to join the crowd of photographers and, holding up a microphone wired to a recorder in her shoulder bag, she asked whether he still felt real love for music or if diversifying into so many other business areas meant he'd lost interest.

'Music was my first love, and it will be my last,' Roux said, holding his hands across his heart.

The line made me smile since I knew the old song it came from and, as I slipped my shoes back on ready to leave the limousine, Con told me he would meet up with Roux and me in the café in about ten minutes, once he'd parked the car.

'And who exactly have you got coming today?' the crop-haired reporter asked Roux as I stepped onto the pavement behind him.

Roux's briefing had clearly been thorough since he effortlessly reeled off the names I'd heard Gwettay give to Aldo earlier and, while he continued answering questions and Con pulled off into the traffic, other journalists from the group by the entrance joined the crowd around us and quizzed Roux about how much money he was worth, why he appeared so rarely in public and whether he had any plans to enter politics.

Seemingly relishing the attention, Roux gave authentic-sounding answers and was in the middle of rebutting one reporter's suggestion that there was a romantic liaison between him and Countess Creola when a number of girls in the queue suddenly screamed and rushed towards the roadway where a white limousine was pulling into the space left by Con.

The rush set off a chain reaction and, within seconds, dozens of the girls from the queue had come to the kerb and begun surrounding the parking limousine, accompanied by two of the bull-necked men in Pointless Café T-shirts. Several of the girls then began banging on the car's side windows and shrieking 'Wylda! Wylda!'

Having insinuated themselves between the pavement side of the car and the crowd of girls, the bull-necked men created a clearing alongside the car's rear section and, once the vehicle was stationary, they pulled open the kerbside door to let out whoever was in the back. The crowd fell silent as a stooping man emerged, dressed in a sleeveless sports top and baggy trousers.

The man then brought his muscular frame to its full six-foot-two height and, adjusting his super-large sunglasses under the peak of his cap, he turned his face to the crowd and was met with a hail of shrieks and whoops. The adulation brought a smile to his face, which he battled to keep down. Then, recovering his nonchalant expression, he waved his tattoo-covered arms above his head and shouted: 'Cool, y'all; yeah! Really cool!'

He then followed in the wake of the two bull-necked men as they cleared a path to the café entrance and, when a girl grabbed him round the neck and kissed his cheek, his suppressed smile broke free, revealing two diamond-studded gold teeth in the upper set.

Turning back to Roux, I saw the photographers had deserted him for the new arrival and only the reporter with the microphone was still asking him questions. She seemed interested in writing a business article about Pointless's commercial operations since she was quizzing him about his reasons for diversifying into so many areas outside the media field. 'Take the Pointless Café as an example,' she said.

Hearing Roux struggle to come up with anything that sounded strategic enough to convince the woman he knew why Pointless had recently set up retail, mineral water, printing and management-consultancy businesses, I put a staying hand on his arm and said to the young woman: 'Can I ask who you're working for exactly?'

Looking put out, the woman explained she was a freelance journalist who'd been writing business features for quality newspapers and trade-press publications for many years.

'In which case,' I said, battling to make myself heard above another round of screams from the crowd, 'could I suggest you send your business card and examples of your work to Pointless's PR team. I'm sure they could arrange a formal interview with Lord Pointer at a later date.' Then, sensing she was about to protest, I quickly explained 'Lord Pointer' and I needed to go into the café now since we were running late.

Her tone hardening, she told me she'd tried several times to arrange an appointment with Lord Pointer but had always been stonewalled by his staff, even though she'd promised to write a quality piece looking solely at his business activities rather than his personal life, which she knew he liked to keep private.

Ushering Roux towards the café entrance, where Wylda Warrior had just disappeared through the revolving door amid a final round of shrieks, I said if she rang the Pointless offices again and asked for Gwettay Oluke, and explained Professor Small had recommended she make contact, then she should be able to set something up.

I felt bad about telling such a lie – or at least what I believed was a lie – but I told myself it was justified if it kept her away from Roux. I then hurried up the entrance steps, protected by a line of bull-necked men and followed Roux into the revolving door and the café.

Inside, the dining space was much bigger than I'd expected with sixty tables set out on the main floor and a further forty arranged on three tiers to the rear of it, the top one of which had a twenty-five-metre-long bar running along its back.

A young man with spiked hair and a Pointless Café T-shirt greeted Roux and me in the reception area then led us between the main-floor tables and onto a staircase running up the centre of the three tiers. Eight tables were set either side of the staircase on the first two tiers, with every table occupied except those in the second tier's left section, which was roped off with purple cord and guarded by a stout man in a dark suit.

The top tier was set with four large tables either side of the steps and its left section was also roped off, although – unlike the area just below – this space was packed with people, most of whom were chatting noisily as they stood drinking at the bar.

Accompanying Roux to the back of the bar crowd, I suddenly felt an ache in my feet and asked if he wouldn't mind ordering me a sparkling mineral water while I took a seat. I then made my way to one of the unoccupied tables and, sitting with my back to the tier's handrail, I slipped off my heels and wiggled my toes in relief.

As Roux tried to catch the eye of the bartenders, I saw several drinkers in the crowd glance at him then nudge their companions to take a look.

Twisting in my chair, I looked at the scene below, where the garish colours of the diners' clothes and hurrying of the waiters was combining with the noisy table chatter and piped dance music to create a gay, high-energy atmosphere. I then heard a booming voice shout something unintelligible from the top of the stairs and turned to see Wylda Warrior, who'd just come through the purple-rope cordon, waving to someone at the bar.

Breaking off from her conversation with two glamorous-looking women at the bar's far end, a long-legged girl waved back at Wylda and shouted: 'My man! How you doin'!' She then moved to meet him halfway up the bar and, after a showy embrace and kisses, she said: 'They let you out on your own then!'

Wylda Warrior confirmed he'd come alone and was met with a coy look and invitation to come and meet the rest of her band. She then linked his arm and led him back to the glamorous companions, one of whom was wearing a low-cut dress that showed her diamond-studded navel and, whenever she leant forward, most of her plastic breasts.

From the conversation fragments I caught, I gathered the girl and her two associates were members of the band MTR, and they, and Wylda Warrior, were enthusiastic about collaborating artistically in some way, perhaps by performing together at a live event. The conversation then drifted to clothes, jewellery and other banalities so I turned round and had another look at the diners below.

As I was watching a waiter weave his way between the tables, carrying a tray of drinks head-high, Roux arrived, a tumbler of mineral water in one hand and a bottle of beer in the other, and I asked how much I owed him.

Placing the drinks on the table, he beamed: 'Nothing. It's all free.' Then, sliding the tumbler in front of me, he added: 'We are the VIPs after all!' He then took a swig of beer and looked up and down the bar, craning his neck to see beyond the crowd.

I asked who he was looking for and – surveying the main floor below – he said: 'Con Dweir. The PR people said he'd fill me in on what to do next.'

Unsure what my own next move should be, I tried to think through with Roux what might be expected of him. We then agreed, since it was likely all the artists knew what Lord Pointer looked like, Roux's immediate job was probably to stop being 'Percy' and simply enjoy his lunch. 'I'm sure when it's time to go, you'll have to put on a show again,' I added.

Looking disappointed, Roux gave a pout then suggested the empty tables just below were probably reserved for us and the lesser members of the stars' entourages while the artists themselves and the real Percy would dine where we were now. I agreed that sounded likely and was just reaching for a peanut from the complimentary dish on the table when the piped music suddenly stopped and a series of deep, staccato notes sounded from somewhere below.

Throwing me a puzzled look, Roux said: 'What the hell's that?'

The music then came again and I realised it was a tuba being played at breakneck speed, rasping out the melody of 'It's Not Unusual': the 1960s song made famous by Tom Jones.

Drums and other brass instruments then came in and, realising the music was being played by a live band, I looked down to see where it was. Most of the diners at the far side of the main floor were now twisting towards the space hidden from me by the curve of the ceiling and I guessed that's where the musicians were.

Then, as I kept watching, I saw a man in a puff-sleeved shirt and leather trousers emerge onto the main floor and start making his way between the tables with a kind of dancing march, setting the time for the music on a bass drum strapped to his chest.

Following in single file behind him came five other men in puffy shirts: one was the tuba player and the other four were playing a trombone, a trumpet, French horn and snare drum with attached cymbal. The percussion made the music's already manic rhythm even crazier and gave the song a whole new feel, reminding me of the ska groups my British psychiatry students used to love.

By the song's second chorus, the band had grouped into two lines of three and begun dancing with synchronised crossing steps where they abruptly dropped one knee every eighth beat, giving the impression the whole group was about to drop to the floor. Several diners nearby stood up and began performing party-style dances, clicking their fingers in the air.

Then, as the song was building to its climax, I saw Con the driver come in through the revolving door and, as he moved towards the staircase, he looked up, caught sight of the now waving Roux and gave a single wave back.

When he arrived by the rope to the bar area, Roux was already waiting to greet him and ask whether or not he needed still to be playing 'Percy'. Sipping my fizzy water, I saw Roux give another of his pouts and guessed the answer was no.

A loud round of applause and whistling broke out below, signalling the band's first number was over just as Con and

Roux arrived at the table. The band then struck up again and, after a few bars, I looked back over my shoulder to see them snaking their way in single file between the main-floor tables, stepping to the beat and making sharp twists at the waist as they delivered Charles Trenet's 'Boum!' with the same manic joy as the first number.

The mad euphoria of the music reminded me of the student parties of my youth and I toyed for a moment with the idea of asking Roux to get me a glass of sparkling wine, but thought better of it. I then noticed a couple of dozen more people had started dancing below, some of them on their chairs, while several of the VIPs left the bar to come and look over the handrail.

Scanning the watching VIPs to see if Wylda Warrior and MTR were among them, I noticed Aldo had suddenly arrived on the tier and was looking for a gap at the handrail, his jacket off, shirt buttons undone and his feet bare. His arm was looped round the waist of a small man with a neatly cropped beard and diamond ear studs, who was laughing as he allowed himself to be propelled by Aldo.

Continuing to look for a gap, Aldo caught sight of me and, after a quick word in the small man's ear, he disengaged his arm and led him by the hand to where Con, Roux and I were sitting. 'Professor,' he said, his eyes shining. 'I want you to meet Raphael Iniesta – MD of the café.'

As I leant across Aldo to shake hands with the small man, I caught the scent of alcohol on Aldo's breath and, after telling Raphael it was nice to meet him, I asked where the pair had just sprung from since I hadn't seen them come up the staircase. Aldo pointed out a 'staff only' door beyond the bar's far end which promptly swung open to allow out a team of four waiters carrying glasses and baskets of tableware.

Remembering Gwettay's warning, I caught Con's eye and said to Aldo: 'You've been enjoying a little free beer yourself then?'

Looping his arm round Raphael's waist once more, Aldo said: 'Not beer, Professor. Champagne!' and, grinning at Raphael, he added: 'Raphael's just hit the million-a-week mark – three months ahead of target.' He and Raphael then sat down alongside me and, as they settled into their places, I caught sight of the team of waiters again, who'd now arrived on the tier below and begun laying the tables.

'How did it go with the paps?' Aldo said. 'Were they a pain?'

Roux said everything had gone brilliantly except a little bit at the end, when a journalist had started asking questions about Pointless's business strategy. 'Fortunately the professor was there to rescue me,' Roux said, nodding in my direction.

'Interesting!' said Aldo, then he thanked me for helping out and asked what form the rescue had taken.

I told him I'd fobbed off the journalist by telling her to contact Gwettay and request a formal interview with Lord Pointer at a later date, but knew full well Gwettay's first instinct would be to block any contact from reporters.

Letting out a roar of laughter, Aldo wagged his finger and said: 'Naughty!'

I smiled and said: 'It was all I could think of.' I then recalled the journalist's question about diversification and said I'd be very interested to know myself what his corporate strategy was, if it wasn't a secret.

Taking a moment to listen to some whooping that had broken out to a chorus of 'Boum!', Aldo leant towards me and said: 'I'd never admit it publicly, but the truth is, I don't believe in strategy.' He then explained how the development of strategic visions was alien to him and it was only once he'd met someone with a business idea that interested him that he even thought about making any sort of plan.

'It's a case of "who" then "what" with me, rather than "what" and who can do it for me – if you see what I mean,' he said. Then, gesturing to Raphael he added: 'Take Rapha, for example.

I had no intention of getting into restaurants until I met him.'
He then explained he'd stayed at an Andalusian hotel eighteen
months previously where Raphael was the entertainments
manager and, after getting to know him, he'd realised he
possessed a genius for throwing parties.

Raphael gave an embarrassed shake of the head and seemed
about to protest, but Aldo continued: 'I mean, tell me this isn't
a great party right now!' And so saying, he jumped onto his
chair and, whooping like a wolf, started dancing to the final
verse of 'Boum!'.

Con threw me a look I guessed meant he wanted to talk and
Raphael caught the arm of a passing waiter and pulled him close
so he could give some whispered instructions which, I assumed
from the little circle he drew in the air, concerned arrangements
for our table.

Slipping my shoes back on, I excused myself then headed for
the ladies', giving Con a surreptitious squeeze of the shoulder
as I passed. He gave a knowing nod and, when I was halfway
to the toilets at the tier's far end, I glanced back to see him rise
from the table and head for the bar with a casualness so feigned
it made me smile.

After washing my hands and patching up my foundation, I left
the toilet and made straight for where Con was now standing,
by one of the wooden posts holding up the bar's canopy. He
twisted round to check on Aldo when he saw me coming then
came forward so he could meet me on the move and veer us
into the handrail crowd, most of whom were now watching
the band perform a slower, Latin number I'd never heard before.

'I'd say we've got another fifteen minutes, max, before he does
something stupid,' he said, once we'd come to a stop. He then
leant close and told me Aldo had a habit of fixing on someone
when he'd been drinking and trying to 'press their buttons' to
make them crack. 'It's like he knows what to say to make them
crazy,' he added. 'Like a kid pulling wings off a fly.'

'I see,' I said. 'You seem to understand him very well.'

Con gave a rueful smile and said he was the father of teenage children and accustomed to knowing when one piece of craziness was about to lead to another.

Taking a look at Aldo, who was still on his chair, swaying to the slower music, I asked Con what he thought we should do.

'You've got to stop him drinking – especially wine,' he said. Then he told me he would make sure he was on hand later, to intervene when things turned ugly. He also said it would be a big help if I could prepare Raphael to spirit Percy away when the trouble started; then, once the dust had settled, have him ready to be picked up from the café's back door.

We then headed back to the table together, which had now been laid, and I said he seemed very sure it was a case of 'when' trouble broke out rather than 'if'.

Holding out my chair for me, he said quietly: 'Wait and see!'

Delaying sitting down, I picked up a place name on my plate and read: 'Lord Pointer special guest'. I then showed the little card to Con and asked if he thought that meant me.

Picking up the card in front of Roux, he showed me that said the same and, looking round the table, he suggested: 'It must be you two; everyone else's has got their name.'

Having noticed Con's card check, Raphael confirmed we were all in the right seats then he looked up at the dancing Aldo and said something to him about a cake I didn't catch fully since the music had become much louder.

Twisting round once more to look over the handrail, I saw the band was now in a line at the foot of the staircase, facing out towards the main floor, their instruments pointed at the ceiling. A flourish on the snare drum then heralded the last few bars of the song and, when it was over, the band members fell into their bows to whooping and whistling.

Aldo was among those vigorously clapping their approval and he only stopped when the band played the opening notes of their next number: 'Zorba the Greek'. He then sat back down and, nudging me, he said: 'Aren't these guys fantastic!'

I agreed and continued to watch the musicians, who, on a signal from the bass-drum player, turned in unison and began making their way two abreast up the stairs, marching in funereal time.

Wiping sweat from his face with a shirt cuff, Aldo said: 'Goodness! – it's hot up here!' Then he looked up and down the tier and said to Raphael: 'Can't we get some more champagne brought up?'

A frowning Con caught my eye and I slid my tumbler before Aldo, saying: 'No more wine now. Have some water before you get a headache.' And pushing the drink closer to him, I looked him in the eye and added: 'These conditions can be extremely dehydrating.'

Aldo's face immediately became serious and he asked if I was trying to nursemaid him. 'I'm just trying to keep you comfortable,' I said, holding his gaze.

A smile dawning in his eyes, he suddenly burst out laughing and said: 'You really are very good, aren't you,' and taking a gulp of my water, he added: 'If I ever need a shrink, you'll be it.' He then told Raphael he thought it would be a good idea if the birthday cake was served before people ordered their meals, since it would promote a party mood. 'They don't actually have to eat it yet,' he added.

Nodding his agreement, Raphael rose from the table and set off for the staff door while Roux announced he was going to get himself another beer and asked if he could bring back a drink for anyone else.

Aldo grinned at me and said he would like a water and Raphael and I would have one too. Con said he was fine, his voice serious.

Keeping half an eye on the band, who were climbing the stairs without wavering from their slow tempo, I asked Aldo if he'd had a chance yet to decide about visiting Gian Paolo to discuss his genetics project.

Finishing off my water and allowing an ice cube to plop into his cheek, he said: 'I'm sorry. I didn't know I was meant to give it serious thought.' He then crunched the cube and added: 'I thought it was just part of his health issue.'

I explained the project was very probably part of a delusional complex, but there was just a tiny chance it wasn't. 'In which case, it could be something absolutely Earth-shattering,' I said and, leaning closer, I added: 'I was hoping very much you could at least talk it through with him and see what you thought.'

Fastening a couple of buttons on the front of his shirt, he said: 'I see – you're serious.' He then smoothed his collar and added: 'I'll get Gwettay to book me an evening to come up to…' and, folding back one of his cuffs, he said: 'Where is it you've got him again?'

'Royston,' I said.

'That's it, Royston,' he said. 'I'm sure I can do something in the next couple of weeks.'

I was about to say how medically vital it was he visited before the week was out when two fashionably dressed young men arrived and, after exchanging warm handshakes with Aldo, fell into conversation about the songs they were recording for their next album.

While they chatted, Roux arrived with three tumblers of water and an opened bottle of beer and said the celebrity guests must have drunk their fill since there had been much less of a scrum at the bar this time.

Thanking him, I took a sip of my water and noticed Raphael had reappeared through the staff door, followed by a woman in a chef's hat pushing a trolley with a huge, candle-festooned cake. The music then took on an immediate quality as the first pair of musicians arrived on the top tier and took up position by the purple cord, closely followed by the remaining four band members.

Driven by the bass-drum player, the tempo of 'Zorba the Greek' then moved up a gear and seemed to catch Aldo's attention since he broke off suddenly from his conversation with the young men and watched the band, his lips slightly apart. He then rose and, without taking his eyes off the musicians, approached them with a sliding, heel-to-toe walk, like a tightrope walker.

Seemingly unaware of his presence, the band played on and, even when he moved to within half a metre of them, they gave no sign they'd noticed. His arms then rose out from his sides and he started clicking his fingers in the way made famous by Anthony Quinn in his on-screen dance in *Zorba the Greek*.

As the music moved up another gear, Aldo performed wavelike movements with his bare feet that took him on a sideways glide, making him look like he was on castors. The finger-clicking then became faster and, as the trumpet-led music quickened even further, he relaxed his arms at the elbow and suddenly launched his shoulders and chest into a high-speed jelly wobble; like a belly-dancer.

The faster the music, the quicker Aldo's wobble became until his pectorals were vibrating at such speed some of the crowd who'd left the handrail to come and watch cheered: 'Go Percy!' The high-speed wobble then continued, with a few positional variations, to the end of the song and, when it stopped, the musicians forewent their bows so they could clap a sweat-saturated Aldo, who was now standing frozen with one hand above his tipped-back head, the other at his back.

The diners on the first tier, most of whom were now on their feet, erupted into whoops while a few people on the main floor shouted: 'Olé!' Roux, who was among the watching crowd, gave a piercing whistle and cried: 'More! More!'

Retaking his seat, Raphael smiled like an indulgent parent and I leant forward and said: 'I don't wish to be a killjoy, but I understand Lord Pointer has a habit of misbehaving when he's been drinking.'

Nodding, Raphael said it was true and he'd seen before what Percy's drinking could lead to. 'Especially last time,' he added. 'My God! Touching all the boob-job girls like that!' He then glanced over at Aldo, who was now shaking hands with the band, and, rising once again, he said he would cross his fingers nothing like that happened this time.

Quickly laying a staying hand on his arm, I asked, if trouble did arise, could he take it on himself to smuggle Aldo out through the kitchens then arrange for Con to pick him up from the backyard.

Sitting back down with a half smile, he told Con to give him the number for the limousine's phone; then, after he'd programmed it into his mobile, he excused himself and set off for the trolley with the cake. A nervous-looking Con thanked me and said it was time he moved to Percy's side.

As he rose and headed towards Aldo, who was now waltzing with an imaginary partner around the trolley where Raphael had just started lighting the candles, Roux returned and said: 'He's some guy that Lord Pointer. I just don't get why he doesn't want to be famous. He seems to like a crowd well enough.'

I gave a small shrug and watched as the still-waltzing Aldo arrived beside Raphael, followed by the band, who then formed a semi-circle to one side, ready for their next number. Raphael finished lighting the candles meanwhile and, with the battery-powered lighter still in his hand, he turned and gave a wand-like signal to the bass-drum player.

Almost instantly, the musicians launched into a crazily fast version of 'Happy Birthday to You' and a few of the VIPs who'd gathered round the cake began showing off by singing harmony. Beaming, Aldo picked up a huge knife from the trolley and began using it to conduct the musicians.

The song then morphed into 'For He's A Jolly Good Fellow' and more of the VIPs gathered round and joined the singing, causing Aldo's beam to widen. He then turned and conducted some of the singers while the woman in the chef's hat bent to the trolley's lower deck and pulled out a stack of small plates and napkins.

When the song ended, with the fastest round of 'and-so-say-all-of-us's' I'd ever heard, the VIPs broke into applause, joined by the band. Aldo looked embarrassed and hastily waved the gathering into silence with the knife. Then he gave a short speech, thanking people for their kindness and saying the future of Pointless Records looked rosy thanks to the fabulous array of talent before him.

A 'hear, hear!' rang out, causing Aldo's embarrassed look to deepen and, quickly looking down, he blew out the candles, prompting a small cheer and a few claps. He then cut the cake in half before handing the knife to the chef, who promptly set about cutting it into slices. The band formed back into three rows of two meanwhile and began making their way down the staircase, playing 'When the Saints Go Marching In'.

Having decided to help the chef hand out the cake, Aldo had just started moving among the VIPs when I noticed him look towards the far end of the bar where Wylda Warrior and the girl with the diamond navel stud were perched on high stools, their heads close together in conversation. And he threw several more glances their way as he continued distributing plates of cake. Then, when most of the VIPs had been served, he made his way to the bar's far end with a slice of gateau wrapped in a napkin.

Noticing his arrival, the naval-stud girl sat upright, her hands rising to cover her bust, and Wylda Warrior greeted him with a nod. Con moved to the canopy post a little way behind and loitered, pretending to be interested in some wine racks while Aldo took an at-ease position and, bouncing the cake in his palm behind his back, he said: 'And how are you, Marion? Meenyonne?'

The girl started to reply but Wylda Warrior cut across her saying: 'Don't call me Marion, man. You know it's Wylda or M.'

'Ah! Of course. Just so,' Aldo said, nodding. Then he fell silent and beamed at the pair, reminding me of the coffee kiosk queue at the station the other Sunday, when he'd stood smiling at everyone as if he was enjoying some private joke.

An embarrassed silence then fell, as it had in the kiosk queue, and Wylda Warrior looked at him from under a scowling brow while Meenyonne folded her arms over her chest. Aldo continued to beam nonetheless and bounce the gateau, then, just as Wylda Warrior was turning back to Meenyonne, Aldo's left hand shot to the back of Wylda's head and the other squashed the cake into his face with the speed of a cat.

Wylda instantly knocked the gateau away and jumped down from the stool, squaring up to Aldo. 'What the fucking hell are you doing, you fucking asshole!' he shouted, bringing his face close to Aldo's, their noses almost touching.

'Ooh, now! Let's keep our cool,' Aldo said and, raising both palms to Wylda, he added: 'You do know you're meant to be the cool guy round here?'

Wylda scowled for a long two seconds; then, his eyes narrowed, he bent to pick up the napkin the cake had been wrapped in and used it to wipe his face. 'Don't fuck with me, Percy,' he said, his voice full of aggression, 'or you'll get a kick in the fucking bollocks – you get me?'

Aldo's beam returned and he said: 'No! I thought you'd be happy to look a bit blacker.'

Still wiping himself, Wylda said: 'What the fuck are you talking about, man?'

'The chocolate,' Aldo said, gesturing to Wylda's face. 'A bit of blacking up is just what you need for the real gangster look.'

His face clear of cake, Wylda screwed up the napkin and tossed it onto the bar. Then he sat back down and, tapping his temple, he said: 'You're fucking mad, man. Your marbles have gone.'

'Maybe,' Aldo said, 'but I'm sane enough to know you need the gangster thing to get your dick up.'

Meenyonne slid down from her stool saying: 'I'm just going to catch up with Taysha a second,' then she headed to the other end of the bar.

Sucking his teeth, Wylda watched her go and said: 'Now look what you've done, man. You've scared the bitch off.'

Aldo moved closer and said: ' "The bitch", yes.' He then looked into Wylda's face and added: 'You think if you play the gangster, you can take charge of women, don't you. Tell them what to do.'

Picking up his beer, Wylda took a swig and glared silently at Aldo.

Con moved closer, his fingers twitching.

'And you've got to take charge and do it to them because if they take control – like they're enjoying it – then they're just whores, right?' Aldo continued.

Starting to rise, Wylda said: 'I don't have to listen to this shit,' but Aldo put a staying hand on his shoulder and, looking into his eyes, he said softly: 'Come on. A cool guy like you can take a bit of banter.'

A look of shock suddenly crossing Wylda's face, he blinked to focus on something in the space immediately behind Aldo and I guessed he must be experiencing a vision.

'I mean, hating whores makes sense if you had a lot of uncles as a kid, right?' said Aldo. He then reached along the bar, picked up a half-finished glass of wine and drained it in one, adding: 'The problem is, it's boring to just keep having it done to you – that's why the only girls who stick it out are the ones after your money.'

'You better shut up, man,' Wylda said, looking unnerved.

'So the sexy, cool guy never actually satisfies a woman and, if he does, he hates her for being a whore and gets the droop,' Aldo said and, turning away, he added in a sing-song voice: 'If only the fans knew!'

His face twisted with rage, Wylda flew off the stool and punched the departing Aldo in the side of the face, sending him to his knees. He then moved round to Aldo's head and seemed to be deciding whether to punch him again when Con bowled into him from the side, knocking him heavily to the ground. Con then got to his feet quickly and moved to stand over Wylda, I guessed so he could block any further attack on Aldo.

A moment's silence then passed before Wylda moved to a sitting position on the floor and said: 'My fucking arm, man!' and, looking up at Con, he massaged the elbow he'd landed on, his face pained.

Con apologised then turned to help Aldo to his feet and steer him towards the arriving Raphael, who quickly supported him with an arm round the back and guided him towards the staff door.

Wylda managed to stand meanwhile, using just one arm, and, having watched Aldo and Raphael disappear through the door, he turned to Con and said: 'You want to have a word with him, you know. All the money in the world won't stop me kicking his fucking face in if he keeps that kind of shit up.'

Con apologised once more – on Aldo's behalf this time – and, as he dusted off Wylda and helped him back to his stool, he turned to the VIPs who'd gathered and told them everything was okay now and they should go to their tables.

I suggested to Roux he and I go over to see if we could help Con, then I pushed my chair back and said: 'Shame about lunch though – I'm starving!'

Draining his beer, Roux set his bottle on the table and said: 'Haven't we at least got time for the starter?'

'I don't think so,' I said, picking up my bag. 'I'll check.' And I left the table and crossed to where Con was standing, still trying to excuse Aldo's behaviour to Wylda Warrior.

When he'd finished explaining, I walked with him to the rope cordon by the stairs and asked if Roux and I needed to accompany him to the car now. He said we did but to give him a couple of minutes' start so he could bring the limousine to the front of the café.

Having watched him exit the café through the revolving door below, I made my way over to the bar where Roux had just ordered another beer and, touching his elbow, I told him we needed to make a move. He looked annoyed and began complaining how Percy's behaviour had ruined everything.

As the barman handed him his drink, he asked whether I thought it would be okay to take the beer with him. I said if the paparazzi were still outside, a photo of 'Lord Pointer' holding a bottle would look awful next to any story they published about the Wylda Warrior dust-up.

Pouting, Roux gave a sigh and promised he'd dispose of the bottle before we went outside. He then challenged whether the press would be able to find out anything about the incident with Wylda Warrior but quickly accepted my view that enough people had witnessed it for some kind of account to reach a journalist.

'Even if they don't publish a story straightaway, someone's bound to write something at some point,' I said, and we made our way down the staircase.

Taking a long swig of beer, Roux said: 'That's the price of being somebody, I guess.' We then headed for the revolving door and, as we passed a table a waiter was in the middle of clearing, Roux surreptitiously placed his bottle on one corner.

As we exited and made for the limousine, which was just pulling up at the kerb, I noticed only one photographer was still waiting by the café steps and the queue of adolescents seemed much more sedate. The dark-suited woman who'd welcomed us was nowhere to be seen meanwhile, so Roux opened the car's rear door himself and we climbed in the back.

Aldo was already inside, semi-recumbent on the bench seat immediately behind the driver's compartment, his bare ankles glowing white between the black of his shoes and trouser hems. He sat up as we slid onto the opposite seat and asked Roux to shut the door. The redness of his cheek where Wylda Warrior had struck him was clearly visible despite the tinted-window gloom.

Once we were belted up and the car was preparing to pull away, he said to us both: 'You think I'm a monster, don't you.'

Roux turned to me, panic in his eyes.

'We're all capable of monstrousness,' I said. 'I'd say you just have more chance to express it.'

Sitting back, Aldo gave a half laugh and said: 'More chance, or more money?'

'Both!' I said and, taking a glance out of the window, I caught sight of several people in the queue peering at the car. 'But,' I continued, 'that kind of behaviour doesn't bring happiness – as I'm sure you've discovered.'

A car horn sounded as we pulled into the flow of traffic and Aldo said: 'And how would you know?'

I explained I'd treated many patients who'd indulged in law-breaking or excess because of the momentary thrills it gave them and I'd learnt such acts were nearly always an attempt to escape a state of depression, which inevitably returned.

Looking into my eyes, he said: 'And you think I'm depressed?'

As I returned his gaze, I noticed a small, but distinct, white spot in the brown of his iris and I was just thinking how unusual it made his eyes look when his face transfigured into a hissing leopard with pinned-back ears.

My heart thudding, I pulled back and blinked to refocus my vision, causing his normal face to reappear.

'I'm sorry, I didn't mean to make you jump,' he said and, placing a hand on my knee, he added: 'I don't really like being observed.'

A crossness rising in me, I said: 'Then don't ask people to judge your mental state!'

Sitting back with a sigh, he said: 'Yes, you're right of course. Sorry.' He then glanced out the window at the people-filled pavement and added: 'And you're sort of right about the depression.' He then explained how, beneath the glamour of his lifestyle, he felt fundamentally empty because the feelings that made himself, Gian Paolo and his late sister different from other people prevented him forming a loving relationship with anyone. 'You see, every time I get close to someone, I end up damaging them,' he said.

I was on the point of asking what damage meant when an echo of the hissing leopard crossed my mind and I said instead: 'So you feel alone – apart?'

'Sort of, but it's not just that,' he said and, a pained look in his eyes, he continued: 'You see, I can never quite forget what I know.'

'What you know?'

'Yes,' he murmured, and propping his head on his hand, he said he knew the truth about the human condition: about how we were actually beams of celestial sunshine trying to light up the world but could only be here by means of our hopelessly flawed bodies. And being constantly aware how our 'sunbeamness' was stuck for eighty-odd years in appetite-ridden flesh, he was unable to avoid an almost continual feeling of discomfort. 'It's like if you walked round with your shoes a size too small and on the wrong feet,' he continued.

I wasn't quite sure what he meant and said: 'So you're depressed because our bodies are flawed?'

'Partly,' he said, sitting back. 'But mainly because of how desolate the world is compared with where we come from.

How we're squeezed out onto a spinning bit of rock that's actually totally alien to us.'

'Interesting,' I said. 'Gian Paolo said that's how you viewed the world when we were chatting on Monday and he told me about "floaty".'

Roux, who had so far been looking quietly out the window, gave Aldo and me a sideways look.

Aldo let his head loll back on the top cushion and said 'floaty' had been Renata's word, and it was very apt for the process he, Gian Paolo and Renata went through in connecting with faraway space. He then laughed and said 'floaty' had always been Gian Paolo's favourite experience because of his escapist tendency.

'Not like me,' he continued. 'I like to grab the world with both hands.'

'Yes, I can see you're much more the realist,' I said. 'In fact, you seem very different from Gian Paolo in many respects.'

Aldo smiled and said people had been saying that ever since he could remember.

'But you do love your brother?' I said.

'Of course,' he said and, suddenly serious, he added: 'Why do you ask?'

Glancing at Roux, whose attention seemed fixed back out the window, I said Gian Paolo had told me Aldo had given him, Alice and Claudio money as part of a tacit agreement they stayed out of his life, keeping only minimal contact.

Aldo nodded and said that was true but it didn't mean he didn't love his family. 'I just want to be free to do my thing,' he said.

'I see,' I murmured and, sitting forward, I said: 'I'm glad to hear that.' Then, looking into his eyes, I continued: 'You see, Gian Paolo really does need you to visit.'

Puffing his cheeks, he said: 'Yes. I've already said I'll find a date.'

'Yes, but I didn't quite explain the urgency,' I said. 'You see, a couple of weeks will be too late.'

Sounding irritated, he said: 'Hang on! Surely a week or two is neither here nor there with mental illness.'

Glancing back out the window, I saw we were approaching the road with the underpass and said: 'Normally, I'd say yes. But there's more to this.'

Sitting upright, he said: 'What are you saying?'

My mind raced to come up with a way to gently break the news to him of Gian Paolo's condition, but I couldn't think how to put it.

'Just tell me the truth,' he said.

As we entered the underpass and descended into gloom, I took a deep breath and said: 'He's dying.' I then put my hand on his knee and told him how sorry I was.

Roux glanced my way then quickly turned back.

'Dying?' Aldo said. 'But how? What from?'

I said the results of all Gian Paolo's tests were not yet available, but he had a brain tumour which, in light of its size, was likely to prove fatal in less than two weeks.

Wringing his hands, he fidgeted in his seat and said: 'But that's impossible. I showed him about mutations; there's no reason...' And, stopping mid-sentence, he flopped back and said: 'Of course!' Then, turning to look out the window, he gave a series of little head-shakes and said: 'Typical Gian Paolo! Escapist till the bloody end!'

'I'm sorry,' I said as we emerged from the underpass. 'I don't follow.'

Taking a quick glance at Roux, Aldo said he'd shown Gian Paolo a technique for manipulating mutating DNA to ensure it didn't produce cancer. He then explained he'd developed the technique shortly after Renata's illness and had been using it at regular intervals ever since.

Wondering if the alcohol had made him delusional, I said: 'Are you saying you have a cure for cancer?'

'Not a cure,' he said. 'More a prevention.' He then told me he had the ability to scan his body in infinitesimal detail and subsequently will individual atoms to reconfigure their molecular relationships.

Roux and I exchanged glances and I said: 'Is that meant to be a joke?'

His eyes darted several times between Roux and me, then he slapped his thigh and said: 'Of course it is! A joke, yes!' and he gave a forced laugh.

But I couldn't help thinking Aldo's technique matched too closely with the 'cyclonic' experience Gian Paolo had told me about for it to be just a joke. I said nothing, however, and returned to looking out the window while he phoned Gwettay Oluke to make arrangements for a helicopter to take him and me to the hospital.

In re-diarising the appointments he had scheduled for later that afternoon, Aldo entered into a dispute with Gwettay about whether or not one particular meeting could be postponed. He then seemed forced to accept her point and, sounding irritated, he finished the conversation by instructing her to call him back as soon as she knew what time the helicopter would be available.

Sliding his phone back into his trouser pocket, he turned to me and said, before we could fly, he needed to return to the office to pick up a laptop loaded with ad campaign materials promoting the Pointless management-consultancy business. 'If I don't sign them off tonight apparently, the marketing team won't hit the TV slots they've got booked,' he said and, turning to Roux, he added: 'Are you okay if we drop you back at the office?'

Roux confirmed he was happy then spent the rest of the journey in silence.

OH BROTHER!

As soon as we were back on the fifth floor of the Pointless building, Gwettay Oluke handed Aldo details of our helicopter flight and, after he'd picked up the laptop loaded with the consultancy business's ad campaign, he took me back down in the lift to the car park where Con was waiting to drive us to the heliport.

The helicopter taking us was much bigger than I'd expected, with a little sofa and yellow wallpaper in its seating area, creating a living-room atmosphere that left me nicely relaxed by the time we touched down on the helipad in the hospital's rear field.

Aldo was first to leave the cabin and he ducked low as he moved out of range of the helicopter blades, even though they were so far above his head there was no risk of injury. He then stood a moment with his hands on his hips and, turning to me, he shouted above the engine noise: 'Which way do we go?'

The late June evening was unusually chill and we walked briskly as I led him across yellowing grass to the automatic doors at the back of the main building. We then made our way along several corridors to the lifts going up to the third-floor cancer ward and, as we waited for a lift to arrive, I warned him to prepare for the upset of seeing Gian Paolo on a drip and physically altered by chemotherapy.

'Isn't that a bit premature?' he said. 'I mean, if they haven't even got the test results yet.'

I explained that, although the precise nature of the tumour hadn't been confirmed, there was enough evidence to suggest it was imminently life-threatening and the process in such circumstances was to begin treatment immediately.

'I see,' Aldo said as the light pinged above a lift entrance. 'That sounds sensible.' And, as the lift's doors opened, he gestured for me to enter then followed me in, saying: 'I warn you now though, I'm not good with illness.'

Pressing the button for the third, I said: 'Yes, Gian Paolo told me you hate suffering of any kind. He also said you hate hospitals.' I then massaged my foot where the shoe was rubbing and added: 'That's why I had to tell you he was dying – even though he said not to. I just didn't know how else to get you here.'

As we left the lift and made our way to the cancer ward, I took my phone out of my bag and switched it off, asking Aldo to follow suit so we didn't interfere with any of the ward's radio-frequency monitoring equipment. He quickly complied and said the hospital seemed well equipped before asking if there were any hospitals in the world where Gian Paolo could receive superior treatment. I suggested private clinics existed where Gian Paolo's stay would be more luxurious but, as far as the treatment was concerned, this hospital was second to none. 'It actually has the highest success rates in Europe for a number of cancer types,' I said.

Nodding, he said: 'And has he used his money to get the best room?'

I smiled and said: 'As a matter of fact, he's paid me over two million pounds!'

Then, in response to Aldo's puzzled look, I explained Gian Paolo had given me the money as a down payment on the research project he wanted to talk to him about – isolating the genes that made their family special.

'Ah! We're back to that,' Aldo said and, as we approached the doorway to the ward, he added: 'Doesn't he understand genius has nothing to do with genes – it's just fluke.'

'I don't think he's suggesting genes make genius,' I said and, opening the door to the ward, I added in a quieter voice: 'He understands genes must be behind your family's "new feelings" so, if you really are the next step in evolution, well... genes do drive evolutionary development.'

Heading up a walking route through the open-plan section of the ward and into a narrow corridor with a dozen small patient-care rooms on either side, we made our way to Gian Paolo's room, which was three-quarters of the way up on the right. Gian Paolo was visible through the room's corridor window and I could see he was awake and watching TV as he lay with the top section of his bed in the recliner position.

Turning to Aldo, I gestured for him to enter first but he stepped back and, guiding me to one side of the window, he said: 'Look, this idea of genetically modifying Man – what do you think?' Then, glancing through the window over my shoulder, he continued: 'I mean, first, is such a thing possible; and, second, does it need doing?'

Giving a shrug, I said: 'I can't answer if it needs doing, but it's certainly possible.' I then made a move for the door handle but Aldo put a staying hand on my arm and said: 'Sorry, but I want to be absolutely clear.'

Wondering what was coming next, I looked into his eyes and, as he held my gaze, I could see he was mulling something over. His face then relaxed and he said: 'What you're saying is nobody really knows whether we should genetically engineer evolution or not – right?'

I let out a half laugh and said: 'I don't know about that! Two billion Christians would presumably...'

'But nobody scientific, I mean,' he said, cutting me short.

Ignoring his abruptness, I said: 'Scientists can only do what legislation will let them, but, no, I think most geneticists have an open mind on some form of human modification.'

Nodding, he murmured: 'Okay,' and, gesturing towards the door, he said: 'Let's go.'

He then went ahead of me into the room and, as soon as Gian Paolo caught sight of him, he broke into a smile, clicked off the TV and swung into a sitting position. The intravenous tube taped to his arm tautened precariously and I quickly moved to the wheeled stand with the tube's drip bag so I could position it closer to him.

'Good to see you,' Gian Paolo said slapping Aldo's hand in greeting. 'I didn't expect you to make it this quickly.'

It looked for a moment as if Aldo was going to embrace his brother, but his eyes darted from the tube to the bag-stand to the monitor in one corner and he contented himself with patting Gian Paolo's thigh, saying: 'What happened to the hair then? Is that the chemo?'

Buffing his cranium with a palm, Gian Paolo said: 'No, I shaved it off so it wouldn't get too messy.' And grinning broadly, he added: 'I always wanted the Buddhist look!'

Folding his arms, Aldo gave a faint smile and, leaning back against the wall, he said: 'And did you shave off your eyelashes too?'

Gian Paolo looked embarrassed and said in a quiet voice: 'No. I guess that is the chemo.'

Nodding, Aldo said: 'Okay,' then, taking a sideways glance at me, he continued: 'So why didn't you do the manipulation?'

Gian Paolo's face became serious and he said he'd made a lot of effort to have me drag Aldo here and he'd not gone to all that trouble so he could listen to a lecture. 'I got you here to talk about a project,' he said.

'I know, I know,' Aldo said. 'But if you'd kept yourself well, we could have talked about it without me having to jump around in helicopters.'

'No, we couldn't,' Gian Paolo said. 'You know you're always too busy.'

His voice rising, Aldo said: 'So what? – you let yourself get cancer just to get my attention?'

Gian Paolo looked thoughtful and said: 'In a way – maybe.' Then he took a deep breath and added: 'But the real reason is, I've had enough.'

Bouncing away from the wall, Aldo moved to the bed, sat beside his brother and said: 'But that's crazy. The student life is so cushy.'

Gian Paolo swung his legs up and leant back against his pillow. 'I suppose it is,' he said. 'It's just I feel I've done my bit.'

'What is it with you?' Aldo said, rolling his eyes. 'Why has there always got to be some "bit" to do? You're just like Renata!'

'What can I do?' said Gian Paolo, shrugging. 'It's just how I am.'

Aldo sighed, then said, given he'd now decided to sponsor Gian Paolo's genetic research project, Gian Paolo would have had a 'bit' to do if he could have kept himself well for the establishment phase, since he would have had responsibility for monitoring the project's initial progress, ensuring its strategic direction was right. 'After all, you're the man with the vision,' Aldo said.

Glancing out the window to the adjacent hospital block, Gian Paolo said: 'It's not my thing, the practicalities,' and, turning back to Aldo, he added: 'Besides, I've already passed the vision on to Professor Small.'

Drawing his legs up so he could lounge at the other end of the bed, Aldo said he wasn't sure if explaining a vision to a psychiatrist really counted as Gian Paolo having done his bit. 'It seems to me,' he continued, 'your real bit would have been to get a worldwide debate going on whether the lifeless wilderness beyond us needs science to put it right or if there's really some heavenly father out there saying don't fuck with it.'

Wondering if Aldo shared Gian Paolo's metaphysical views, I said: 'And you would go along with there being no heavenly father, I suppose?'

'What do you think!' Aldo said; then, quickly realising his answer was rude, he added: 'Look, I've been what you would call "floaty" thousands of times and I can tell you there's nothing out there.' He then glanced towards Gian Paolo, who was busy plumping his pillows, and said: 'Not unless you count the odd bit of moss on a few icy rocks.'

A laugh escaped me and I said: 'I'm not sure whether I'm meant to take you seriously.' Then, in response to the glare he gave me, I added: 'I mean, this "floaty" thing, even if it's real, surely it can't have enabled you to look round the whole universe.'

'No, that would be impossible, but I've seen enough to know billions of miles of creation around us are completely desolate,' Aldo said. 'No sign of heaven!'

'I see,' I said; 'and you're convinced you and your brother are best placed to do something about it?'

Moving to a cross-legged position, Aldo said, if he was honest, he'd have to admit, until now, he'd felt confident God would somehow sort it out, but the more he thought about it, the more he found himself agreeing with Gian Paolo's idea that Man was required to do the sorting.

'So the pair of you agree on one thing at least: it's Man's job to be the builder of creation,' I said.

Aldo glanced at Gian Paolo and said he didn't agree Man's role was to be a builder. 'I see us much more as a pair of chunky gloves,' he said. 'Like the ones scientists use to handle radioactive stuff in glass cases.' And, pointing to his temple, he added: 'Without the gloves, scientists can't make use of what's in their heads, right?'

'Yes,' I said. 'I see what you mean.' Then I suggested that, if he and Gian Paolo saw God as this mind without hands, pervading the whole universe, didn't that mean there must be some sort of repository made up of all the bits of God that weren't in the world – which would presumably be the huge majority? And, if so, wasn't that repository more capable of improving creation than the two of them?

'Do you want to answer that?' Aldo said, looking towards Gian Paolo once more. 'I mean, you are the philosopher!'

Gian Paolo moved to a cross-legged position, mirroring his brother, and said I needed to move away from the time-and-space-bound thinking of seeing God as being made up of bits that could be physically located in one place or 'repository'. 'That's what's led to your beardy bloke on a cloud in the first place,' he continued.

'You mean the idea of God the Father?' I said, slightly nettled.

'Yes,' he said, 'the idea of a god with a personality you can pray to.' Then, exchanging grins with his brother he added: 'Only persons have personality!'

My nettled feeling growing, I took a moment to study the brothers as they sat bookend-like on the bed, their raised chins oozing confidence. I then thought how misguided I'd been to see them as having nothing in common simply because their looks and approaches to life were so different. Studying them now, I could see their whole demeanour exuded an identical self-belief and assumption of superiority that actually made them alike as two peas in a pod.

Moving away from the bed, I paced slowly round to the other side of the room and said: 'You boys really are something, aren't you!'

They turned surprised faces towards me and I continued: 'You go round like you've got all the answers: all the understanding the rest of us are just too stupid to have.' And, as I saw their surprise increase, I found myself enjoying such a luxurious feeling of release I couldn't help telling them they needed to challenge themselves on whether it was perhaps their ideas that were misguided: whether the shipwreck of their early family life had given them an inflated idea of how much of a special case they were.

'And before you say it, Aldo,' I said, 'I know you're a self-made billionaire.'

'Double actually,' he said. 'By the time I was twenty-six!'

A desire to shriek flashed through me and I looked out the window to hide my anger, my feeling of release shattered.

A long silence then followed, which was only broken by Gian Paolo saying: 'What's your real take on me then?' And, as I turned back to him, he added: 'On us.'

'My take as a psychiatrist or as a Christian?' I said, still angry.

'Either,' Gian Paolo said.

'Both,' said Aldo.

Their faces were now fixed in my direction and, even though I was determined to stand up to them, I found I couldn't hold their combined gaze so I began pacing the room again while I told them my psychiatric opinion was they didn't believe in a Christian God because their parents' divorce meant their father had left the familial home at a time when their Oedipal complexes would have been actively driving them to do away with him so they could possess their mother. And, because their childish eyes would have seen their father's departure as successful realisation of their Oedipal wishes, they would have grown up believing they possessed a super-potency which – combined with their need to combat the guilt arising from the 'murder' of their father – would have spawned a number of complexes.

Among these would have been a superiority complex that now, in their adult lives, was driving them to remove God as creator of the universe and install themselves in His place – in a replay of the original Oedipal ousting of their father.

A roar of laughter escaped Aldo and he spent the next half-minute slapping his thighs and guffawing. He then managed to catch enough breath to say: 'I'm sorry; what a load of bollocks!' and, bringing himself under control, he added: 'Psychobabble just kills me!'

'It's a theory,' Gian Paolo said, throwing Aldo a stern look. 'But I have another,' and he went on to suggest the absence of their father in childhood could have resulted in the voices of authority that develop superego thinking being considerably weakened and, consequently, the brothers would have grown up free from much of the anxiety people experience from the ego failing to live up to the superego's diktats.

This freedom from anxiety would have allowed them to explore the meaning of existence with greater fearlessness than other people and consequently grasp more of the truth about life.

'My God!' Aldo said, laughing again. 'I forget you speak psychobabble too!'

Ignoring Aldo, I said: 'So you're saying the pair of you know so much about the secret of life, you can make God's decisions for Him.'

Aldo was about to speak, but Gian Paolo silenced him with a look and said, first, there was no 'Him' to make decisions for and, second, he wasn't arrogant enough to suggest his and Aldo's insights gave them the right to dictate to humanity.

'Truly huge decisions have to be made collectively,' he said, 'personally involving as many people as possible.' He then went on to suggest collective decision-making was not about a mass of people taking a vote to follow one path or another, but involved myriad groups of individuals discovering the right thing to do by taking part in acts that gave them a shared, glad-to-be-alive feeling.

'It's the alive feeling,' he continued, 'that tells you when what you're doing truly needs to be done.' He then told us of a story he'd read once in a magazine concerning a bunch of men who'd rescued a small group of wild horses that had run onto a beach and become trapped in wet sand as the tide was coming in.

Efforts to pull the horses free by hand were useless and it seemed inevitable the animals would either drown where they stood or be swept out to sea in the middle of the night, at high tide.

The men, nearly all of whom were strangers to one another, devised a plan that involved tying long ropes to the horses and, working in teams of three or four, they battled through the night to keep each horse upright and prevent it being washed out to sea. The incident had taken place in early winter on an unusually dark night, leaving the men gripping their ropes with frozen hands in pitch blackness for many hours.

At the first signs of dawn, the tide had receded far enough for the men to begin digging out the horses that hadn't been freed by the tide's action and, by the time the winter sun was fully risen, the men had succeeded in saving every one of the animals and were able to dry their coats and warm them with blankets before returning them shaken, but unharmed, to the wild.

A local café owner who'd been part of the rescue team subsequently invited all the men back to his shop for a free, cooked breakfast and later told the journalist writing the magazine story that the comradeship and selfless compassion he'd experienced during the action had made the night the greatest of his life.

'You see,' Gian Paolo continued, 'the struggle of the men united them and gave them the strength to achieve something noble. And that's what felt so beautiful.'

'It's a lovely story, Gian Paolo,' I said. 'But I don't see what it has to do with decision making.'

'It has everything – can't you see!' Aldo butted in. 'When a group of people have a beautiful experience, you know God is in the world – in super-concentrate!'

'Yes,' Gian Paolo said. 'It's an intensity of God that can only come about if people are on the right path – doing the right thing.'

Returning to the window, I took a moment to think about what they were saying but felt a deep unease that a beautiful feeling rather than conscience should decide rightness. 'But,' I said, 'what about when people get together in some kind of debauch or drug rave: aren't they having a shared beautiful experience?'

'No, not if next morning they can't truly say "that was one of the most beautiful nights of my life",' Gian Paolo said.

'I see,' I said. 'And is it down to conscience to say if someone's being truthful about their night?'

'I'm not sure what conscience is,' Gian Paolo said. 'I just know, we can all tell when we're kidding ourselves.' And watching Aldo rise from the bed, he added: 'And anyone who thinks a night they can't remember was truly beautiful is definitely kidding themselves.'

Arrived at the bedside table, Aldo selected an apple from a bulging paper bag sitting between a jug of water and Gian Paolo's table clock and, holding up the fruit, he said: 'You don't mind, do you?'

'Help yourself,' Gian Paolo said. 'I've enough for a lifetime!'

Polishing the apple against his chest, Aldo arched an eyebrow at Gian Paolo then returned to his place on the bed. He then took a crunching bite and said: 'Yes, it's going to be hard not having you around.'

'Good grief!' Gian Paolo said. 'It almost sounds like you'll miss me!'

Aldo glanced round at the paraphernalia being used for Gian Paolo's treatment then, looking into his brother's eyes, he said: 'I will. You know I will.' And, leaning back on his elbows, he made a vague gesture with the apple, adding: 'Although I won't be sorry to see you escape all this.'

'That's for sure!' Gian Paolo said; then, turning to me, he added: 'Not that I'm not grateful. It's just I'd quite like the treatment to stop – which I guess it can, now the project's going ahead.'

'Stop?' I said. 'I don't think you should give up just yet, Gian Paolo. There are plenty of other things to live for.'

'I don't agree. Not on Earth. Not for me,' he said, his eyes fixing on mine.

The firmness in his voice made me think there was little point trying to persuade him to do more to fight the cancer and I said: 'It seems pretty clear you've made up your mind,' and, moving to perch on the corner of the bed by Aldo, I added: 'But doesn't that rather put a hole in your theory of good decisions and people being glad to be alive.'

Gian Paolo laughed loudly and said: 'Professor! I never thought you'd be guilty of sophistry!' and, swinging his legs off the bed so he could sit next to me, he patted my hand and added: 'But I'm flattered you don't want me to die!' He then said, the truth was, he was genuinely very glad to be alive and looking forward immensely to continuing life unencumbered by his body.

The sincerity in his eyes contrasted starkly with the sickly appearance of his puffy face without lashes or brows and I felt touched. 'Well, I must say, you seem very calm,' I said. 'It can't be easy.'

Patting my hand again, he said there was no reason to be anything other than calm since there was no such thing as death, just the passing of the funny little bundle of idiosyncrasies that was his person. 'And you can't look on that as death,' he continued, 'in the same way you wouldn't say the eight-year-old child you once were is dead, or the smooth-skinned college girl. They're still alive in you although, in reality, they're long gone.'

'I'm not sure I understand,' I said. 'Are you saying you'll live on through your soul?'

'No, no, no!' Gian Paolo said, vigorously shaking his head. 'No "me"! No soul!' He then said the idea of eternal, individual souls was the product of Man's vanity and what actually happened in death was the life, love, consciousness, truth, beauty and creativity that had flowed through people's minds and bodies in life simply stopped flowing into the world and remained floating in God, like sea water waiting to evaporate before falling again as raindrops. 'The idea the raindrops will forever keep a personal identity is ludicrous,' he said.

'But if nothing remains of the person after death,' I said, 'doesn't that make our lives pointless?'

The brothers exchanged grins once more and Gian Paolo said no Earthly life was pointless because God used its experience of materiality to learn what to do next. 'If you think about it,' he continued, 'God could have had no experience at all of material being until the universe happened, so it's having to build creation through pure trial and error. That's what evolution is.'

He then said I needed to think of God as mind as well as spirit to appreciate how every idea any of us ever thought, and every experience we'd ever known, exists eternally in God's being in the same way the memories of the children we once were exist in us.

'It's the idea of the boy being the father of the man,' Aldo said. 'The creation becomes the creator's creator!'

Gian Paolo threw his brother another look and told him not to overcomplicate things. 'The point is,' he said: 'There is no "you", only a present version,' and he went on to suggest wherever a human being was in its development – whether a wide-eyed child, insecure adolescent or adult in its prime – each of us was just a continually transforming channel for the thing looking out through our eyes, which, conversely, was constant and unchanging; or at least unchanging for the span of our lifetime.

'But if God is just this personality-less abstraction pushing itself into a world it can't physically control – at least not in real time – why do so many people believe in an almighty God?' I said.

Gian Paolo sucked his lower lip and said: 'Okay. Say you've got a six-year-old boy who's just lost his mother to cancer. What can the father say to ease the pain?' And he went on to suggest the best consolation would be to say 'Mummy was alive and well in heaven, waiting until God called them to Him too; then they'd all meet up and be a happy family once again'. 'That's how the fairy story began,' Gian Paolo said. 'Because it has to end happily for children.'

'It's not the first time I've heard the fairy-story argument,' I said. 'But your view of God offers no salvation from death at all.'

'Because there is no death,' Gian Paolo said. 'That's what I'm trying to show you.' He then turned to his brother, who was busy tucking into his apple, and added: 'Give us a bite will you, Aldo. My throat's really dry.'

Note to Publisher

And so, that's how it ended. Gian Paolo was dead six days later, on 4 July 2010, and Aldo formally pledged the next day to make funds available to set up the research project, isolating the genes he believes are behind his extraordinariness and that of his late brother and sister.

He then asked me to help him find a managing director for the project, so I briefed Michael Servo on Gian Paolo's vision and, in the middle of that July, introduced him to Aldo.

The two of them hit it off straightaway and Michael became completely fired up about the vision. Not just because of the scientific challenge of trying to create the Homo superior: but also because he fell in love with Gian Paolo's idea that transformation of the barren space between planets would come about through development of a plant that could convert dark matter into particulate energies. (Michael's passion for the idea comes from an overwhelming hunch he has that a particle-generating plant is not only thermodynamically feasible but that the technique for its creation already exists in the manufacture mechanics for synthetic organisms.)

By the end of July, Michael had met with a lawyer, finance director, facilities manager and human resources specialist from the Pointless headquarters and, having named his salary to take on the project's directorship, he set about recruiting a project team.

The budget at his disposal made recruitment of the best brains relatively easy and, as early as March 2011, Michael's team had identified a strand in the DNA of Aldo, Gian Paolo and Renata that contained an atomic configuration outside anything identified through the human genome project or any other research. Then, a fortnight later, the team discovered another genetic anomaly, unique to Aldo – although God knows which of Aldo's strangenesses it's responsible for.

By the summer, Michael's team was focused on designing trials to identify what characteristics these genes would produce in living creatures and, just last month, he told me data from all the experiments with mice were irrefutably demonstrating animals modified with the anomalous DNA behaved differently, spending much more time apart from their groups and gathering straw and other materials then arranging them into patterns which they would subsequently rearrange dozens of times a day.

What the mice behaviour actually proves, I'm not sure, but I have a strong hunch it means Michael is on an inexorable path to genetically engineering human beings that will possess the supposed 'new feelings' of Aldo and his family. The question is, do those feelings – if they are real – represent an evolutionary step or is Michael actually working to create a creature that will so anger God, He'll make sure it dies off quickly in the natural world?

Before I met Gian Paolo, I would have had no hesitation in saying God's anger would be roused, and the work was doomed to failure, but my experience of treating him has left me with an underlying anxiety about the sustainability of the world and the soundness of Man's design and now I'm not sure who's best placed to solve these issues.

That's why I'm asking you, as a publisher, to bring Gian Paolo's case to as wide a public as possible who can decide if our only chance of survival is to correct creation's shortcomings through science, or whether we should simply continue to wait in joyful hope for the coming of a saviour.

Perhaps you could find a way to encourage readers to give me their thoughts and hopefully offer their own insights. If so, my email address is: prof.joysmall@virginmedia.com

Best wishes

Professor Joy Small
Head of Psychiatry
Pasteur Hospital

March 2012